# SILENT
# ECHOES

# SILENT
# ECHOES

---

*Story of a Man Torn Between*
*Duty and Conscience*

# Gene Baldwin

Revised 2011

**To order additional copies of this book, contact:**
Xlibris Corporation
1-888-795-4274
www.Xlibris.com
Orders@Xlibris.com
10270

# CONTENTS

*For those who were there*

*When I consider Life and its few years—*
*A wisp of fog betwixt us and the sun;*
*A call to battle, and the battle done*
*Ere the last echo dies within our ears.*

Lizette Woodworth Reese (1856-1935), *Tears*

# 1

## March 1963

I never wanted to wear a suit and tie and go to an office everyday, with its stifling sameness. There was never a doubt what I wanted to do. As long as I can remember, the goal was always there, drawing me toward it. Some people have an obscure dream of what their future will be. Mine was crystal clear. I wanted to be an Air Force fighter pilot – not just a pilot – a fighter pilot. I realized that dream. I experienced the exhilaration of becoming one with the aircraft. As my body merged with the fighter, we became one machine, one life form. There was an intoxicating euphoria darting next to clouds, rolling effortlessly over their tops with a slight touch of control pressure and climbing to dizzying altitudes. It was in an element foreign to most humans, and inexplicable to those who could never experience it.

I had recently been assigned to a new F-4 unit at Mac Dill Air Force Base. This was the top operational fighter in our inventory, and I relished flying it. The powers that control officers' lives are sometimes arbitrary and capricious in their decisions. In my case, they decided I could best serve my country as an assault airlift pilot – "needs of the service" – I was told. That's how my world of flying changed abruptly. It altered more than my time in the air when I began flying the C-123 at Pope Air Force Base, North Carolina. I was not happy flying the assault airlift mission and for the first time and I was having doubts about my chosen profession.

When I hung up the phone, I knew. A no-notice briefing contained a clear message – another deployment. Rumors had flown around the base for weeks that it was imminent. The bar talk didn't put a date and time to the rumors. Speculations flowed as freely as the happy hour drinks.

"Who was on the phone?" Leslie asked.

"Operations. I have to go to the Base for a briefing. Hope it won't be too long."

"Dinner will be waiting when you get back."

"Thanks." I zipped my flight jacket, kissed her cheek and shot through the door.

As I left the briefing, the wind swept across me, accentuating the damp cold. March has never been my favorite month. It's that god-awful transition from winter to spring that comes in so awkwardly. This year it was trying to be more unpleasant than usual. I plodded down the gravel walk as the stiff wind whipped at me in unpredictable gusts. The chill accentuated what I had just been told. As I thought about the briefing, I mulled over the consequences. The impending deployment, just announced by Squadron Operations, swirled in my thoughts. The slight shiver I felt could have been from the news or the cold. Either way it didn't matter.

"Hey, slow down." Zack tugged at my arm. "Lucky us, huh? Whatcha' think about that great news we just got?"

I glanced in his direction, not wanting to listen, not wanting to talk. I needed some space, time to think about the things happening so rapidly they were impossible to assimilate. I forced myself to stop and give Zack my full attention. "Thinking was a luxury I dispensed with rather quickly the day after arriving at Pope Air Force Base." I shook my head. "Zack, just why the hell do ya' think maintenance has been putting in Benson tanks and armor plating under the front seats for the last two weeks? It doesn't take a damn genius to interpret that."

"I just figured the odds might be with me—with us—not to be on this one." He scowled. "You know, by damn, the Wing could've given us a little more notice. A briefing tomorrow morning is pretty short notification." He kicked at the loose gravel. "I had a two-week leave starting next week. Everything planned—right down to an oceanfront view." He slowed, turned his back to the wind, and lit the cigarette dangling from his mouth. He exhaled and the smoke dissolved in a wind gust. "Hey, Coach, it took me three months, a bunch of damn expensive dinners, not to mention sitting through 'Porgy and Bess', to get her committed to this trip." He drew deeply on the cigarette, letting it out slowly in an upward thrust of his chin. "By the time we get back, I'll have to start over with her."

"Do you think with anything above the waist?"

He stood there, staring at me, as the wind whipped at us. The few seconds seemed to turn into an eternity before Zack spoke. "You're gettin' better at cheap shots."

"I had a good teacher."

He moved his collar up to shield his face from the wind. "What th' bloody hell's really wrong with you? I know this thing's not sitting too well with either one of us, but as you said—we knew it was coming." His penetrating gaze never left me. "Now, tell me, what's really got your jaws so torqued?"

"Nothing."

"Something's got your boxers in a bunch—let's hear it."

"Let it go, Zack." I turned quickly and walked on down the path.

I heard his footsteps as he walked faster, pulling up on my left side. "Hey, we don't do this." He yanked on my sleeve. "Dammit, talk to me."

I nodded toward the cigarette. "You know those damn things'll kill you?"

"No doubt," he said. "But you gotta go with something." He held the cigarette out looking longingly at it. "This is as good as anything."

"See ya' tomorrow." I turned back down the walk. Glancing back, I saw Zack still standing there watching me. There was no way to tell him what I was feeling. Why should I bother him with things I can't understand? I wandered toward the parking lot, thoughts about the deployment mingled with those of Leslie. I stopped at the blue VW and leaned on the cold metal. Looking out onto the vast concrete ramp, I studied the forms moving about the aircraft, busy in readying the C-123's for the mission. I didn't want to go.

It had only been a few months since I sat in southern Florida, waiting for the "go" signal to land 82nd Airborne troopers in a cane field in Cuba. *These goddamn deployments are coming at the wrong time in our lives. It drains us. It saps our emotions down to the raw.*

As I leaned against the cold metal, my mind generated snapshots of the past. Radiant images of the last seven years with Leslie flew in and out of view. The scenes evaporated as quickly as they came, and again, I watched forms moving on the flight line. *Goddamnit, not now!*

My mind refused to focus as I drove. My stomach churned as I turned onto the driveway and looked at the house where we moved last month. Paint cans and a ladder beside the drive indicated there were a few final touch-ups to be done. The balled shrubs lying tilted awkwardly on their side, waiting to be planted, were on my list for Saturday. The grass was barely showing through the dirt, green shoots casting a light verdant hew across the barren churned earth. I turned off the key and sat there, wondering why life has a tendency to tease you with expectations and dreams, only to snatch them away as if mocking you.

As I moved from the car along the curved walk, thoughts swirled in my head about the things left undone here. I stopped at the door, looking around me. *If I just had a few more days – just a few more days.* I grabbed the doorknob, holding it tightly in my hand, not wanting to go inside. Slowly I opened the door.

"Oh, you're home?" Her voice soft and calm as always. I couldn't quite grasp whether it was a statement or a question. When her voice lowered and the words came out in monosyllable tones, the meaning was usually detectable.

"Yep," I answered. "That quickly-called meeting at Squadron Ops took more time than I thought. Sorry."

"I left some spaghetti in the oven," she said. "I wasn't sure when you'd be in, so I went ahead and ate a bite. Hope you don't mind." As she brushed past toward the bedroom my eyes followed her to the doorway. There beside the door was a large box, half-packed, a sweater drooped over the side waiting to be placed inside. It was conspicuous testimony to her decision. There had been times when she was unhappy enough to close the bathroom door and weep. But somehow we would end up in bed, making apologies, making love. The next few days following those make-ups would be like it was when we first married, but that happiness was fluid, elusive.

She returned to the kitchen, and wandered over to the counter. She leaned back against the sink, watching me pick at food, which was not on my mind. "The realtor said she'd run the ad tomorrow." She moved closer. "Sorry the spaghetti isn't hot but I didn't know when you'd be back." She instinctively pushed the butter toward my hand as I broke off a piece of bread. "You want me to warm it up? It'll only take a minute."

"This is fine."

"We'll have to wait and see how long it takes for the house to sell," she brushed at her hair. "You know—to finalize things."

I looked up from the spaghetti. "Leslie, come over here, sit and let me tell you the latest." I dropped the fork on the plate, and watched her move toward the chair. She sat quickly, a questioning expression on her face.

"You've got a strange look. What's the matter?"

"The Wing's deploying a squadron to Vietnam day after tomorrow—I'm on the list. That was the hot news they called us in for."

"My God, that's sudden." She impulsively moved toward me. "For how long?"

"Six months."

Her hand touched my arm. "I don't know what to say—Lord, David, I'm stunned."

"I knew it was coming, but not this sudden two-day notice. So I can't get too damned concerned about selling this house. I've gotta get my stuff squared away and try to concentrate on what I'm supposed to be doing. My mind can't deal with this other crap right now." I didn't mean for it to sound so abrasive.

"I'm sorry—really sorry." Obviously, no offense was taken at my insensitive remark. Her hand moved lightly down my arm and her eyes met mine. She squeezed my arm. "With you leaving, I'll stay here till the house sells. I wouldn't leave you with that responsibility; you've got enough to think about now."

"Everything hits at once." I tried to drop my edgy tone. "Look, there's no need to interrupt your plans—maybe just delay 'em a while. The house should sell quickly. It's new, a solid plan, and in a good neighborhood. I'll have a power-of-attorney drawn up tomorrow so you'll have no trouble closing."

"Look, I've got no definite plans. I'll stay as long as it takes. Mama won't mind; she hasn't yet accepted that I'll be coming home for such a long visit." Her voice lowered. "She doesn't always understand my decisions anyway."

"Mothers never do."

Her hand moved self-consciously toward a tear. "David, I wish this deployment hadn't come up now. We needed some time to . . ." She shook her head.

"Maybe it's out there somewhere for you, Leslie."

"See, that's what I mean." She moved away and slammed the washcloth into the sink. "You just don't communicate. Why, the devil, can't you let go and say what you really feel. Can't you get down to those gut level emotions just once? Instead, you snap back with some inane comment like that and keep your feelings bottled up." She glared at me. "Just look at the way you sit there, arms folded across your chest, making sure nothing will penetrate that impregnable exterior."

"Sorry. I'll try another stance."

"Damn." She swirled around, shot through the door, and down the hall.


She came by her independence and self-confidence quite naturally in that small Texas town. Leslie Ann Herrington was comfortable in a mantle of allegiance that came with the acceptance and love found in small southern towns. Possessions and money were irrelevant and always subjugated to one's roots. The important thing was, and always would be, ones' family. As it turned out, Leslie had both. While her piquant character was being developed, finely honed at home, by a doting father and mother, her friends provided further endorsement. She became self sufficient with the latitude of decision-making virtually unknown to her peers. Leslie grew up happy, independent, and loved. Leslie Herrington knew who she was.

Being the youngest and only daughter, she was given more leeway than her older brothers. She took to the horse farm with much more enthusiasm than her siblings. There was a genuine love of the rippling green pastures and the horses that frolicked there. It nurtured her. She was a natural horsewoman at age eight and, by age twelve, became the Texas junior jumping champion. Her brothers, Todd and Frank, developed other interests. They never felt close to the ranch or their father. Todd, the oldest, graduated from Duke and became an English professor at the University of Virginia. Frank went straight to New York after college and was making his way slowly as a stockbroker and financial advisor. They returned to Deerfield only twice after graduation. The first visit in June 1953 for their father's funeral, and the second was for Christmas that year, at their mother's insistence. The whole family would never be together again at Deerfield. Leslie and her mother reconciled that this would probably be the boys last visit to Killeen.

Leslie gradually grew closer to her mother, but both knew no one could replace her father. It took the remaining two months of that summer to shake the depression and feeling of total abandonment. Her loss was almost irreconcilable. By the end of August, with much encouragement, she went back to Austin and completed her senior year at the University of Texas. That summer she came home to stay. She was determined to take over Deerfield and manage it; it felt preordained.

It might have been preordained, but no one told the Richland Bank and Trust. When Walter R. Herrington's last will and testament was read, his estate consisted of $100,000 life insurance, $32,000 in stocks, $4,450 in savings, $1,100 in checking, and a mortgage of $487,000, not to mention various other debts. The reality of the situation was all too obvious and Richland Bank and Trust had never been known for its patience.

Gus Hardy, the family attorney and friend, provided the only logical alternative—sell Deerfield. By doing this, Leslie's mother could save the home and ten acres of land. This would satisfy all debts, the mortgage and provide enough cash for a livable investment income. Deerfield sold for $683,450 in July 1954.

Leslie, at first, found it difficult to accept. It was as if her mother had betrayed her father's memory. There was a sudden realization it was only land and a few horses, and that people are the only important assets in life, she rebounded with her usual resilience and quickly forgave her mother. She managed to keep two horses; one was Rambler, the horse she rode in the junior jump championship. At the end of the summer, Leslie packed her bags and accepted a teaching position in San Antonio.

I watched her close our bedroom and then turned back to the cold spaghetti.

The briefing room was a buzz of incoherent conversation, small groups gathered around analyzing the upcoming mission, discussing the latest rumors, and exaggerating both. Zack was leaning against the wall checking the door. He glanced my way and quickly waved me over.

"Sidle over here and let me tell you the latest and greatest from rumor central." He stared at me for a few seconds, analyzing my facial expression. "You in a better mood this morning?"

"Not really, so don't make any sudden moves." I smiled.

He laughed as his eyes darted around the briefing room. He looked as if he expected to gain more information from the crowd of aircrews milling in every direction. "Listen, I just found out Lieutenant Colonel Adams isn't our CO any longer. They've picked some desk jockey from Wing Personnel for Squadron CO." He moved closer. "And get this. We've got Major Lynch from Wing Plans as Operations Officer."

"Who?"

"Remember about a month ago at the Wing party? You were in one of your irascible moods – a wee bit lit really. When this guy at the bar in the tan sports coat told us to quiet down; you told him to piss off. Well, Coach, he's now our damn Ops Officer for this gaggle."

"Maybe he's forgotten."

"You hope."

"Why the hell isn't our CO taking the squadron over?" I asked. "I counted on Colonel Adams to lead the deployment." I looked at the back of the room at the officers waiting to come down the isle. "Let's hope these guys can lead sixteen C-123's from North Carolina to DaNang."

"Don't you just love the infinite wisdom of Wing Headquarters?" He leaned closer. "This Composite Squadron is made up of guys from every squadron on base. We'll be part of the First Air Commando Group once we're there—a completely new unit designation when we get to Nam."

"Ten Hut!"

Everyone rose to a position closely resembling attention while Zack remained slouched against the wall anticipating the "As you were" command. Lieutenant Colonel Douglas Patrick Norwood, however, was enjoying his newly found power. His smug look and strutting walk gave off an air of authority. He waited until he stepped onto the front stage to give the command to take seats. He smiled as if he were the bearer of great news. A half-smile flared his nostrils. He shuffled the sheets of paper in front of him, glancing up to see if he had our rapt attention.

"Gentlemen, we've been given a difficult, but important mission. I hope you look upon this with pride because of the absolute confidence that's been placed in your ability. That's why each of you was selected. Tactical Air Command was tasked by the Joint Chiefs of Staff to place tactical airlift support for Special Forces, operating in I Corps area, as soon as possible. This Wing has been given that mission—and you're the aircrews hand-picked to get it done."

"Handpicked, my ass," Zack whispered. "We were victims of luck of the draw."

"Shh." I frowned in his direction.

"I want you to carefully read the aircrew assignments included in your mission folders." Norwood continued. "There's no crew integrity that's guaranteed from your unit. This is a composite squadron, made up from crews from every squadron in the Wing. We've changed some crew positions for reasons of equalizing experience and we're placing augmented pilots on each aircraft. To make up for no autopilot on the long legs three pilots have been assigned to each crew. The third pilot, on each crew, will return to Pope with the C-130's." A loud groan rose from the audience. Norwood glanced up from his notes, looked out on his captive group, and then continued. "Aircraft numbers have been assigned so that flight engineers can start checking things over. Read over the list, check your gear, and make final arrangements at personnel for wills and power of attorneys. I want all crews back here at exactly fifteen hundred for a detailed briefing of this mission." There was a rustling of papers as notes were being rapidly being taken. "Navigators, bring your charts. Pilots and copilots, bring radio facility charts for the U.S. portion. Engineers, have a reading on all write-ups on your aircraft. Loadmasters have the weight and balance forms filled out with the appropriate fuel loads. Any questions?" His head moved side to side, scanning the audience. "Okay, see you at fifteen hundred."

I searched the sky for the sun as a few rays slid through the gray overcast. I was hoping it would push through and add some warmth to the cold March air. I craved warmth. The spirit sometimes responds to such things.

The noise of the Officer's Club rebounded through the door as it opened, focusing my thoughts on the day. Walking among the noon chatter and clattering, I slid into a chair beside Zack, taking quick note of the occupant next to him. A hand shot across the table and a voice was heard above the cacophony of blurred sound. "Chuck Stone. I'm your augmentation pilot for the flight over."

"A third pilot'll come in handy with no autopilot." I grasped his hand. "David Barfield. Glad to meet you, Chuck."

"He's smiling cause he gets to turn around and come home on one of the C-130's," said Zack. "We get to stay."

"Hey, I've already done a few months over there—your turn, guys." Chuck sipped his coffee. "It'll pass fast." He held the cup in both hands, looking back and forth at Zack and me. "Frankly, I was down in the Mekong Delta. I hear the flying up in I Corps area is tough – all mountains and short LZ's."

"Thanks for the encouragement. You're gonna build up our morale all the way to DaNang?"

"Not quite, Sport. I get off at Clark Air Base in the Philippines. You guys can take it alone those last six hours." He chuckled. "I'll take in a few massages, some great food, and whatever else goes with that scene. Clark Officer's Club has become a swinging place since World Airlines started flying into there. Those stewardi are frappin' unbelievable."

"You're one sweet fellow." Zack lowered his glass. "Keep it up, Chuck. Make me feel real good."

Their conversation flowed as my mind dwelled on leaving Leslie. Vietnam, flying in mountains, and the Viet Cong were irrelevant at this moment. I could only think of not being in her presence, hearing her voice, being in her universe—*damn*. The sounds of Zack's voice drifted through my contemplation. I gradually focused on my name being called out. "David. David, you still with us, Coach?"

"What?" I said, glancing at Zack.

"Chuck just asked you if you were one of the Flight Commanders. You are, aren't you?"

"Reckon I am. Don't know who else would be in the flight though. I'll leave that to our illustrious leadership." I dropped my napkin on the table, sliding the chair back. "I've got to get movin' to get things done by that fifteen hundred briefing. See ya' there."


The Base theater parking lot was full. One spot looked appealing on the far end. It meant parking on the grass, which each blade was considered sacred by the Base Commander. It was never to be walked on, much less parked on. I pulled up onto the greening turf and shut the motor. *To hell with his damn grass.*

Sunlight finally burst through the clouds as they floated in almost recognizable shapes toward the northeast. The cold front was pushing the clouds out ahead of the frigid air. Wintry weather was moving in rapidly, underscored by the arrogant wind. Gusts scooped up damp leaves, casting them about the cars and people. I zipped my flight jacket toward the collar and moved reluctantly to the door.

"Captain. Captain, Barfield." My name was being shouted to my rear. I slowed and turned toward the sound. A tough-looking Master Sergeant was jogging toward me. He came to a stop, gasping for breath. I couldn't help but notice the pugnacious look of a guy who must have put some time in the ring. His nose was bent slightly to the left as if it had connected well with a hard-thrown right. His squared-off jaw was further evidence of my analysis. His heavy-lidded brown eyes expressed an undisguised sadness, as if they have seen too much human folly. He was talking even before he dropped his salute. "Sergeant Picardo, Captain. I'm gonna be your Engineer."

"Well, I don't think so, Sergeant. My engineer is Tech. Sergeant Wall and my loadmaster is Sergeant Franklin. Except for a navigator, I've got a crew."

"Not anymore. We got a copy of the crew list down on the flight line this morning before it was posted. That's when I saw I was on your crew. Just thought I'd let you know who I am before the briefing." He looked at my astonished expression. "Hell, Captain, they've changed up most of the crews."

"Okay, Sergeant . . ." I looked at his name plate. "Picardo. We'll check this out right after the briefing." I turned and continued toward the door. There was a buzz of conversation and rustling of papers as I moved down the aisle looking for Zack. A hand shot up and motioned me toward a seat on the right side about four rows from the stage. Zack stood as I slid by him and plopped in the seat. "You had to get right down here next to the stage?" I asked. "I figured you for the back row."

"I would've, but I just got here too. Lucky just to save you a seat."

I snatched his sleeve, pulling him closer. "Our crew has changed. Let me give you a bit of friggin' information. I just got stopped by 'Igor' outside here and he tells me . . ."

"Ten Hut."

"Tell you later." I said.

Lieutenant Colonel Norwood, Major Lynch, and his entourage moved down the aisle toward the stage. His handpicked staff sat behind the podium as Lt. Col. Norwood moved to the mike. "Take your seats, Gentlemen. We've got a maximum amount of info to put out in minimum time. There are some crucial points to be made about this deployment. In the back of the room is a table with folders, labeled for each aircraft commander." His arm extended toward the back. "In your folder is a schedule of tomorrow's take-offs, and a prefiled flight plan to California. You already know your aircraft number for this mission, and your crew list is included in your folder." He looked around at the staff behind him. " I'm turning this over to Major Lynch to cover the details of the mission. If you've got questions, I'll take 'em at the end."

"Excuse me Colonel." I stood quickly. He turned back toward the mike and scowled as he glared at the Officer who would dare interrupt his planned briefing. "I wanted to ask about crew positions. I've heard there have been changes made from our regular crews. I hope that was just a bad rumor."

"Captain." He strained forward trying to read my name on the flight jacket.

"Captain Barfield, sir."

He straightened up, as he seemed to be filing this intruder's name in his memory. "Barfield, I'll take a little of our valuable time to tell you this. Major Lynch and Captain Allen, the Admin. Officer, made the final decision on crew assignments based on many factors. This is not the time to rehash their decision. We've got a lot of info to dispense in a short time." He looked out over the assemblage. "I'm not concerned with who your friends might be or who you flew with in your previous unit." His eyes narrowed. "Understand?"

I settled into my seat as Zack made no effort to stifle his laughter with his hand covering his mouth. "Understand?" he whispered. "I've always told you to keep a low profile—just blend into the maelstrom of humanity." He chuckled. "You just painted a big-ass bull's eye on the back of your flight jacket."

I gave him a withering look. Zack looked back, his head still nodding.


Major Lynch placed his notes on the rostrum, looked nervously out at an auditorium filled with experienced flight crews. They sat silently waiting for the crucial information that would get them and their aircraft to our destination. He cleared his throat. "First let me say that I'm pleased to have been selected for this assignment. I hope all of you are as eager to accomplish this mission as I am." Muffled laughter, groans, and whispers provided him a reaction he didn't expect. "We'll take-off individually tomorrow morning, beginning at 0430. Check your schedule for engine start, taxi time, and take-offs with ten-minute intervals between aircraft. We've blocked out altitudes, alternating aircraft between seven thousand and nine thousand feet all the way to California. We'll follow the southern route to California, then north to McClellan Air Force Base." He looked out again over the group for indications of agreement. Getting no feedback, he continued, "The Benson tank will provide ample fuel on the first leg. It'll take full Benson tanks to make the next couple of legs—with none to spare. That means you'll be taking off from California with gross weights exceeding sixty thousand pounds." Groans were heard from the theater.

"Damn, Major, the maximum gross weight for take-off in the C-123 is fifty-eight thousand pounds." A lanky lieutenant rose in the back of the auditorium. "Christ, if you lose an engine on take-off, or anytime during the first few hours, you've had it."

"Then hope to God you don't lose one. Has anyone said there was no risk at all associated with this deployment?"

The lanky lieutenant shifted his weight back and forth but didn't relinquish the floor. "Frankly, Major, this mission has all the ear marks of being outside the envelope." He placed his hands on his hips.

"Whose infinite wisdom and extraordinary knowledge of the C-123 capabilities planed this one?"

Lt. Col. Norwood sprang to his feet ready to move to the rostrum and extricate Major Lynch from the grips of the question. At that moment, Major Lynch continued, surprisingly maintaining a calm demeanor. "I know this is pushing the limits of aircrews and aircraft but Tactical Air Command thinks we can do it—and do it we will. Listen up carefully, each and every one of you, we're gonna put sixteen aircraft in DaNang in ten days, ready to support Special Forces in I Corps area." There was a silence among the group that comes with apprehension and skepticism. Ninety-six people sat in awe of the mission assigned them by some unidentified General in TAC Headquarters. A mission conceived by an anonymous staff who operated on theory, not pragmatism. The planning procedure for this mission was slowly sinking in. It was abundantly clear that it was unimportant to an anonymous staff up at Langley Air Force Base that this would be pushing the envelope, maybe outside the envelope, for aircraft and crews. Col. Norwood slowly settled back into his chair.

"This is beginning to sound more like a Tasmanian cluster fuck every minute," Zack said.

Before I could reply, somewhere in the center of the group, a slight humming began, then a barely audible sound of: "*M-I-C-K-E-Y M-O-U-S-E, Mickey Mouse*" was being sung. Major Lynch stopped and strained to hear the sound. Suddenly, a few more picked up on it. Some were singing, a few whistling, and several humming the strains of the Mickey Mouse Club song.

Major Lynch pounded the rostrum for silence, glaring out at us. Col. Norwood rose and strode toward the front, then stopped abruptly. "Okay, fellas, that's enough," Said Major Lynch. And then there was immediate silence. The Colonel glanced at the Major, turned slowly and sat down. He must have sensed the group's mood. I could feel the apprehension in the auditorium; it was an uneasiness that traveled like electrical energy. It had to be obvious to those on the stage. The Mickey Mouse song was a way to break the tension that was building among the crews.

Major Lynch, having gathered his composure, began as if nothing had happened. "Every crew member turn in your military passport to Captain Allen when you report to the flight line tomorrow morning. We'll place all passports in a footlocker on one the C-130's for safekeeping."

My hand shot into the air. "Major, don't you think we'll need our military passports if we have to divert to some foreign base? Not to mention the fact you could lose all of 'em if something happened to that C-130."

Lt. Col. Norwood jumped to the rostrum, already stirred by the lack of respect shown in the singing and now the audacity of this captain. "Captain, do you plan to question every decision on this mission?" His eyes narrowed. "You're certainly making a good start."

"Sir, I just wanted to mention a possible problem. It wasn't meant to question your authority."

"The hell it wasn't," whispered Zack, almost audible to those on stage. I kicked his shin.

The Colonel's stare bore into me. "That'll be all, Gentlemen. You're dismissed."

As we stood, Zack slapped my back. "Yep, a big ole bull's eye right there."

"Captain Barfield." I turned to see Lt. Col. Norwood moving toward me. "Captain Barfield, could I talk with you a minute or two?" He glanced at Zack. "Will you excuse us for a minute, Lieutenant Williams?"

"Zack, go on up and grab our folder and a copy of the crew list. I'll catch up with you."

Zack formed his fingers in the shape of a pistol. "Bang." He glanced back twice as he walked on.

I turned back to Colonel Norwood. "Yessir. You want to speak to me?" Two lieutenants moving with the flow of bodies bumped me to the side. Both of us flattened our bodies against the seats, out of the way of the surge.

"Let's move down there out of the way." Colonel Norwood pointed toward the front row of seats. I followed as he moved swiftly to the front row. I glanced up to see Major Lynch, still on the stage, staring at us. He quickly averted eye contact. Colonel Norwood turned sideways in the seat, looking at me with a generous smile. "I like to get to know all the senior people in the unit, especially the Flight Leaders. Tell me about yourself, Captain. You know – how much flying time in the C-123 – your past experience."

"I've got about a hundred forty hours logged in the 123 now." I said. "Most of my previous experience has been in fighters. I started with the F-94 and a combat tour in Korea, flew the F-86, F-89, F-102 and ended up in F-4's."

Norwood rubbed his chin, taking on a perplexed countenance. "You know, we usually have Flight Leaders with more experience in the bird than that." He cleared his throat. "This is going to be a difficult mission. Do you feel confident in the C-123 with only a little over a hundred hours flying time?"

I could see where this discussion was going. Now was the time to head off being summarily replaced as "B" Flight Leader. "Historically, Colonel, Flight Commanders are determined by rank and seniority. Of course they have to be checked out as an aircraft commander." I made sure we had eye contact. "I'm probably the ranking captain in the group, Colonel, and I've been checked out as an aircraft commander. As for confidence, I've got more than enough. Flying fighters guaranteed that."

"Good." He glanced up at the stage to see if Major Lynch was still there. "I'm sure you'll do well as a senior member of this squadron." His eyes narrowed. "And I'm sure I can count on you to always give me your support – loyalty is a very high priority with me – David. It is David, right?"

I knew right then that he and Lynch had discussed this. He didn't even know my last name when I asked the question. "Yessir, it's David. I understand your priority, Colonel."

"That's good," he said, rising from his seat. "We'll talk again later."

I motioned with my hand for Zack to follow me as I headed straight for an exit. The splash of cold air against my face, as we stepped outside, cleared some of the anger that was seeping into my thinking.

"What was that all about?" Zack asked.

"Nothing really. He just wants to get to know his Flight Commanders." I didn't want to tell Zack the true meaning of the conversation. No need to get him agitated, considering his very low flash point.

"Well now, Coach, you looked like the 'Lone Ranger' down there to me. Where were the other three Flight Commanders? I had it pegged about that 'bull's eye', right?"

I glanced at the roster of aircrews just placed in my hand, several names from my squadron showed up who would be in my flight. Only two engineers, one pilot, and a navigator were unknown. My eyes settled suddenly on the navigator assigned to my crew. Zack was glancing over my shoulder, reading names. "Good Golly, Miss Molly. Our damn Nav is a butter-bar, Second Lieutenant." He reached for a cigarette, twirling it in his hand, not anxious to light up. "Now, how th' hell did we luck up and get a brand-new navigator assigned to us; he's probably just outta training?"

"Zack, ole boy, you better hope he studied well in Nav School. He's gonna take us all the way across the Pacific—not to mention finding Wake Island out there—that little speck in the middle of a great big Pacific Ocean."

"If it turns out he can't find the latrine without detailed instructions, just remember, your butt's along for the ride too." He laughed as he flipped his lighter open. "Hope you're still so full of good humor about six thousand miles out, wondering about how far you can swim." He lit the cigarette, exhaling hard into the wind. "Lord, what a freakin' experience this is gonna be."

"We've got enough problems without worrying about our navigator. Do me a favor. See if you can get the others listed in—flight together for a quick briefing at Operations at 1615. I'd like to cover a few things before we launch tomorrow."

"I'll round 'em up," said Zack.

"Zack." I didn't continue, not knowing how to ask the question. It was probably better left to another time, though it was obvious that I had committed myself.

Zack stopped. "Yeah, David?" He stuck his hands on his hips. "Well, what did you call me back for?"

"Just a silly-ass question. How does Col. Norwood know you – he called you by name?"

"He must have read my name tag on my flight jacket."

"Okay," I said. Watching Zack take-off to gather the flight, my mind whirled around Zack's explanation. I knew there was no way for Norwood to have read his name from that far away. *Why would Zack lie about it?*


Eighteen crewmen sprawled around the edge of the Ops briefing room. "Looks like the gang's all here, Coach," said Zack.

"Not quite, we're missing somebody." I glanced around, counting heads. "Who's not here, Zack?"

"Excuse me, Captain, my aircraft commander's a little late. He said he'd be here soon," Lieutenant Piotrowski stated matter-of-factly.

"Just who the hell's your AC, Gary?" I asked.

"His name's Lieutenant Merc—Phil Merc. He's from the 76th Squadron."

"Okay, fellas, I'm Captain David Barfield—your Flight Commander. Most of us have been together in the 78th. For the new guys, I just wanted to get everyone together so we know who's in—Flight for this wingding of a show. We've got six new faces in this flight. We've all got lots to do before we leap off tomorrow, and I don't intend to waste what little time you've got left. Take it upon yourselves to get acquainted fast. Good luck on this first leg. The others will definitely be different. I'd like a quick word with the three—well, *two* other aircraft commanders."

The slamming door announced the entrance of a tall first lieutenant, as the other crewmembers passed him at the doorway. "Sorry I'm late. Needed a quick stop at the exchange." He sauntered toward me, as I examined his face. His head was square, a high, bony forehead. A shock of maple-colored hair fell across the high forehead as he flipped off his hat. "Did I miss anything, Chief?"

"Dave'll do. I tell you later what you missed." Turning back to the other two first lieutenants, "This'll be pushing all of us to get this mission done. I just want you to know "B" Flight's not going to be the one making things go wrong. Let's make sure we stay on top of everything. And for God's sake, if you've got a problem, let me know first." I watched the bobbing of heads and two thumbs up. "See you guys at oh-dark-thirty tomorrow."

Lieutenant Merc moved closer as the other two left. "Watcha' got, Chief?"

"What's your first name, Lieutenant?"

"Phil." He put his foot in the chair, looking around the room.

"Okay, Phil, I'm David—not Chief. Next, if I ask—and I always ask—members of this flight to do something, I damn well expect them to do it. Everyone else made the meeting. We don't need to get off on the wrong foot, so we'll forget this one, Phil."

"Yes Sir, Captain." The sarcasm was obvious.

"Phil, If you want to play it that way—fine. I can be one ornery son-of-a-bitch. It's up to you."

"Okay." His foot hit the floor from the chair seat. "You made your point." He moved toward the door, glancing over his shoulder. "Anything else?"

I shook my head. "No."


The smell of roast beef hung like a cloud in the kitchen. The aroma drew me across the room to the stove. I cracked the top of the other containers, smelling and savoring their contents. "Hi," she said into my right ear. I dropped the lid as if burned. "Sorry," she added, "didn't mean to startle you like that."

I turned toward her. "Hey, that's some meal there. You didn't have to do all that."

"It's your last night. I didn't want to send you off with an empty stomach."

"Thanks, I appreciate you doing this—really do."

Leslie moved to the sink without a comment, an utterance, or gesture—anything to build on, to pick up the start of what could've been a conversation. I wanted to go to her. Instead, I threw my hat on the chair and walked down the hall. I stopped at the scene in the room. She had neatly laid out my flight suits, uniforms, underwear and socks. The two B-4 bags sat beside the bed as reminders of the inevitable.

"Thanks for getting my gear together," I said as I reentered the room. "That's lots of help—or maybe you're anxious to get me on the road."

She spun around. "You couldn't let it go with just a 'Thanks'?"

"I was kidding—just kidding, Leslie."

"By the time you shower, dinner will be on the table," she said.

*My God, why try*, I thought. My gut ached with the realization we couldn't pierce the defenses, couldn't relax the verbal shield – not even on this last night. I turned and ambled down the hall.

We ate with occasional glances, with a carefully thought-out comment punctuating the dinner's composed atmosphere. I complimented the food, she retorted with a mild "thank you." We approached, but couldn't, or wouldn't, breach the wall. It was there waiting to be scaled, but instead we resorted to the safe, the unemotional.

"All the important papers are there on the desk, along with a general power of attorney, so you can make any decision without my signature."

"I'll file them in the metal box." She looked up, her eyes saying more than her voice. "Look, if you think it best, I'll wait until you get back to sell the house."

"No need to wait. I'm sure you can handle everything."

She touched my arm. "What's bothering you about this deployment, David? I've known you too long – you're worried."

"I'm not worried exactly – just got a bad feeling about the leadership. I've seen absolutely no camaraderie this time." I forced a smile. "It'll be okay."

"Make sure nothing happens to you. I couldn't take that."

"Remember one time, long ago, when I told you I was indestructible?"

"Remember, that I said I wasn't? And quite frankly, you aren't either Captain Barfield – don't take any chances over there." Her hand squeezed my arm.

"No sweat. I don't do that anymore. Hey, thanks for that great dinner. I'll wish for some of that roast in a few days." Sliding the chair back, I squashed the impulse to take her in my arms.

"Can I get you more tea?" She smiled.

"No thanks. I'm about to explode."

"I'll clean up here." She leaned against the counter, her eyes as penetrating as ever, but softness to her voice. "I know how unhappy you've been here at Pope. You've been a different person since the day we arrived. This deployment certainly isn't making it any easier for you."

"I'm a damn fighter pilot, Leslie. I've got an appreciation for the assault airlift mission, but it's not me. I couldn't talk that idiot Major at Tactical Air Command Headquarters out of changing my orders. I should still be at Mac Dill or going to Nam flying F-4's." I swallowed hard. "I'm a fighter pilot."

"I wasn't unhappy to see you stop flying fighters. But now I see what it's done to you." Her body cringed slightly then a smile slowly appeared. "You need to get all your things together so you don't forget something." She chuckled. "You usually do."

"Yeah, but you always remind me just in the nick of time." My eyes were fixed on hers and my hand tightened on the tea glass. "Listen, if something happens to me . . ."

"I don't want to hear any more of that. You're going to be fine." Her hand wiped at her eyes, as she turned away and I headed toward the bedroom.

Everything was in the two B-4 bags, one zipper left open for a shaving kit. I placed the bags beside the door and turned to see her come out of the bathroom. Her face was beautiful in the soft light, even without makeup. The pajamas were a fuzzy flannel, buttoned to the top. Her hair was rolled tightly. For her to wear a sheer black nightgown, faint makeup, and hair slightly flowing over her shoulders would be playing a game. 'Love me as I am', was always the message. It was especially clear this night. She sat on the edge of the bed, glancing over her shoulder. "I'll drive you to the flight line tomorrow. You'd have no way to get your car back."

"I hate to ask you to get up that early."

"I'm glad to do it. We'd better get some sleep." She lay down, pulling the covers tightly to her chin.

The lamp went off with a flip of the switch. I lay there, staring at the slim streak of light from the bathroom nightlight. It arched in a dim half-moon sliver of light on the ceiling. It was something to focus on. Listening to her heavy breathing, I let my mind drift back to other nights—nights when I should have taken her in my arms. I turned my head toward her, almost reaching across that barrier to hold her. My arm moved toward her. It almost touched her shoulder, as it reached further toward the soft white skin. I gradually pulled it back, once again not able to clear the top of that damn wall.

Leslie reached for the heater knob on the VW floor, eager to get some warmth inside the car. She shivered as she pulled her collar up close to her face. "Brrr, it's cold as the devil this morning." She exhaled a mist as she spoke.

"You're just not used to these crack of dawn take-offs. It's always damn cold at 0400."

"Anything else you want me to do—anything at all while you're gone?"

"Yeah." I turned toward her. "Tell your mother I'll miss seeing her this year. This'll be the first summer I haven't been there to do all her minor fixing." I laughed as my breath clouded the windshield. "She usually has quite a list of things for me to do. But, Lord, she sure did feed me well." My voice dropped, "I'll miss that Texas barbeque."

Her hand found my knee. "I know." She patted my leg. "Mama'll miss you too. She loves you, David."

"Why not, she lucked out with the perfect son-in-law." Her head swiveled my way and I saw her smile in the faint light.

She braked the VW to a halt in front of Operations as flight crews milled around in different directions. Aircraft engines roared in the distance as ground crews checked and rechecked the C-123's. The cacophony of sound echoed across the runways as the noise penetrated the darkness. It was a cogent sound, heard so many mornings of my life. It had become a melancholy melody announcing another detachment from all that warmed my soul. I dragged the bags out of the car, dropping them on the ground. As I reached down for the handles, the VW engine stopped. The sound of the door closing and her footsteps made me glance up. Suddenly she was there, a breath away, looking into my eyes.

"Be careful. Please be careful. There are those who love you, you know."

"I hope you're counted in that number." She smiled, giving me the answer I needed. "I love you, Leslie." She gave no further indication of hearing the assertion, as I continued, "And not to worry. I'll be some kind of careful—need to eat some more of Miss Ellen's home cooking." I looked at her as though I could transmit my thoughts. She gradually placed her arms around my neck and kissed my cheek. I took my hand and softly turned her face to me. I kissed her mouth, pulling her close to my body. I was not about to leave on some benign kiss to the cheek. Not this damn day. "Bye. Take care." I released my hold.

"Bye. I'll miss you and –." She stopped mid-sentence and ran to the car. The taillights disappeared into the blackness, leaving me with a strange, hollow sensation. I watched the lights until they disappeared in the darkness.

# 2

## Leslie

I returned to the States, and San Antonio, in June 1953, one month before the Korean War ended in that disaster of warfare blended with misguided politics. We lost over 50,000 men, 8,000 still missing, and proved nothing. In spite of the ambivalence of our country, we came back with our confidence and spirits intact. After all, we were fighter pilots.

The adjustment to Randolph Air Force Base was excruciatingly slow. This was "West Point of the Air", not some outback air strip where uniforms, as well as customs and courtesies of the service were relaxed. This was tradition at its finest. It summarily replaced camaraderie and the "tiger instinct" I had come to rely upon as a way of life. This was a pilot training base and not an operational fighter wing. I reluctantly accepted my duties and responsibilities as instructor – not to mention role model. It took months.

The fall days evaporated with flying and ground instructions. Patience, however, was never a virtue of mine, and this was particularly true with my students. Errors were slammed with verbal abuse, emphasizing how quickly they could make themselves a crispy critter. "If you're going to be a fighter pilot – a live one – there's no room for errors in judgment," I screamed. "Stay ahead of this aircraft." I hoped they listened.

Evenings, after flying, usually found instructor and student at the officers' club stag bar. My best instruction took place over a drink as some story unfolded that supposedly made an important point, or provided insight to being in a skin-tight cockpit traveling in excess of mach 1. The young officers hung on every word, looking at us combat veterans as infallible sources of knowledge. I didn't have the heart to shatter their misplaced devotion.

The biting cold snap came early, in the first week of November. A Saturday. I decided to visit the "River Walk" and its enchantment of boats, people and scenery. La Fiesta grill had become my favorite spot to order three tacos and watch the maelstrom of humanity from a vantage point of the patio.

As I wove my way through the throng, the darkened clouds released their moisture without warning and a cold rain began to fall. People scrambled for the cover of awnings and entrances, riverboats docked while passengers ran for cover.

It was a biting, wintry rain that fell across south Texas that afternoon. I dashed under the awning, dodging into the doorway to escape the downpour. The heavy rain was rippling the water of the River Walk. Shaking my head dislodged some of the accumulated water. The cold filtered through my body. *One more block and I would have made the cafe.* I removed my jacket, shaking it vigorously to get the water off.

"Please, watch the water," she said jumping back quickly.

"God, I'm sorry," I said. "I didn't know anyone was behind me."

"It's okay." She continued to brush droplets from her face.

"Here's my handkerchief. I really am sorry."

"It's okay—really. I've been wetter than this and didn't melt." She laughed, as she looked me up and down. "You're the one who's soaked."

"Thought I could make the cafe across the bridge over there before I drowned." I glanced over toward my original destination. "Reckon I misjudged that deluge."

"I'm going over that way," she said. "Be glad to share the umbrella."

"Hey, thanks."

She flipped open the green umbrella and moved it toward me as I steadied her hand. We walked, stooped over, while the rain pelted the umbrella. Neither of us said anything as we made it across the connecting bridge on the River Walk. I took the umbrella, folded it, shook off the water, and handed it back to her. "Let me buy you a cup of coffee for sharing your umbrella and saving me from a drenching."

"Thanks, I'm just going through here to do some quick shopping—and you didn't stay that dry anyway."

"Hey, it'd only take a minute. A hot cup of coffee will take the chill out."

"No, really . . ." A smile wiped across her face, "Well, okay. It does sound pretty good."

She flipped off the hood, revealing her shoulder-length brown hair. She moved her head swirling it loose around her face. It was a face that seemed chiseled with high cheekbones and full lips. Her deep brown eyes sparkled with animation. When she slipped off the raincoat, the tight blue sweater and plaid skirt optimized her figure.

"By the way, I'm David Barfield."

She stuck out her hand. "Leslie—Leslie Herrington."

It was difficult to take my eyes off her to look for a booth. I tripped over the leg of a chair, stumbling slightly before regaining my balance and composure. "Let's sit here." I pointed to an empty booth toward the back of the long room. "How about a bite to eat? You can take a little more time and the rain may slack off."

"Hey, remember, I'm the one who's got the umbrella. But – yeah, a bagel and cream cheese would be great."

I thought that an odd request at a great Mexican café.

She sipped the coffee, looking up occasionally. "I haven't seen you around these parts before. What's your reason for having a mid-afternoon snack here on the River walk?"

"I had an afternoon off and I love to come down here to browse." I leaned back against the soft cushion. "I'm stationed at Randolph—I'm an instructor pilot out there."

"Oh, where's home?"

"Little ole wide spot in the road—Bogalusa, Louisiana. And you?"

"Killeen, up near Waco. How long have you been visitin' the great state of Texas?"

"Just got here from the 'Land of The Morning Calm'."

"Korea?"

"Yeah."

"That wasn't too good—was it?"

"Well, it could have been worse. Most of my pilot training class did a tour over there." I laughed. "That's history now. We'll have to wait for the next war."

"That's not particularly funny." She looked at me questioningly, making me wonder what she wanted to ask. Sliding to the end of the booth, and standing hastily, she smiled. "Thanks for the coffee, bagel, and conversation. Gotta go deplete my checking account."

"Thanks for keeping me dry—but we just began what could've been an interesting conversation. What're you doing tonight?"

Her hair flowed gracefully as she shook her head, indicating her answer before she spoke. "I've got a date. But thanks for asking." She turned and started walking quickly toward the door.

"Wait." She didn't turn around. I ran after her, taking her arm gently. "Okay, I buy that about tonight. What about tomorrow?"

She cocked her head, taking on a look of exasperation. "I'll probably be seeing the same friend tomorrow too. Besides . . ."

"Don't say 'no' so quickly." I interrupted. "Look, I'll settle for another cup of coffee and a chance to finish our conversation."

"The conversation was finished. You just didn't hear the last period—and exclamation point."

"Not funny. How about meeting me here Saturday?" I glanced at my watch before finishing the sentence, "Saturday at two-fifteen."

She gave a fleeting look at the door as if to leave without answering. She looked over her shoulder, her eyes sparkling, a smile slowly emerging. "Okay, Saturday. Two fifteen." The smile evaporated. "I can only stay a few minutes." She vanished in the assembled crowd.

Saturday I arrived an hour early and strolled around the River Walk to make sure I didn't miss her. I walked next to the water and the colorful riverboats winding their way through the canal with gawking tourist taking in the sights. I constantly looked around, thinking I might catch a glimpse of her as she approached. The crowds moved about, talking, laughing, and basking in the sun. It was a warm feeling after three gloomy days. Scanning the people as they moved by made me conscious that I was becoming happier with my new assignment. Something had obviously encroached upon my thinking. Turning back toward the bridge I'd just left, I saw Leslie standing there at the top of the steps, looking incredibly appealing.

"Hey there," she said.

"Hi." I felt rather foolish with such an effusive beginning. *Why couldn't I come up with something more original than that?* I walked deliberately toward her.

"I only have a few minutes. I promised to meet someone." She looked intently at me. "You do understand?"

"Sure. Just glad you could spare a few valuable minutes from your busy, busy schedule."

"If you're gonna be a sarcastic ass, I can go now." The glint in her eyes, along with the body language, indicated a quick temper.

"Just trying to be funny—obviously it didn't come across that way. Let's start over, okay?"

There was no comment as she moved through the door going straight for a table off to the right. "This alright?" There was coolness in her question.

"Sure." I pulled out the chair for her. "What would you like—maybe a taco, one of their great burritos, or something?"

"Just a coke—lots of ice, please." The glance at her watch was too obvious.

We sipped our drinks, an occasional glance at the other, nothing more. The silence was awkward. I waited for an opening, a remark, or a gesture from her. *Enough of this crap.* "Why are you in San Antonio?"

"Long story," she said. "I figured I'd be training horses in Killeen these days, but plans change, people change." She chuckled. "I'm a teacher at Brainerd Middle School."

"Glad to know you're not just here on a visit."

"Well, for this year anyway. I may move to Dallas this summer." She looked up. "Why the Air Force?"

I shrugged. "Hard to explain." Her look told me she was truly interested in the answer, not just making conversation. "I love to fly—really love it."

"It shows in the way you said that." I listened closely to the answer to my next question. Her explanation about growing up in Killeen brought a surprising animation to her voice, disclosing her considerable attachment to the town and its people. I was enthralled with her detailed descriptions of Deerfield and the horses. It promptly assured me it was more than just the place's geography that affected her energy and enthusiasm. The influences of her family, especially her father, must have been decisive in formulating her personality—they were obviously responsible for creating the person sitting opposite me. Until that moment, I never appreciated how environment could be such a dominant component in establishing one's individuality. As I listened, it was obvious that the inhabitants of Deerfield shaped, configured, and delineated Leslie Herrington.

I answered her questions about Bogalusa, delving into my younger days, and circumstances I found important in life. We were engrossed in sharing, listening, digesting narratives that chronicled our past and accounted for the present. Time had no meaning. The disclosure was guileless, each imparting a piece of us, devoid of defenses. It was comfortable.

Leslie touched her watch, looking shocked at the time. "Good lord, we've been here almost two hours. Where did the time go?"

"It had no meaning with this conversation." I touched her hand. "Don't go."

She was already standing, pulling on her coat. "I really have to."

"You mentioned you were going home next weekend. I've got to go to Carswell Air Force Base that weekend. I'll be up there in Fort Worth for a week of simulator indoctrination. Being that I'll be driving very close to Killeen, could I drive you home?"

"Frank has already planned on taking me home. Sorry." She grabbed her purse and started for the door. Unexpectedly she stopped, as if deep in thought, then turned and moved toward the table. "Frank has to hurry back here to prepare a law brief. If you really want to see more of Texas—and you really want to stop by, I don't have any plans Saturday afternoon."

"Great. See you about three o'clock. Is that too soon?"

"I'll tell Mama you're coming—she'll expect you for supper."

"Sounds pretty good to me. See you Saturday." She opened her purse, took out a small note pad, and jotted down an address with a few basic directions. Her hand shot out with the paper, which I took immediately. When I glanced up again, she was gone.


Saturday was a magnificent day, but the weather had absolutely no bearing on how I felt. The dark clouds obscuring the horizon and cold blustering winds would normally have a debilitating affect on a very upbeat attitude. Not today. I was on my way to a new flying experience, mixed with unknown possibilities of a new relationship. The challenges of both were electrifying. I glanced at the road map beside me, getting a better picture of the next checkpoint on U. S. Highway 191. Having never been to Killeen, I wanted to make sure of my navigation when I deviated from the major highway that would take me in to Waco.

The turnoff loomed ahead as I swung a hard right past the sign that read "Killeen 2 miles." I drove toward the edge of town on a drive lined with ante-bellum houses, arrogant survivors of years of semi-neglect, and contemptuous weather. There were a few replacements for those that could not survive either—mostly Victorian architecture. As I got further out, the country opened up with fewer houses and more country-like. The sun was almost behind the trees; light flickered through the leafless branches in staccato bursts. I shielded my eyes from the glare, when I unexpectedly saw the brick gates and a large weathered sign, the lettering still prominent – Deerfield.

The house was a long ranch type, with a porch running the length of the front. It was a combination of stone and board-on-batten. The cream-color wood accentuated the Texas fieldstone. I could see the stable off to the right inside another fenced area.

The bell rang for some time before the door opened. I noticed her eyes first. They were confident and luminous. The sparkling sharpness remained even as they narrowed with her broad smile. Her hair was long and dark, pulled back in a bun, with gray highlights giving it a defined softness. She was statuesque, with softly chiseled features, and a complexion as snow white as a japonica. She reached out to me, saying, "You must be David." The statement was made in a slow-speaking voice, mannered, with prolonged vowels. I felt the calluses in her palm, a contrast to the softness of the top of her hand. "I'm Leslie's mother. Come on in out of this cold. We've been expecting you."

This was my first encounter with Eleanor Herrington, one that made a pronounced imprint upon my memory. Her charm and gentleness were infectious. I liked her immediately, feeling comfortable in her company as if we'd known each other for a long time.

"I see you two've met." Leslie appeared in the room, wearing a faded blue sweatshirt and jeans. "Come in and have some coffee." She moved toward the dining room, gazing back to make sure I was following. "You seemed to like coffee so much the first time I saw you, I figured today's certainly one for a hot cup."

"You read my mind. It's cold as blue blazes out there."


Mrs. Herrington poured the coffee, placed the sugar and cream close by and quickly excused herself. Leslie took her cup in both hands, cradling it as she peered over the top, staring across the table as if analyzing me. I said nothing as I studied her face. Lowering the cup into the saucer, she smiled. "How 'bout I show you around the place?"

"I'd like that." "It won't take long. When we had to sell off the ranch last spring, we planned to keep ten acres. As it turned out, we kept almost twenty. We got lucky in the price and were able to keep enough pasture for the horses."

We ambled out to the stables. Leslie eased open the door and flipped the light switch. Horse sounds and smells were evident. A large black head, with a prominent white streak running down the center of its forehead, shot through the opening. Leslie came alive. "Hi there, fella." She rubbed its nose and kissed it. "Meet Rambler. He's been my horse for thirteen years."

I patted his nose. "Hey, Rambler. You're a beautiful horse."

She smiled at me, then him, and gave Rambler another hug. "I love this animal." She spun around. "Now, how 'bout a quick tour of Killeen?"

"Okay, with me. I went through it pretty fast and didn't see that much."

"Killeen is pretty dang small – you didn't miss much."

We drove and talked, settling into a relaxed feeling about each other. Leslie was vivacious in descriptions of her world. She would stop in the middle of a comment, without warning, and pop a question about some portion of my life. She digested the answer, usually following it up with another question. She seemed particularly interested in the Louisiana bayou country. Just as hastily, she would spin around and point out another landmark of her growing up. Suddenly, she would roll down the window and shout a greeting to someone as they waved back. There would be a speedy explanation how they fit into her life.

Her expression changed abruptly. "You have yet to explain why you decided to be a pilot. Was it some burning challenge—maybe just the thrill of bucking the odds?"

"God, you have a way of asking a question that immediately puts me on the defensive. I told you once before—I love to fly. That answer's not good enough?"

"Oh, wow. Aren't you touchy on that subject?"

"No more so than me asking you why you have such an unnatural affection for your home town and horses."

Her eyes flashed fire, as she glared back. There was silence for several minutes. She looked straight at me. "At least you recognize what's important in my life—there's absolutely nothing unnatural about it—even if you do have that distorted view."

"Why the devil do you set me up like this?" I shook my head. "I shouldn't fall into that trap so easily."

"You didn't fall —you plunged."

"Truce?" I asked with a vague smile.

"Okay. Truce."


Dinner was honey-baked ham, rice, lima beans, and candied sweet potatoes, followed by the most delicious pecan pie I ever tasted. The conversation matched Mrs. Herrington's cuisine—homemade and down-home good. I dabbed my mouth with the napkin. "That was delicious, Mrs. Herrington. Thanks for having me."

"David, everyone calls me Ellen—short for Eleanor, which I hate. Mrs. Herrington sounds like what someone I don't know very well, or like very much, would call me."

"Okay, 'Mrs. Herr . . . Miss Ellen."

"Lordy, you just won't do, David.

"I reckon. And by the way, that pecan pie recipe should be copyrighted."

"It is," she said, "the original is in the safe in Atlanta along with the Coca Cola recipe."

I looked up rapidly at the comment, and then realized her quick wit was one more attribute passed along to her daughter. The evening was not at all stilted or awkward. I was surprised at how thoroughly I was enjoying being there, laughing and making small talk about every subject that popped up. Long after the meal had ended, we sat around the table, sipping coffee and talking about Southern idiosyncrasies.

I glanced at my watch. "I've enjoyed the evening but I'd better head out to Fort Worth—it's getting late."

I pushed back my chair, as Mrs. Herrington reached over and took my hand. "So glad you could stop and spend some time with us, David. We'll expect you back soon." Her eyes cut toward Leslie and back at me. Leslie stood there with a smile and no comment, and then moved around the table until she was standing beside me.

"Thanks again, Miss Ellen. I'm glad that pecan pie recipe is locked away. That's way too good to fall into the hands of Yankees."


Leslie and I walked slowly to the car. With her that near, the night air lost some of its chill. She glanced up as I reached for the door handle. "It's only about two hours to Fort Worth. You won't be too tired when you get there."

I stood there looking at her face in the dim light of the porch lamp. She was beautiful—absolutely beautiful. Suddenly, I put my arms around her and pulled her close. Our lips met as she reached her arms around my neck, pulling me even closer. I nuzzled her neck, still holding her close to my body. I didn't want to let go. I knew I had never felt like this in my life. My mouth was near her ear, as I whispered, "Funny things happen when you share an umbrella with a stranger."

"Should I be more careful in the future?"

"You never know the consequences of these things"

"That's very true."

I held her tightly, and there was no effort on her part to leave. Gradually I released my grip, holding her at arm's length. "Can I see you next Saturday, when I get back?"

"Yes," she said softly. "Call me."

"Okay. See you next week." I left her standing there, then suddenly swiveled around. "Wait. I don't know your phone number."

She laughed. "Wait just a minute." She ran back into the house then reappeared with a small piece of paper. "Here, now don't lose it in Fort Worth."

"Don't worry." I leaned over and kissed her quickly.

As I drove off, I looked into the cold dark night just beyond the dancing headlights. At that moment, I realized I found something very special in Leslie Ann Herrington.


I finished the Carswell simulator course before noon on Friday. Feelings, like that of a teenager anticipating his first date, kept me in an energized mood as I drove. The miles disappeared magically with thoughts of seeing Leslie. I drove too much above the speed limit, but I made it back to Randolph by late afternoon

I rushed through the door of my BOQ room and dropped the bag. I grabbed the phone and dialed the number on the piece of paper held in my other hand.

"Hello."

"Hi there. I just got back from Fort Worth and wondered if I could interest you in some Mexican tonight? I know just the place."

"Sorry. I already have plans."

"Change 'em."

"Frank is taking me to a Pops Concert, after that –." There was a period of silence, then, "Why the devil am I justifying this to you?"

"Could it be because you gave me your number on this piece of paper I'm holding, and the fact you told me to call – that you'd like to see me when I got back?"

"Saturday. Check your calendar, Mister Aviator, it's only Friday."

"Sorry. Didn't know I'd have to get in a long and unruly line to see you. I . . ." There was only a dial tone on the other end.

My ego was flattened. Holding the buzzing phone, I couldn't make up my mind if I was mad as hell, or bewildered. It was obvious Leslie wasn't sitting by the phone in anticipation of getting a call from me. I decided to be mad as hell.

Saturday morning the sun beamed through the window, rousing me from a satisfying sleep. I stretched awake anticipating the day. My thinking was in a more buoyant mood than last night. I glanced at my watch to make sure it was a decent hour for calling, tipped the phone off the hook and dialed Leslie's number.

"Hello."

"Thought I'd give it another chance. Something seemed wrong with your phone yesterday."

"Oh, it was working fine. It hangs up automatically when there's an asinine idiot on the other end."

"Sorry it can't detect humor. You'd better get it tweaked. Now, before it cuts off again – how about dinner and a movie tonight?"

"Well . . . Okay. About seven-thirty?"

"Seven."

"Okay then, seven."


We were together constantly during the next nine months, and Frank was never mentioned again. Spring came and left unnoticed as the months flew by. We were too involved with living to perceive changes in the seasons. Under that façade of snappish wit, Leslie was the most vivacious, intelligent and caring person I had ever known. Feelings that took over my thoughts that first night I left her at Deerfield never varied. I was in love with Leslie Herrington, but I felt her hesitation at the most intimate times. Even though warm and sensual, there was an enigma about her. I felt this keenly when we were at Deerfield. There were ghosts there, changing her into a more diffident personality. I felt less close to Leslie at that ranch than anywhere else. Deerfield's roots anchored her to that piece of earth, and freeing her only when we could escape its gravitational-like pull. Geographical separation caused a noticeable transformation in her personality, yet she was never aware of this.


As summer came, there was a change in Leslie as noticeable as the season. She opened her heart and mind to our closeness. That was when I knew we had achieved the closeness that defines love. I remembered it as a warm August afternoon. The kind that glides across your being, a carefree feeling that life is as it should be. I was consumed by the feeling of complete contentment. We were at the Gulf, near Corpus Christi, walking along the dunes, digging our toes into the loose sand, listening to the gentle crash of the waves. We turned and strolled slowly up the boardwalk toward the resort. We walked in silence, as if any utterance would break the spell. As we approached the steps leading to the tall porch, I pulled her close and held her tightly. "Will you marry me?" The gray spindles of moss hanging from the live oak's low-lying branches formed the backdrop for the question. I wanted this moment, these surroundings, to be indelibly imprinted on my mind. It would be hard to forget this place or the moment she whispered, "Yes."

The drive back to Killeen was a blur of emotions, both of us immersed in our own contentment. It made the drive seem much shorter than the four hours it took. The gravel and dirt on the drive crunched beneath the tires as the car slowed to a stop beside the house. Leslie jumped out and ran around the car. She took my arm as we walked down the walk, her hair swinging, and a constant smile there every time I glanced at her. For that moment my existence was complete. We walked arm in arm to the door, as Mrs. Herrington came out to welcome us.

"How was the trip back?" She gave Leslie a hug and took my hand. "I know you enjoyed the old city and the Gulf. The bay is a wonderful sight this time of year."

"Great trip," said Leslie.

"Come on in and tell me all about it over a cup of coffee." She motioned with her head as she held open the screen door.

Leslie held tightly to my arm as we walked to the dining room. We glanced at each other as if we couldn't contain ourselves. I pulled the chair out for Mrs. Herrington at the head of the table, as Leslie bounced around to the other side. She was vibrant, full of energy, and moving constantly. Then she sat and stared at me across the table as I sat next to her mother. It was easy remembering Leslie's face, those crinkly wrinkles at her eyes as she smiled. Her glance warmed my insides. Mrs. Herrington smiled knowingly as she looked back and forth. She straightened all of a sudden. "Leslie, would you do me a favor and please take Lou that cake I baked this morning." She glanced at her watch. "Lord, I almost forgot and she'll wonder what happened to that cake." She looked at me. "She's having the women's auxiliary or some such thing this afternoon."

Leslie jumped up. "I'll only be a minute; Aunt Lou's just a mile and a half down the road. You two can talk while I'm gone." Leslie looked back, smiling as she left through the arched doorway. She winked and slid around the pocket doors, only her hand still visible. There was a wave of her fingers before her hand too disappeared.

Mrs. Herrington set her coffee cup down, looking questioningly at me. "You look like you have something you want to talk about, David. Am I right?"

"Well, I thought we'd be into the third cup of coffee before you hit me up with that kinda question." I looked straight at her. "I'm sure you've probably guessed by our foolish actions what I'm about to say." I shuffled in the seat, wishing the subject hadn't come up so rapidly. But Mrs. Herington had her own timing in mind and that was that. "You probably guessed I asked Leslie to marry me when we were at the Gulf?" I looked for the response, hoping she'd pick it up from there. She smiled, took a sip of coffee and let me twirl helplessly in the statement without comment. I swallowed hard. "I realize Leslie's twenty-four and this seems a little Victorian to be asking your permission. Reckon I just think that way—I—well, it does make a difference to me what you think."

She carefully placed the cup in the saucer, reached over and patted my hand. "David, I've known you for almost a year now. I had a good notion, a long time ago, about what kind of character was there. The point I want to make right now is important. It'll tell you more about Leslie and me than just the simple statement it is." She straightened back against the chair, looking very serious. I abruptly had visions of hearing the worst. My imagination was out of control as I waited for her to continue.

"Leslie's made her own decisions since she was a young girl; her father was responsible for that. Fortunately, for all of us, she always made the right ones. There were two things that resulted from the way she was reared: she became a self-reliant, independent person, and I came to trust her judgment explicitly." I waited for a change in the serious expression, a look that would tell me what I needed to hear. But the smile didn't return. "David, when Leslie told me she loved you, there was no endorsement or character witness, by anyone, that would tell me more. If Leslie is in love with you, then I approve." The smile appeared like magic.

"Thanks. Naturally that's what I wanted—what I expected to hear. But I still needed to hear it."

"That's why I've always liked you, David. You're embodied with that ole southern gentleman instinct that's fast disappearing. Not only that . . ." The door opened rapidly, interrupting the sentence, as Leslie bolted into the dining room.

"Looks like you two finished your coffee while I was gone." She smiled as she looked back and forth at us. I began to feel close to Leslie's mother that afternoon, that minute. Our relationship continues to transcend the usual mothers-in-law's relevance.

We were married in the First Methodist Church of Killeen January 5th 1956.

The last time I saw Miss Ellen was during our short leave before reporting to Pope Air Force Base. Moving every two years, demands of Air Force living and those miniscule snares of life slowly and insidiously drove a wedge between two people. It crept upon us over the last two years because we let it. Apathy was the enemy.

Deerfield was supposed to be a relaxing leave, but there was the usual anxiety in a military move, combined with the fact that Leslie hated leaving Florida. The tension was slow to abate during that week. Leslie became reticent at Deerfield and I reinforced her silence by saying things that were better left unsaid. When we talked, we snapped at each other over trivial things that should have been overlooked.

That Sunday lunch was the last meal before leaving for North Carolina. We finished the pork loin, scalloped potatoes, butter beans and sliced tomatoes and let our backs fall against the dining room chairs. Miss Ellen pushed the dessert plate away. "You two go rest before you leave. You've got lots of things to gather up and get together – it's along drive ahead of you."

"Nonsense, Mamma. I'm going to clean up here – no arguments. You two go sit on the porch and catch one of those breezes."

Miss Ellen and I walked to the porch, the door banging shut after us. She plopped down in here favorite rocker and I stretched out in the swing. We sat silently as the soft wind blew across us. She stared at the large rose bushes as if analyzing each branch. "Those old things should have been trimmed back a long time ago." I nodded. She turned her head my way, a smile across her face. "David, I can see you're both on edge. You and –."

"Miss Ellen, "I interrupted. "We've a lot to figure out right about now. This move didn't help. We'll work it out and things'll settle down as soon as we get through this blasted move."

"I'm sure it will. You know, David, I've always wondered why it's the little things that are so difficult to cope with in life. We stiffen our backs and handle the big problems when they come our way – with a resolve we usually didn't know we had." She looked at the roses as if she were talking to them. "But pesky little problems wear us thin and cause us the most bother." She cocked her head, still staring at the large flowering bushes. "I think I will cut those things back this fall. Don't you think that'd be the thing to do?"

I chuckled. "Yes'm, those bushes definitely need trimming."

Leslie bounded through the door, waving me to follow. "I want to ride Rambler one more time before we leave – want to come with me?"

I jumped up following her toward the barn. "I reckon I'll ride old what's his name."

"Velvet," she said.

We saddled the two horses and rode down the rutted trail to the creek. I'd never felt at ease on horseback, but rode occasionally to pacify Leslie. We stopped by the shoals where the water rippled over the rocks, and let the horses drink. We lay back on the cool grass and were quiet. I thought about Miss Ellen's comment, and knew it was up to both of us to break this cycle. *Reach out, you simple ass. Make a move – do something.*

I rolled toward her, taking her hand. "Why don't we do better in talking things out?"

"Sometimes you shut me out."

"Not intentionally."

"But you do."

"I reckon I get defensive."

"I do the same thing," she said. "My protective instinct takes over."

"I'll rephrase it. Let's both make a better damn effort."

"It won't be easy, David. We've done some damage."

I squeezed her hand. "We can try."

"I wonder if it's possible," she said.

"Anything's possible."


Later, we loaded the car and went back to tell Miss Ellen goodbye. She hugged Leslie for a long time, and then took my arm at the door. She leaned into my ear as Leslie walked on to the car. "You two know what's important, don't you?"

A grin spread across my face. "I certainly do."

We waved out the windows as we drove down the gravel drive. The house grew smaller in the rear view mirror, Miss Ellen standing by the porch, still waving.


Adjusting to the move was difficult for both of us, especially Leslie. She was left to deal with the movers and utility companies while I was flying every day. For several weeks I was deployed with the 82nd Airborne Division on Swift Strike Three exercise and left her with all the decisions on the house we were building. Leslie was the most organized human I had ever known, and was right on top of every detail. She managed the house, negotiated getting all utilities setup, and ran for President of the Officers' Wives Club. She won.

Four months later, as we planned a leave to spend two weeks at Deerfield, I got a call to report to operations immediately. The sudden national emergency required three squadrons to take off within four hours. I left Leslie again, as we said goodbye beside operations. It was a way of life for us. For the next 32 days we sat in South Florida waiting for the "go signal" that would have us land in a Cuban cane field with the 82nd Airborne Division. The waiting worked on our patience and anxiety. Every day we anticipated a launch into the unknown of fighting on a small island. We sat for hours on the tarmac; auxiliary power plugged in, radios on, troopers loaded, ready for what we believed was the inevitable.

We didn't invade Cuba in the fall of 1962 and Leslie and I never got to Deerfield.

These separations were taxing on emotions and constancy, and I was convinced the mathematics of our marriage made quantum physics seem simple by comparison. These deployments kept me in a cynical mood, and Leslie bore the brunt of my frustration. We carried on our lives in robotic fashion, watching our relationship crumble, slowly, and steadily. We were not able to breach the wall we crafted so skillfully. Instead of reaching out, we reached for another block for the wall. We were caught in a vortex and couldn't grab a lifeline that would save us. It happened insidiously.

# 3

## Hawaii

The interior of the fuselage was a mess. There were bags of all shapes strapped down, a bulky green Benson tank, took up most of the interior, a fifty-five-gallon drum of oil strapped to each side, and a hammock strung diagonally across the top of the Benson tank. I stood looking at the general disorder around me, wondering just how ridiculous this looked. "What's with the damn hammock, Sergeant Franklin?" The Loadmaster leaned against the Benson tank, exhaustion showing in his face. He was in no hurry to answer my question.

"Sir, this stuff's all strapped down for weight and balance. It wasn't easy figuring our load with this damn thing half-full of one hundred-thirty octane." He slapped the tank. "The hammock was my idea. You'll appreciate that thing before this trip's over."

I smiled at the Sergeant, watching his expression change to one less tense. Jocko Franklin had an expressive mouth, large and flexible, that he used to wrap around words that always stretched into extra syllables. He spoke fluent Tennessee hill country. His expression was one of profound melancholy, changed only by his broad smile. I watched as the smile wiped slowly across his face with my obvious acceptance. "You did good, Jocko. We'll use that damn hammock you've rigged." I slapped him on the back. "But let me tell you, if I roll outta that friggin contraption, you're in for one very long trip." His laughter roared through the aircraft.

Zack jumped onto the aircraft and made his way to the copilot seat. He busied himself checking radio settings and completing the take-off and landing data card. The "TOLD" card was vital information. It told you at what airspeed to rotate, the expected airspeed at liftoff, total runway before airborne, and most importantly—when to abort. Zack looked the card over one more time then placed it in the center of the console. He wheeled around. "Hey, David, it's ten minutes to start engine time. You ready?"

"Be up front in a minute." I was too busy looking at the youthful second lieutenant climbing on board with an unwieldy briefcase and four sacks he kept shifting from hand to hand as he scrambled up the ladder.

"I'm ready to go, Captain. Got all the charts for the over-water legs and a few things here to supplement those in-flight rations we were issued."

"Well, Nav, you can rest on this first one. It's all airways to California. Lieutenant Johnson, your work'll begin when we leave the States." I looked him up and down. "What's your first name, Lieutenant?"

He fumbled with his load as two sacks hit the deck. Cookies, candy bars and Slim-Jims scattered across the deck. He bent down, grabbing at his cache, glancing up in my direction. "Tom, sir," he blurted, as Jocko bent down to assist in his retrieval. Chuck Stone leaped on board, followed by Sergeant Picardo. Jocko pulled the door closed and latched the lever, sealing us in the flying fuel tank.

"Everything checked fine on runup this morning, Captain," Picardo stated as he moved toward the cockpit.

"Well, reckon we can start engines." I quickly checked my watch, noting six minutes until we were to begin this mission that had taken over our existence. Specific start engine times, followed by taxi time, and a precise time to line-up on the runway had been spelled out. I threw my hat onto the seat beside Chuck. "I'll take the first leg. How 'bout we rotate every two hours?"

"You're the AC, David. I'm just along for the ride." He threw his feet up on a B-4 bag, leaned back against the canvas seat and pulled his hat over his eyes.

There was a methodical use of checklists as the engines revved to life, and taxi instructions received. I cocked the aircraft into the wind as we completed the run up, listening for anything abnormal. Zack called off items in a rhythmic manner, with me quickly providing the correct response. Zack's finger slid down the list. "Mixture—rich; props—full increase rpm; rotating beacon—on; boost pumps—high; cowl flaps—open; flaps—twenty degrees; radios—set departure frequency."

He closed the checklist and pointed his gloved finger at me. "Waiting on the tower, David."

"Chalk five, Pope. You're cleared onto the active and hold. Departure in one minute."

"Roger, Chalk five holding."

I brought the throttles forward to sixty-two inches manifold pressure, flipped both water injections on, getting a positive indication. Zack nodded. I brought the throttles up to sixty-three inches of manifold pressure as the aircraft vibrated its recognition of the raw power.

"Chalk Five, Pope. Cleared for take-off."

"Roger, tower, Chalk five rolling," Zack snapped back.

I released the brakes, letting the engines take charge. The aircraft roared down the runway, leaping into the air at four thousand feet. A quick check of instruments showed all in the "green." "Gear up." I stuck my right thumb in the air. "Flaps up. Climb power set."

"Roger. Gear up, flaps up, cowl flaps trail, oil cooler doors trail, water injection off," Zack responded as his head swiveled in a crosscheck of instruments. It was a good feeling having Zack in the right seat. I smiled in his direction and he grinned back.

We banked hard right out of traffic and I glanced down for one more look at the lights of the Base. I watched them growing dimmer in the early morning darkness. The faint illumination abruptly disappeared as we were engulfed in the dense cloud layer, climbing to altitude.

Chuck banked right over the center of Los Angeles taking a northerly heading along the published airway to Sacramento and McClellan Air Force Base. Zack called in our position report to Los Angeles control as Chuck loosened his straps, lifted the armrest, and moved out of the left seat. He bounded down the ladder and arched his back in transition to standing again, as I brushed past him on the way up. "I'll take it on in." The seat was almost comfortable as I strapped myself in for the last part of this leg. Zack banked hard left. "Hey, get a load of those houses down there. Does everybody in Southern California have a swimming pool? I don't think we had one blasted pool in the whole town of Chadron."

"I always wondered if you folks had indoor plumbing up in that corner of Nebraska. If someone actually had a pool up there, it'd most likely freeze over in July."

"Back in Bogalusa, Louisiana, you guys probably swam in the local swamp—didn't need swimming pools."

"You're right, Zack. But every now and then, we had to move over, swift-like, for a 'gator. It made for some fast swimmers and weeded out the slow ones. In fact, fourteen of us boys started school together and only ten made it to high school." I grinned, "But those ten could swim like Tarzan."

Zack smiled, slapping me on the arm. "Glad to see you can still initiate a chuckle." He squinted. "Is this deployment getting to you? Something's been working on you."

"Nothing that won't straighten itself out."


Tall, wiry, sandy hair and a large boyish smile, Zachary Sullivan Williams immediately intrigued me. His 6 feet 2, well built frame was carried with a relaxed self-consciousness, avoiding being too military. It was a brutally cold day back in November when we first flew together. He was more instructor than co-pilot, having six hundred hours in the C-123, but he never let his superior knowledge of the aircraft become apparent. Instead of a comment or even a suggestion, he would gently adjust a throttle, turn off a switch, or make an alignment of the prop controls, as an incidental action, while talking away. He subtly honed my skills as an aircraft commander. His wit and upbeat attitude were infectious. Every facet of Zack's personality indicated he was an enemy of the ordinary. As we built up flight time together, we thought about flying in the same way, instinctively, naturally, always anticipating each other. He made my transition from being alone in a fighter back to multi-engine tolerable. Zack was fundamental to my ability to think as part of a cohesive unit, instead of the loner concept of an F-4 cockpit.

After landing, the aircraft lined up in designated spots. Fuel trucks circled in close, waiting to unload into the belly of the C-123's, and then fill the large wing tanks. Busses lined up for the aircrew. Word spread rapidly down the line for all pilots and navigators to assemble in two hours for a briefing.

"Glad they gave us all that time to check into the BOQ and shower. Maybe we'll even have time to eat before we take-off tomorrow." Zack grumbled.

"Dip into one of those sacks Tom's carrying and you probably find a full meal."

"Tom may have to resort to one of those cold in-flight rations tomorrow. He won't have a chance to refurbish his gedunk stash before we take-off."

Aircrew, dressed in civvies, looking like a bunch ready for a tailgate party, filed into the large briefing room. "Do Navigators take their briefcase of maps to the latrine with 'em?" Zack asked, as Tom sat beside him and unloaded the unwieldy case. Tom looked surprised at the question, not yet knowing how to take him. Zack's sardonic wit was obviously lost on the young lieutenant. A quick judgment of Tom's personality made me guess it would take us at least to Wake Island before he got a handle on Zack's nature. I hoped he'd last that long.

Lt. Col. Norwood cleared his throat. "Major Lynch will cover a few specifics, but before he does, I want to emphasize a couple of points. Sixteen aircraft will leave the States tomorrow at 0530 I intend for all sixteen to land at DaNang on the twenty-ninth. Safety, of course is paramount, and I realize there's some inherent danger to this mission—but I don't want aborts along the way for trivial write-ups. I don't intend to look back at the completion of this gaggle and find aircraft scattered between here and the Philippines. I'm sure each aircraft commander understands the importance I place on this subject." He looked across the room for reactions and seeing none, said: "Major, it's all yours."

"Take-off is at zero five-thirty, ten minutes between flights. This is where it gets more difficult. There's little wiggle room in aircraft performance. Take-offs from here, and on into the Philippines, will be with full Benson tanks. You'll exceed gross allowable weight by several thousand pounds. This is where we'll be pushing the envelope. Even though you'll be exceeding aircraft limitations, the data furnished by Fairchild states it's still within the bird's capability." Major Lynch glanced around the room, as if he was hesitant to bring up the next point in his briefing. "There's a two-hour span of time on these two long legs, where you can't make it either way on one engine. The point of no return becomes quite long. If you have an emergency, I can't tell you aircraft commanders how to handle the situation. We do know there's never been a successful ditching of a C-123." His sphinx-like expression changed, his brow puckered, giving him a resolute look. "I have complete confidence in you experienced aircraft commanders – that's why you were selected. I know damn well we're asking for the maximum from crews and aircraft, but we'll get it done. Flight commanders take over. Good luck."

Zack continued to stare at Lynch, his elbow nudging me. "Yep, that man's definitely emotionally constipated."

I shot a look of disdain toward Zack. "B Flight, I'd like a minute over here in the corner." I shouted, pointing to the corner by the door.

They gathered quickly, a motley looking group, most in loose-hanging sweatshirts, jeans and loafers. I glanced around to make sure we had everyone assembled. "Just got a couple of things to cover. I'll fly lead in the third launch, with Rusty on my wing. The second element will be Phil, with Rick flying his wing. I recommend we change lead every four to five hours to give the navigators a break. Each element will be virtually on your own to reach Hickam. A reminder on take-off tomorrow—make sure you use as much runway as needed to get your airspeed higher than normal rotation speed. In case you lose an engine—you'll need it." I glanced at Phil Merc, off to one side, looking toward the door. He wasn't listening or responding to anything said. "Any questions?"

"Yeah, David, reckon we've got time for a drink before the cutoff. Maybe stretch it a bit with just a couple for dinner?" Rick Hafenback asked.

I glanced at my watch. "You'd have to be eatin' right now. You know the rules—no alcohol twelve hours before take-off. Rick, I'm not about to lead you guys by the hand. You know the rules. Okay, see you for another sunrise." I glanced at Phil. "Could I see you a minute.

After the others left, Phil stayed behind. He leaned against the wall and stared at me.

A thick silence followed as we measured each other.

"Okay, Phil. Let's get the problem out in the open. Your attitude was obvious to the rest of the flight."

He glared at me. "I don't need someone explaining the intricacies of an overweight take-off, how to make an adjusting turn in weather formation, or what to do in emergency procedures." His eyes narrowed. "I just finished a tour in Alaska, and have logged twelve hundred hours in this bird. How many you got, David?"

"Enough for these silver bars to say I'm your Flight Commander." I aimed a finger at his chest. "You've got an attitude problem, but from now on you best act like you're part of the flight."

"Damnation, there goes my self-esteem. I did so live for your approval," he sneered.

I moved to his nose, "You better damn well hope for my approval or stand by for what I told you on day one—I can be one bad-ass SOB if that's what you want. Tell you what – when we get to DaNang, make sure you request reassignment to another flight. Until then, shape up your act – and damn quick-like. Understand?"

"Loud and clear," he shouted as he moved to the door.

Zack sawed into his filet, never looking up. "How'd you handle it with our bad boy, Phil? I know you could hardly keep from chewing him a new one during the briefing." He placed the bite in his mouth and started chewing as he looked up for my answer.

"That might be the trouble spot in this flight." I sipped my coffee. "There appears to be some big-time resentment of his low-time Flight Commander from an Alaskan bush pilot, with loads of time in the C-123."

Zack's knife and fork hit the plate, as he leaned toward me. "That bastard has some nerve. You've got more time upside down, at thirty-five thousand feet, in a fighter, than he's got in the goddamn Air Force. I'll set him straight, Coach."

"I'll handle it, Zack—but thanks for the support." I glanced at my watch. "I'm like Rick, wish we could've had time for a couple of bourbons."

"A couple of drinks would've taken the edge off." Zack's face lost its perpetual smile. "You definitely need the edges honed a bit. "Something's eatin' at you and it sure as hell's not Phil—you could have him for breakfast." His mouth drew into a straight line, his jaw flexing muscles, as his eyes narrowed. "What's really bothering you, David?"

The room swirled as I thought about Leslie. I had almost blocked it out with thinking about the mission at hand, and didn't need Zack bringing it up now. "Christ, you won't let it go, will you?"

"Nope, Coach, sure won't. I've got to live with your butt up there in the left seat for a long time. You could be having epileptic fits for all I know."

I couldn't help but laugh. "Okay, you inquisitive SOB. Leslie and I may be getting a divorce."

Zack's stunned look was sincere; he was unprepared for the statement. "No way. You sure as hell knew how to cover it around the rest of us." He stared hard at me, thinking about his next question. "David, are you messin' around or something?"

"Hell no." I frowned at him. "Frankly, it's something that might be beyond us—the two of us just not capable of getting there." I took a sip of coffee and looked at his grimace. "I know you have no idea what the hell I mean." I put the cup down. "Now, did you call Christy tonight, before we leap off tomorrow? And, by the way, how's she taking that lost vacation on the beach?"

"Jane."

"Who?"

"Jane, not Christy. We ended that several months ago. Jane's a doll, sharp as a tack, with an awesome personality."

"God, I can't keep up with you. That's how you describe every woman you go with. You time relationships like a stick of gum—spit it out when the flavor's gone."

"Good shot there, Coach. You're gettin' pretty damn good at low blows."

"I had a good instructor." Reaching down, I drained the last few drops of coffee from the cup. I watched carefully for his reaction. "Zack, did you know Lt. Col. Norwood before the briefing yesterday?"

He slid his chair out. "Tomorrow's coming quick. Let's get some sleep."


There was a faint glow above the mountains to the east, the indefinite light showing softly above their shoulder. The bus jostled half-awake crews toward the long line of aircraft. I knew the interminable day of flying would take us into the night. The thought of seventeen hours in the air was bewildering. The repetitious sea and clouds would provide too much time to think, the last thing I needed. The bus jolted to a stop and four of us moved sluggishly toward the front, swinging bags in front of us. Jocko was busy inside the aircraft, his solemn expression unchanged, checking tie-downs. Sergeant Picardo met us with the aircraft forms in hand. "No major write-ups, Captain, just a slight oil leak on number two—nothing to worry about."

I took the forms, signing off on the minor discrepancies, then threw my bag up to Jocko. In a spreading sunrise that began to light the area, we positioned ourselves for the rest of this day and a half, enclosed in the innards of a cylindrical aluminum tube, accompanied by one very large fuel tank. The roar of engines down the flight line became a din of noise. Checking my watch, I nodded to Chuck for the checklist. We started engines and taxied behind Alpha four. He set all the radio frequencies, completed checklists, and we began our run up. I checked the mag drop on the number one engine and began the number two check. As I flipped the mag switch to left and then to both, I took a second look. Switching to left mag again, I saw Sergaent Picardo's head shoot in beside mine. I flipped the switch again to both and then to left. "That's almost a one hundred drop on the left mag." Picardo nodded, then reached his hand up and repeated the procedure.

"That's really more than the seventy-five max allowed, Captain. We're way over gross weight and losing an engine would –."

"I know that."

"Changing a row of plugs could correct the problem," said Picardo, "but we'd have to abort for maintenance."

"There's a lot of ocean out there. Hate to become a marathon swimmer today," Chuck said.

"Bravo five, you're cleared onto the runway, hold there." The tower snapped into the headset.

"What's it gonna' be, Captain?" Picardo asked. "Do we abort?"

"No. Complete the checklist."

Chuck stared at me, "Are you sure?"

I knew that I had just made a decision that could get this crew killed. Yet, my gut instinct said we should go. "Complete the damn checklist." I looked over my shoulder. "Hey, Nav, give me our first heading to set in the remote compass."

"First heading is two five seven degrees. I'll give you changes about every twenty to thirty minutes—depending on the winds aloft."

"Chuck, follow me through on the throttles. The TOLD card shows rotation at ninety knots. Call eighty knots and five thousand feet remaining—take a good look at the number two engine 'cause there's no abort pass that point. If we lose an engine, all we can do is pull off the good one and go in straight ahead—with this gross weight we can't fly on one."

"Roger. Take-off check list complete." He switched to tower frequency, and announced we were ready for take-off.

"Roger, Bravo five, McClellan tower, you're cleared for an immediate departure, winds two niner zero, gusting fifteen, altimeter two-niner point three four. Right turn out of traffic, contact departure control on 126.5 immediately after take-off."

"Roger. Bravo five rolling." As I brought the throttles up, I couldn't ignore the gnawing feeling in my stomach. The C-123, loaded to more than three thousands pounds over maximum gross weight, vibrated laboriously down the runway. Airspeed grew steadily but not rapidly. Runway evaporated in front of us as the engines strained with all the power asked of them.

"Eighty knots. Let her roll – no fuckin' abort now." Chuck exclaimed.

My eyes shot back and forth at the airspeed indicator and disappearing runway in front of us. The airspeed indicator inched toward ninety knots as I pushed harder on the throttles. Chuck's voice snapped the announcement. "Ninety-five knots." I hauled back on the controls as the C-123 grabbed at the sky. We were flying. We looked into pure azure as the nose came up past the horizon. The engines labored toward nine thousand feet, as I adjusted my seat back a notch. As altitude increased, the churning in my gut decreased with every foot of sky we put between the ground and this cylindrical fuel tank. It took longer to get to altitude than usual but it was a reassuring sound to throttle back, setting cruise power. I glanced past Chuck to watch Bravo six join in formation.

"Hi, y'all." Rusty called out on UHF. "Take me to Hawaii, Bravo five. My navigator's already asleep."

"Negative perspiration, Bravo two. We've got us a hotshot 'Butter-bar' Lieutenant that can put us right across Waikiki beach," Chuck announced.

There was a quiet time, absolutely no conversation. Chuck sat quietly, adjusting mixtures for maximum range. He tweaked the prop controls to get both synchronized. After about fifteen minutes, he turned to me, leaning on the armrest. "Could I ask you a question, David, and you won't take it the wrong way?"

"Fire away."

"Why didn't you abort with a healthy mag drop on the number two engine? Did Colonel Norwood's words about aborts cloud your thinking?"

Instead of answering immediately, I stared straight ahead at the horizon. My head swiveled toward Chuck. "I thought the mission called for a go – it was my call."

"Listen to me. Don't let Norwood affect your judgment as aircraft commander or pressure you into a bad decision. There's something I know about Colonel Norwood that I believe you should know." He tapped my arm. "This is something only a very few people know about. It's an earth shaker, David. The good Colonel was involved in something that tells you a lot about the man. He pulled this –."

"Hey, Chuck, ready for a break?" Zack interrupted.

Chuck winked at me. "Later." He lifted the armrest and swung his leg over the console. "It's all yours, Zack."

Hour after hour the engines droned their voice of reassurance. The din finally became annoying, driving the sound past the earphones, deep into the brain. Zack and I both constantly tweaked the prop controls. Even in synchronization, the engine noise penetrated the subconscious. Fatigue, its ally, worked its way into the spirit as we looked over a panorama of water. The surf blended into sky in a veil of haze. My thoughts took me away from the tedium as I remembered other times, other places. Leslie filled my dream state.

The droning engines penetrated my momentary cerebral backlash. "Hey, Nav, how about another heading change?"

Sergeant Picardo's unmistakable laughter permeated the headset. "He's in the back, Captain. He's been pukin' his guts out back there, off and on, for hours." He laughed harder. "Reckon the in-flight rations didn't set too well with him."

"How long has he been sick?"

"About the last ten hours—even when he took breaks—if that's what he called 'em. He'd take a fix, then run back to the rear, then come right back computing heading and winds."

"Why didn't he say something? We'd let Bravo two take the whole leg."

"Well, that tells you something, Captain—he is a plucky one."

I looked at Zack, who must have been thinking the same thing I was. There was more to Second Lieutenant Tom Johnson than met the eye. "Ease up on him a little bit now, Zack."

"C'mon, don't spoil him now, just as I'm gettin' him broken in." He chuckled. "Now he knows what the rest of us already knew—those in-flights are your basic third-degree colon cleaner."

"You're a hard case, Zack."

Just as I was ready to swap off with Chuck, the intercom came alive. "New heading two-eight-six, ETA Hickam, twenty-one thirty-five."

"Hey Nav, you sure about that ETA? We're gonna shave about twenty minutes off this leg."

No reply from Tom as I looked over my shoulder to see if he was darting for the back again. He leaned forward, his thin, gaunt face scrunched up tight. Pale, haggard eyes looked out from reddened lids like a bullfrog. "You can call me, Johnson, Lieutenant, Tom or SOB—but for God's sake don't keep saying 'Hey, Nav'. I hate that."

"Sorry, I didn't know it bothered you."

"That's okay, Captain, I just don't feel too good. As for the ETA, it's good. We've had a shift in the winds to a quartering cross-wind for the last couple of hours."

"Hey, Nav, that heading was two eight six, right?" Zack's voice crackled.

"Shit. What's the use?" Tom's voice trailed off.

The lights on the horizon were faint and indistinct, but we knew Oahu was dead ahead. The lights of boats became more numerous, like incandescent spots on the dark ocean. The weariness of 17 hours in the air was abating rapidly with thoughts of Honolulu and Waikiki Beach. Chuck, sitting in the right seat, swiveled around, bearing a broad smile. "Listen, I've been through this drill before. I learned the hard way the last time. If we land number five, there are crews ahead of us for everything. I've got a suggestion." He looked at me waiting for some indication of acceptance.

"Whatcha' got in mind?" I asked.

"As soon as you cut engines, we won't wait for transportation—Tom and I'll bolt to the passenger counters inside Base Operations. They have representatives there for Fort De Russy and rental cars. I'll arrange reservations at Fort De Russy while Tom hits the rental car desk. You and Zack can fill out all the forms at the aircraft, get the baggage on the crew bus, and when you get inside, we'll be all set for a night on the town."

"Sounds like a winner. Tell me about Fort De Russy."

"It's a choice piece of real estate, right on Waikiki, owned by the Army. It's their R&R hotel for officers. It beats the hell outta' the BOQ on base. The kicker is the size—there's only so many rooms. See why we gotta beat these guys ahead of us?"

"Okay, tell Zack to get his butt up here in the right seat for landing and brief Tom. We'll handle everything on the flight line and get refueling started. It may take us thirty to forty minutes to get inside ops on the crew bus."

"No sweat, we'll be standing there with reservations and a set of car keys while these other dudes are trying to find their butts."

I filled out the forms, noting the mag drop and oil leak on number two engine. Sergeant Picardo sidled up beside me wiping grease from his hands with a red rag. "That was a brutal seventeen hours," I told him. "You and Jocko can catch up on some needed rest." The lids of his eyes were not fully open. "By the way, I've written up the oil leak on number two. Have maintenance check it out along with the mag drop."

"Roger. I think we got lucky on that engine, Captain."

The squealing bus brakes announced its arrival. I knew by his remark that Sergeant Picardo didn't agree with my decision on the mag drop.

"We'll have a briefing tomorrow night for an early morning take-off the next day. If you have any trouble with quarters or chow, give me a call at Fort De Russy." He responded with a thumbs up as Jocko threw the last bag on the bus. He ambled back to the aircraft to make his day even longer. Zack and I scrambled aboard, moving quickly to a seat. The night air felt good streaming through the open window. I rested my head back and closed my eyes.

"Got us two rooms at Fort De Russy," Chuck exclaimed as we entered Base Operations. "Let's go check in, shower, and hit a couple of bars in Honolulu—I'm ready to drink some booze from those coconuts and pineapples." I looked back at the person making the statement with mouth agape. *Chuck was obviously delirious. Maybe this first long leg got to him.*

"Man, we've been up twenty-one hours now—and you're talking about gettin' smashed?" I asked. "Get serious."

Tom ran up dangling a set of keys before Chuck could reply. "Got us a four-door Chevy, guys." He looked around the room. "Where're my bags and map case."

"Holy Moly, Tom, were we supposed to bring your bags too?" Zack asked.

I put my hand on his shoulder. "Don't sweat it, Tom, he's just messin' with your mind. They're outside with ours, waiting on us." I looked hard at Zack, who just shrugged.

It was comfortable settling into the back seat, as Tom drove, and Chuck gave directions. The wind from the open window was warm and moist. There was a faint sweetness to the air, provided by the abundant island flora. I tuned out the drone of conversation around me, as the soothing breeze almost put me to sleep.

"Hey, David, you agree with that plan?" The words suddenly brought me back to the motion of the car and its occupants.

"What? Guess I was dozing there for a minute."

"Soon as we check in, shave, shower, we'll meet in the lobby for some food and drink."

I ran my hand over the stubble covering my face. "Shave would be good—and a shower. Sure we'll get some great Hawaiian food. As for the drinks, it'll take about two to put me in la-la land."

We walked into the room and Zack and I crumbled across the beds. The softness enfolded around me, as I pushed the pillow under my head. My eyes took in the accommodations, blinking in their effort to remain open. The room was more than just adequate. It contained the usual furniture, clean, and most of all, I was in it. I stretched every muscle, enjoying the sensation and giving in to the desire to curl up right there and sleep. But the gnawing phenomenon in my belly was a stronger urge than sleep. "Zack you wanna shower first while I shave or vice-versa?"

"I'm on my way, Coach." He rolled off the bed, grabbing a towel. "That hot water may knock me out. If you hear a gurgling sound reach in and turn off the water."

"I'll call Tom to do it. After the grief you've given him, he'd hold your head under." I sat up. "Don't you think he's initiated now? Cut him some slack."

"Okay, I'll try, but damn, he plays right into every punch line." He stopped suddenly, turned my way, looking like a small boy caught in the act of behaving badly. "Okay, I'll try." He stood in the doorway and continued to stare at me. "David, why didn't you abort this morning?"

"Because I thought the mag drop was still okay – and the mission called for pushing the envelope more than usual."

Zack slowly walked into the shower.

The street was beautifully lit. There was nothing gaudy or obtrusive. People moved about casually in the reflection of the multicolored lights, talking and laughing. We blended into the surroundings, hopefully not looking like tourists. We walked four blocks before Chuck turned into the doorway of the Tropicana Lounge. He held the door open with a sweeping gesture of his arm. The black leather-covered bar, immediately to our left, was crowded, but the dining area had a few vacant tables. To the right a waterfall cascaded down the irregular sloping rock into a pool of swirling water. The dim lights added to the illusion of a tropical paradise. "Four in your party?" she inquired.

"Yes." Zack stated quickly.

"Right this way." We followed her to the table, as she bent over lighting the candle. "Your waitress will be over in just a minute to take your orders." She disappeared into the crowd. I perused the menu, reading carefully the ingredients of drinks pictured as pineapples with little umbrellas protruding from the top. The food selection was extensive, listing a multitude of seafood, various pork dishes covered in outlandish sauces, and things I could not decipher. I was starving.

We sat sipping drinks we'd never order in the States, laughing about the Air Force, airplanes, women, and life. Sitting there in this strange exotic environment, engaged in idle chatter with three guys about nothing, I could push all problems into oblivion for the moment. We ate, we drank more, laughed even more, and our weariness slowly dissolved into a state of suspended animation. It took only two drinks for the slight buzz to begin. I rather enjoyed the numbing of the senses. After one too many drinks the room took on a surrealistic impression, alluring lights merged into a collage of vivid colors, and surrounding conversation was unintelligible. I forced myself to tune back into the talk around me, trying to comprehend the words.

"Let's go walk the beach," Chuck suggested. "It'll be some kinda fantastic with the moon glistening off that sugar-like sand. And we all could use some fresh air."

"If you were only a different sex, Chuck, it'd make it a lot more enjoyable." Zack added.

The sound of the waves rolling onto the sand was exhilarating. The moon glistened off the white foam washing ashore. The wind in my face began to clear the cobwebs. I looked at my watch, straining to see the illuminated dial in the moonlight. It was almost 3:00 A.M., and the beach was deserted, giving us exclusive rights to the area. Even though tired, I wasn't ready to crash into bed. The atmosphere was too exhilarating to let sleep become a priority. Yet, I knew in about 27 hours we'd be back in the air, yearning for sleep. When I stopped dead in my tracks, the others turned to face me. "Just remember we're having a briefing in fewer hours than you can imagine." I said.

"Maybe not," said Chuck. "While we were waiting on you two in Base Operations, I checked the weather. The forecast winds are for a nineteen to twenty-knot head wind to Wake Island. I heard Major Lynch tell his co-pilot we'd have to delay with winds that high. Seems we can't make Wake, even with Benson tanks, with headwinds over eighteen knots."

"Hot damn," Zack yelled. "Two more days before we leap off."

"You're speculating on some idiot weather forecaster," I said. "Better check weather yourself tomorrow before you get to celebratin' too much."

"Hell, it *is* tomorrow!"

"Now you're gettin' the picture," I said.

"I'm gonna walk our friend up the beach for a while," Chuck said as he strained to keep Tom upright. "He needs some air – quick."

"Okay," Zack said as he kicked off his shoes, pulled off his socks, bent over and rolled up his trousers. "Right now, I need to feel that water."

I sat and leaned against a large coconut palm, watching Zack kick at the rippling water, then run swiftly up the sand ahead of the next wave. He dashed farther into the surf and retreated rapidly, daring the white caps to overtake him. He laughed as he managed to stay only ankle deep ahead of white caps as they broke over the beach. He finally tired of 'feeling' the water and dropped down beside me. He stuck his sand-covered feet out in front, wiggling his toes as if admiring them. He glanced at me. "Have you gone maudlin on me again?"

"Naw. Just sittin' here lapping up the ambiance—and watching a grown man make a fool of himself."

Zack rolled with laughter. "Not one shred of evidence supports the notion that life is serious. I hope to always be a little irrational. It defies any monotony in life."

"Is that why you try for maximum variety in women too?"

The smile left quickly. "You know how to get right down to the guts of a matter, don't you?" His face was solemn. "I wish I knew the answer to that question—I wish I knew." He looked down at the sand, and his voice lowered. "This time's different." He looked hard at me. "You've been in combat before. Do you ever get a bad feeling in your gut about going into something like Nam?" He looked at his feet, avoiding eye contact. "Every now and then I get a hint of that bad feeling somewhere down here in the belly." He rubbed his stomach. "Maybe it's because of my feelings for Jane – or maybe it's just that pork dish I just ate."No doubt that the rum had reduced his inhibitions. This was the first time Zack had ever spoken seriously about anything that delved into his emotions except for the opposite sex on occasion. It was a subject seldom discussed among pilots – we usually assume the fear factor exists to some degree in all of us. But if it's not discussed it stays at bay – locked deep in the psyche – always under our domination.

"Zack, we all have little flashes like that. It just means we do our job that much better. Attachments, like Jane for instance, make you think about things you didn't dwell on when it was only you to consider. Now, since you bring up things that bother us. This afternoon, Chuck was about to tell me some deep dark secret about Colonel Norwood when you stuck your head up there and relieved him. It sounded petty ominous. I can't shake thinking about that."

"I wouldn't doubt anything in that bastard's past, Coach."

"That's the second time you've referred to him as a 'bastard'. Zack, there's definitely something missing here. You ready to tell me about it?"

He jumped to his feet. "Here come Chuck and Tom, just in time to change this goddamn conversation."

"We need to hit the sack anyway," I said.

"What th hell, we can make up the sleep tomorrow night," said Zack. "Those winds aren't gonna suddenly die down."

"You better pray they don't. We'd be hard-pressed to get in a cockpit with four hours sleep in three days—even if we catch a few winks tomorrow night."

"Tonight," Zack emphasized. "This *is* tomorrow."

The sun felt good on my face. The endless breeze wafted through the patio, rustling the plants back and forth. I sipped on the Bloody Mary, looking around the terrace at people in various moods of relaxation. The atmosphere was infectious. The delicious-looking Eggs Benedict waited to be consumed. I noticed Tom, sitting across from me, watching my every move, as if fascinated by the way I drank a Bloody Mary. His eyes shifted as we made eye contact. I wondered what he was thinking. *Was he wondering about this crew that had been thrust upon him, finding he'd become part of something he doesn't understand. After all, we were going into a combat area, having to rely on each other for survival. Wonder what he's thinking?*

He looked up again. "I like that shirt." I laughed at the comment. "What's funny, Captain?"

"Nothing really, Tom." I pulled it out in front of me. "It isn't bad." Tom couldn't be more than twenty-three, maybe twenty-four. I suddenly remembered my twenty-third birthday, flying a fighter in Korea. *Tom, old boy, you're about to age rapidly. You're about to enter another world, one that'll test your insides.* I thought about Zack's question this morning. It made me wonder if I could meet the challenge again. Did the others feel this way too, or was I only placating Zack with my axioms?

"Where're you from, Tom?" I asked.

"Hattiesburg, Mississippi. Grew up there and went to Mississippi Southern, right there in town."

"How'd you happen to become a navigator?" I was curious about what capricious circumstances brought us together at Pope Air Force Base.

"Air Force ROTC. I had a scholarship and selected for the pilot program." He looked embarrassed. "I found out my senior year I was color blind—that only left navigator training if I wanted to fly and –."

"Fly? Zack interrupted. "You sit back there staring at those charts and trust your life to the likes of us?" Zack asked. "You should've gotten a ground job and done your four years in personnel or something."

"Zack talks tough, but he's really got a heart of stone," I said. Laughter resounded around the table. "And now, Tom, we're sitting here in Honolulu eating brunch at a four star restaurant, teamed up for whatever adventure might lie ahead of us." Tom looked serious, maybe a slight pallor to his cheeks. The thought of what may lie ahead certainly registered with him.


The beauty of the backside of Oahu was dramatic. Unlike the sugar-sand of Waikiki, the western side of the island sloped from rolling declines to shear drops where the terrain fell precipitously onto black lava-rock beaches. Towering waves smashed against the dark beaches with a fury. We stood there, engrossed in what nature had acquired from eons of lava flows combining with the assiduous onslaught of the Pacific. I thought of the first natives to settle here from other Pacific islands, finding a paradise beyond their wildest dreams. Man, in his drive to tame and conquer, had transcribed only a portion of this enchantment into a modern city. There remained a flavor of the indigenous, a segment of the unspoiled in this fragment of the original island.


We stood silently at the Battleship Arizona memorial, a place for solitude, for poignancy, for emotions to take over. There, barely beneath the surface, were the entombed from December 7, 1941. My emotions were a dichotomy, ranging from reverence to anger. *The price of war, any damn war, is too high. Unfortunately, sometimes we have no choice. The problem is knowing when the option exists. Man is basically a stupid animal.*

We walked silently back to the car. It was as if we were making sure we were out of earshot of spirits that may still be listening.

"Hey, guys," Chuck said, as he checked his watch. "We better head back, turn in the car and double check weather. We barely have time to make the briefing."

As we entered the BOQ, the news was already out. The winds were forecast at exactly eighteen knots. It was a "go" for a 0500 take-off tomorrow morning. Zack slammed his fist against the wall. "Damn winds were forecast for more than eighteen knots. What damn weatherman ever hit a forecast anyway? Colonel Norwood and his freakin' adjutant will be sleepin' quietly on one of those C-130 while we're at the mercy of Major Lynch's decision for a 'go'."

"Let's get to the briefing and then try to catch a couple hours sleep," I said. "We were pretty damn stupid to count on forecast winds."

Tom slouched against the wall, unwilling to comment. Chuck looked at me, a sly smile on his face. "You do whatcha have to do—was our little interlude worth it?"

The darkness surrounding the flight line hid my discolored eyes, bloodshot from six and a half hours sleep in three days. I didn't think I could focus on an instrument panel for the next seventeen hours. There was only so much response I could expect from this body. This would certainly be past that measure. Zack ambled over under the ramp lights, looking at me as the light washed across his face. It had 'pain' written all over it. Chuck and Tom were no better. I knew immediately we'd all have to do what our bodies told us we couldn't. No one spoke of his feelings. We moved robotically to get the aircraft into the air with a minimum of conversation.

The altimeter read nine thousand feet as I set cruise power, called for the checklist and stared blankly at the churning sea. I swilled a cup of hot coffee and considered the delicate white wisps of clouds, glowing pink with the rising sun. Above were alto cumulus layers of various shapes. A jumble of billowing cloudlets running in parallel bands of ragged towers dotted the horizon. They were merging into dark storm clouds farther out.

# 4

## Fatigue

We darted in and out of formless gray clouds, the horizon usually lost in the gray tumbling vapors. Sporadically we'd break into an area of partial clearing, where we could see the ragged edges of towering cumulus out ahead. They announced the invisible thunderstorms, imbedded, waiting for us. Hour-after-hour the cloud-deck grew thicker and darker, until it swallowed us.

The rain's intensity increased to a crescendo across the windscreen, obliterating anything outside the cockpit. With both hands on the controls, I fought the turbulence, while lightening ripped the sky ahead. My shoulders ached with the determined control pressure needed to keep the aircraft attitude within limits. Maintaining a constant heading was out of the question.

Chuck adjusted the mike in front of his mouth. He glanced at his notes and began the position report, shaking his head. "Well, that was purely a guesstimate. Tom hasn't been able to take a fix for hours."

I nodded, glancing only momentarily in his direction. My eyes were constantly crosschecking instruments that seemed in state of perpetual motion. Chuck, turned my way again, leaning close. "Let me take it for a while."

"Thanks." My hands dropped to the armrests. I closed my eyes to rest them from the strain. *I need just a moment or two. Just a little rest. God, I need sleep.* I slapped my leg, snapping the feeling back. I knew Zack would be relieving Chuck in ten minutes. I would have to stick it out for two more hours after that. "Christ, I wish this weather would let up."

"At least this damn turbulence is gettin' easier." Chuck smiled his reassurance. "We'll break out of this crap soon."

"No telling where Bravo two is."

"Somewhere out there in that murk," Chuck said. "Hope to hell he's got separation since we're gyrating back and forth on our heading."

"Just as long as we aren't gyratin' in the same air space."


The hue of the clouds changed slowly, brightened by the sun beginning to penetrate their density. Unexpectedly, we broke into a clearing between layers. The thin layer above gradually gave way as we flew west. The clearing weather boosted my sagging body enough to take the controls while Chuck spun out of the right seat to take a break. Zack slipped into the vacated seat, strapping the seat belt and shoulder harness into place. "I'll give you a break any time you want me to take the controls."

"I'll hold her for a few more minutes."

My crosscheck of instruments flashed a message, a subconscious, instinctive sensation. I scanned more slowly, as my eyes focused on the oil temperature on the right engine. It was climbing slowly. I glanced at the oil pressure; it was low, moving slightly below the red line. "Damnation, we're about to lose number two." I slapped Zack's shoulder. "Look at the oil temp and pressure."

"Damn, Coach, that doesn't look good."

The engineer's head poked between us, peering at the instrument panel.

"The damn oil temp is close to the peg, Sergeant," I snapped. "That engine's almost gone. I should . . ."

"Hey, David." Tom interrupted. "We're still too far out to make it on one engine. We're still in that point of no return—either way."

"How good can you swim, Tom?"

"That's not funny worth a damn."

"Goddamn oil pressure's still dropping." I glanced back at Sergeant Picardo. "I can't wait much longer to feather the damn thing—it'll seize if I don't."

Picardo never looked at me nor did he respond. His eyes were still scanning the instruments.

My hand reached for the red feathering button. It hesitated, knowing this meant going into the water. As my finger touched the button, I felt cold inside. My hand shook as my fingers closed slowly around the feathering button. I felt the abrupt pressure of Picardo's left hand. He clasped his hand over mine in a vice-like grip, holding my fingers away from the feathering button.

"Gotta feather it now, Sergeant," I shouted at him. "The engine's about to seize."

Without comment, his right was reaching for a switch. I saw him moving the oil cooler switch to the open position. The oil temperature suddenly showed a small decrease, then gradually started down in a slow but steady pace. There was a positive indication of oil pressure for the first time.

"Somebody accidentally hit the oil cooler switch to the close position," Picardo announced with no inflection in his voice. "That'll take care of it, Captain."

I glared at Zack. "You dragged your friggin' chute harness across that switch when you got in the seat."

"You reckon'?"

"Don't be so damn flippant about it," I snapped. "You damn near put us in the drink."

He glared at me, with a look I'd never seen before. "What the hell's with you? We're all tired, but I think you took an 'asshole pill' with that last cup of coffee." His eyes narrowed. "You want me to get on bended knee and ask for your goddamn forgiveness?" His neck veins protruded as he spoke."I want you to act like a professional—or is that unreasonable?"

He stared back angrily, his eyes narrowed and penetrating. "You've had your knickers in a twist since we left Pope." His neck veins pulsed visibly. "Tell you what." His cheeks now crimson. "Soon as we get to Nam, you switch the crews—maybe you can find a professional out there in this flight." He yanked a paperback from his leg pocket in the flight suit and opened it quickly. His face turned toward the book and silence fell in the cockpit like a door slammed shut.

Chuck's head appeared to my right. "You ready for a break?"

"Oh yeah," I said. "My butt feels like it's glued to this seat."

Slowly rolling from the left seat, I glanced at Zack, who took the controls without comment or a glance in my direction. I hesitated for a moment, almost saying I was sorry. Instead, I moved down the ladder, knowing I really felt no remorse at all for my comments. Whatever resolution of our last conversation was to take place, it wouldn't be now. *Was fatigue clouding my thinking? Funny, but I don't know or really give a shit. That subject's just not a priority right now.* All I could think of was closing my eyes for a while.

I stretched outraged muscles into supporting my body. As I straightened upright, I saw the swinging net in front of me. The hammock I had avoided on the first leg, suddenly looked appealing. I straddled the Benson tank and rolled my body onto the netting. Surprisingly, it felt good as I swung gently in its grasp. My eyes closed automatically, lids burning against the retinas. There was no discernable demarcation from awake to drifting into another time and place. I was no longer in an aluminum tube with wings, somewhere out over the Pacific.

I felt the hammock move as someone called my name again. "David, Chuck could use some company up front." Zack's voice came through on the second try. I shook my head, clearing out the cobwebs of that last vision. Stretching muscles into action was more difficult than I expected. I moved up the ladder to the flight deck, still smiling at the illusions of the last hour.

Settling down, checking instruments, and stabilizing the fuel flow took only a few minutes. "Tom, what's our ETE to Wake Island?"

"Wait one—let's see—estimate Wake in two hours and ten minutes." He cleared his throat. "New heading two seven two degrees."

I set the new heading in the reference marker and eased the aircraft two degrees left until the remote compass indicated the new heading. A large muted orange sphere sat right in front of us, almost touching the horizon. The picture of the sun dipping slowly into the ocean was mesmerizing. It was an awesome phenomenon, one that never ceased to amaze me. Even after the sun slipped from sight, the colors continued to illuminate the skyline. The muted crimson hues changed gradually until all light was wrenched from the sky. Sky and ocean merged in the darkness. It was easy recognizing the tattered band of the Milky Way, as the stars began to show themselves against the blackness. The heavens continued to maintain their mystery.

"New heading two niner two." Tom's voice startled me.

"Bull shit, Tom." I glanced over at Chuck, who arched his eyebrows in disbelief. "That's a twenty-five-degree correction."

"That's the heading. I must have been off on that last fix."

"I'd say. That's some kinda *off* out here trying to hit a mile-wide island in the middle of the Pacific Ocean." I waited a few seconds. "You sure about this heading?"

"Positive."

"Well, our ETE now is about one hour five minutes—right?"

There was a long pause as Chuck and I looked at each other with a shrug. Tom finally came out with an answer. "ETE is now one hour and forty-two minutes."

"What?" I shouted. "Over an hour ago, you said we had two-ten to go. Now you give a heading change of some twenty degrees and we suddenly lose thirty minutes. Do you know where the hell we are, Tom?"

"Goddammit, Captain, that's the new heading and ETE—that's it."

"Okay, Tom. We'll go with that." Chuck was shaking his head and smiling at me. I wondered what he found so funny at a time like this. *Well, hell maybe ole Tom did have a bad fix he's just gettin' around to correcting. God, I hope so. There's a lot of ocean out there.*

An hour later, Chuck set in the frequency for the Wake Island Tacan radio beacon. There was no indication as the needle swung randomly in a circle. "Can't pick up Wake," he said. We should be close enough."

I looked at the fuel gauges. "We've used all the fuel in the Benson tank and are already down to slightly over a hundred gallons in each wing tank." I shrugged, glancing over my shoulder. "Tom, let's have another fix. We should damn well be close enough to pick up Wake TACAN, and we are gettin' absolutely no signal."

"Okay, I'll try, but these clouds make it difficult."

Minutes went by as we watched the fuel going down. Chuck slapped my arm. "If we miss Wake, we only have about thirty minutes fuel left at the rate I just calculated." There was a hint of concern in Chuck's statement. "You'd better start asking for a DF steer – if we haven't missed the damn thing already."

"Captain, I know the heading is right and the ETA still holds – damn it, I don't know why you can't pick up Wake," Tom said. "There must be some atmospheric interference."

The TACAN needle swung hesitatingly toward the top. It oscillated s few degrees either side – fluctuating back and forth a few seconds – settling down right on the nose. Chuck glanced at me as I laughed for the first time. Tom had us right down the middle of Wake Island. I felt a little sheepish at my comments about his heading change. *Pretty good for a brand damn new Second Lieutenant.* "Good job, Tom."

Twenty minutes later the approach lights and runway lights were dead ahead and we were cleared for a straight-in approach.

"Let's get this thing on the ground before my ass turns to jelly," Chuck said.

The tires skimmed onto the surface, as I lowered the nose, grabbed both throttles, pulling them into reverse thrust. My left hand moved instinctively to the nose wheel steering, searching ahead for the next taxiway. As I turned hard left, I glanced at Chuck. "Tell 'em we're clear of the active, Chuck—let ole Rusty's crew get their butts on the ground." As Chuck made the transmission, I peered ahead looking for the lighted signal for parking. Abruptly, two elongated lights, moving in rhythmic motions, guided us into a slot beside four other C-123's. The nose bobbed up and down as I hit the brakes in response to his arms crossed with the lighted signals. "After landing check list." The engines whined down to a stop as Chuck and I sat there, limp, searching for the strength to get out of the seats.

"Hot damn, this was one helluva long day," Jocko exclaimed over intercom. "Can't use too many like this."

While we walked tentatively into Base Operations, our bodies were getting used to solid ground again. We staggered through the door, tossing our bags into the pile over in the corner with the others, and moved toward the line of personnel to wait for transport. Unexpectedly, Tom grabbed my arm, spinning me around. I started to bark some response at his brusque matter of getting my attention. But before I could say anything, Tom was exploding his message. "Captain, you better get over there to the Ops desk. The Colonel and Major Lynch are talking to Phil Merc."

"So? What the hell's wrong with that? They should be about ten minutes out."

"They're not." Tom continued to sputter his statement. "I was getting mission data for tomorrow and heard the Colonel on the speaker phone. Phil's still at Hickam. They lost an engine and turned back." He took a breath. "That's the big flap—you better get over there."

I ran up to the desk as Lt. Col. Norwood glanced in my direction then back into the speakerphone. His look left no doubt that he was unhappy with my intrusion. Major Lynch never looked up or acknowledged I was in the area. He continued to stare at the speakerphone as if anticipating it coming to life. Phil was still talking as I eased closer to hear.

"Colonel, the engine change is almost finished. We'll definitely need a check flight to test this new engine. That's standard procedure and we . . ."

"I don't give a happy damn about what you consider standard operating procedure. You've been in crew rest while the engine change took place. Now top off the tanks and get that damn aircraft in the air."

I stepped closer and interrupted Norwood's most direct order. A cardinal sin with this man, but I had no choice. "Colonel, Phil's right. He needs to complete an ops check on a new engine—certainly you need to do that before crossing a goodly portion of the Pacific Ocean."

His eyes showed me his contempt and anger even before he spoke. "Captain, I don't need you to explain operating procedures."

"I'll just say this, Colonel. We'd better hope that engine doesn't give any problems out there about the point of no return."

He swung around facing me, his voice lowered as it took on a slight quiver. "What did you say, Captain?"

"Just stating a fact, Colonel. That crew's part of my flight—I believe I have the responsibility to express my opinion."

Colonel Norwood moved closer. "Step over here a minute, Captain Barfield." His arm extended in a jerk, pointing toward a corner of the room. We walked quickly to a secluded spot. His face was still crimson. "I want you to understand something right now. That damn aircraft will catch up with us by the time we get to Clark—whether you realize it or not, this mission precludes ordinary ops checks." His eyes seemed to actually spark. "In the meantime, Captain Barfield, if I need your considered opinion on how to get this squadron to DaNang, I'll ask for it. You came damn close to insubordination just now." Every word seemed charged with electric meaning. "I told you, back at Pope, I expected your support and definitely your loyalty. So far, I haven't seen either." He stopped abruptly, eyes boring into mine. "I would have thought by now your co-pilot would have briefed you on my behavior when truly mad. Be very careful, Captain Barfield – very careful."

He turned and walked swiftly back to the ongoing telephone call. His voice reached another octave as he ordered Phil to take-off. I headed for the door. My rage, along with total fatigue, would have taken over any control I had barely maintained for the last few minutes. The guilt I felt for not standing firm for one of my crews, combined none too well with my resentment for Norwood. The biggest question tormenting me was his statement about Zack. There was something there in the past, ominously lurking there.

Some deep-seated connection existed between these two, and Zack was more than reluctant to tell me what that relationship was. After our conflict today about the oil cooler switch, I may never know. My stomach churned and my head pounded.

Two hours later, as I lay on the uncomfortable mattress, staring at the ceiling, fatigue had been replaced by anger and self-flagellation. Sleep was being held fugitive by my inability to let the event dissipate. My mind swirled with the thought I needed to let go. I closed my eyes and tried to focus on happier times, on some tranquil scene. Somewhere during this disorganized array of introspection, sleep mercifully took over.

# 5

## Apologies, Catharsis, and Consternation

With a second push, the Officers' Club door swung open onto the scarlet-tiled patio. The cool night felt invigorating, as the onshore breeze washed across me. Being alone was most enjoyable, detached at last from the din of conversations inside. I walked to the edge, looking out over the harbor of Agana, Guam. The moon cast a soft glow on the water and the stars formed a canopy of diminutive lights. Looking out over the bay, I regarded the water stretching in all directions. *Oceans are humbling as they dwarf us mortals. There's no doubt it places our singular significance in proper perspective. We're so damn infinitesimal and extrinsic to the workings of this planet.* Looking hard over the ocean, I squinted hard trying to locate where sea and sky merged, to ascertain exactly where the stars converged with the water. The futile attempt directed my thoughts back to more mundane things. *Tomorrow we'll be in the Philippines. Three nights and two whole days to relax at Clark Air Base before we go on to DaNang. A short rest will . . .*

"Mind a little company?" Zack's voice startled my thoughts as he walked up behind me. "If you'd rather be alone, I understand."

I continued leaning on the concrete balusters, still scanning the water. "Just contemplating the night, the significance of that big ocean out there, and how damn inconsequential we are."

"That's too goddamn philosophical for a comment."

I turned and faced him. "Glad you came out here. We've been avoiding something we need to talk about."

"Maybe nothing needed to be said. Have you thought about that?"

"Just to clear the air—I was completely out of line back there before we hit Wake—about that oil cooler switch. I'm sorry for coming at you like that. If I ever saw a professional in the air, it's you, Zack. I never should have made that stupid remark."

"Don't sweat it. I blew my stack for the same reason you did—we were both exhausted." His hand shot out and slapped me on the back. "There're some folks I would've felt like opening up a large can of 'whoop ass' for, but I know you too well. That happened to be a David who was too damn tired to think straight. Let's forget it happened."

"Thanks."

Zack leaned back against the balusters, looking out in space. "There's another reason," Zack said. "We've all got our hang-ups—things that rattle our cage completely out of all proportion. You just happened to rattle mine real good. It brought back memories of a real bad time in my life. You sounded like my father – and that ripped it." His voice faltered. "Something happened when I was sixteen that has a lot to do with why I reacted so quickly—other than being so ragged-out tired." He stared into the sky, then back at me. "When you came at me with that comment about hitting the oil cooler switch, I saw red. It made me relive things I've bottled up for the last twelve years."

"Sure you wanna talk about this?"

"Yeah, I do. Something that happened when I was sixteen had quite an effect on me." He slapped the hard surface of the railing. "This isn't exactly easy. It . . ."

"Maybe this isn't the time." I interrupted.

"Yeah, yeah it is." He turned to face me. "It happened during a football game—with our biggest rival. My brother was the loved-by-all quarterback, a senior, highly recruited by several colleges, including Nebraska. Man, talking about havin' it all going for you—he was the star of the team, had the best looking gal in school, and—" Zack smiled, "the sonofagun looked like James Dean." His voice lowered. "Not only that, my father idolized him. I was two years younger—knew I'd never measure up to Ron—and I could live with that." He looked at me for emphasis. "I never minded being in his shadow. Hell, I was proud just being part of the team, sittin' on the bench watchin' him. But in a matter of seconds it all changed." He shook a cigarette from the pack, flipped open his Zippo for a light, then let the smoke out slowly.

"Zack . . ."

"No." He moved his upturned hand toward me. "Let me finish this or I might not get it out. Guess I've had just enough to drink tonight to tell you this little ole story. Christ almighty, it's about time I got this outta my craw—you might even find it interesting, Coach."

Zack had never exposed this much of himself. The revelation, unfolding readily, was totally out of character. He took another draw on the Marlboro, and sent the smoke out again. It was obvious he wasn't through with this catharsis. He had to get it out—to regurgitate some bottled-up brooding that had been gnawing at him. Listening, I could tell it had been consuming him, a little at a time, eating away at him for years.

"It was one of those things nobody really understood." He shook his head trying to explain. "There were exactly twenty seconds to go in the game, we had the ball on our twenty-two yard line, fourth down and six. We were leading by two and the other team called a time-out to stop the clock. The coach didn't want to chance a blocked punt. I heard him tell Ron, 'It's their last time-out, they can't stop the clock again. Take as much time off the clock as possible; run a keeper and kill the time.' Ron rolled right, faked a pass, then tucked the ball in and broke in the open." Zack's look betrayed his emotions as he talked about it. I could read the agony in his eyes as he continued the story. "He all of a sudden stumbled and fell forward. We thought he took the time off the clock and just went down as time expired. We stood there cheering our lungs out—Ron never moved. Mumbling started throughout the crowd as the trainer and two coaches ran onto the field. My father ran down from the stands and knelt beside him. He looked back at the bench as if pleading for some miracle. Christ, I'll never forget the look on his face. Finally the ambulance came and took Ron to the hospital. By the time Mom and I got to the emergency room, Dad was walking toward us. He had this ashen look—you know?—like he was in shock. He glanced at us with this blank stare, eyes glazed over; jaw fastened shut, mouth drawn tight. Mom took his hand, but he didn't look at her, he didn't take her in his arms, he looked straight ahead and said, 'Ron's dead'. He said it very calmly with no emotion." Zack took a long drag on the cigarette and looked out over the water.

"What the hell happened out there on the football field?" My attention was riveted on what he was telling me. "What caused his death?"

"The autopsy said it was heart failure—his heart picked that instant to stop beating." His head lowered. "Right there on the twenty-eight yard line. It just stopped beating. A congenital condition, they said." He turned toward me. "I wondered how the hell someone in his physical condition could have anything wrong with his heart. For twelve years, I've mulled that one over and over."

"Zack, it's one of those things in life we can never understand—or accept."

"I think Dad's heart stopped beating that night too. Oh, blood still pumped through his body, but there was no real heart beat after that night."

We stood there looking at each other. Words were too inadequate to express my thoughts on Zack's pain. He continued his search of emotions, dredging them tediously to the surface. I realized he had to force this out in the pallid light of this damn island, this night. I was merely the conduit.

"Dad and I were never close. Ron was his life. When he died, Dad and I became more alienated than we already were. Most of the time, he just ignored me. When he did talk to me, it was usually a rebuff or some putdown." His eyes squinted as he looked at me. "Your statement out there, about not being a professional, sounded like it came right out of his mouth."

"That'd be tough to take—lose your brother and then your father's . . ." I couldn't say it. It stuck in my throat. "I can't even comprehend how you felt—or how you feel right now. It's something you'd have to live through, Zack. I just don't –." Faltering as I spoke, changing the tone, I continued, "What's your relationship with your dad now?"

"There *is* none. Mom couldn't accept his sullen, brooding attitude that permeated everything in his life after that night. She tried. Oh, God, she tried. But she waited until I left for college to get the divorce. If she waited that long just for my sake, she could've saved that much more of her sanity. I haven't seen Dad since the day I walked out the door to go to college." Reflecting in the dim light, I saw the tears in his eyes. "The thing was—he never had any idea how much I loved Ron—how much I missed him too. That was the one thing I wanted to tell him." His faced took on a scowl. "I wanted to grab him by the collar, pull him close and tell him that he wasn't the only one who loved Ron—Goddamnit—I loved him too."

I put my hand on his shoulder, knowing there was nothing I could say. As we looked at each other, I could only hope Zack knew I felt some of his anguish and pain, but was helpless to alleviate it. As we stood there under the stars on Guam, I realized he'd probably never told anyone this story. For some reason he picked tonight to do it, and I was chosen to hear it. That was most humbling.

"David." He leaned back against the baluster. "I did know Colonel Norwood before this gaggle started. You've already figured that out. It was before you got to Pope – a long time ago."

Eight hours after leaving Anderson Air Base and Guam, we were approaching Luzon. The VOR needle sat dead on the nose, the DME indicated 38 nautical miles to destination, and the anticipation of the promised crew rest surged through my thoughts. The cotton candy clouds zipped past under us and jocularity was spewing forth over the intercom. All of us were looking forward to Clark Air Base and a break.

Once again we taxied up in the long line of parking C-123's. I reached up pulling off both mixtures as the engines whined down. Sergeant Picardo's head appeared between us. "Any write-ups, Captain? We better get all the maintenance we need before Nam—it'll be scarce on parts over there."

"Everything looks good." I glanced at Zack. "You see anything we need in the way of maintenance"?

"Yeah," he snapped. "They can jack up this airframe and drive under a C-130. I'd like four turbo jets out there for a while."

"You wish," I added.

"Wait till you see some of those LZ's over there, carved out of a mountain, laughingly called a 'landing zone'," Sergeant Picardo added. "You'll be glad you've got the ole C-123 to get you in and out."

"Ah, the voice of experience," said Zack. "Forgot you've already served a TDY tour over there." He wheeled around. "How the hell did you luck out again?"

"I volunteered."

"You *what*?" "Another Sergeant was on the list and his wife was just diagnosed with MS. Even in the early stages, he should be there with her." He looked at Zack. "It's only six months for me, Lieutenant. For him it'll be a lifetime."

Zack glanced at me, then started walking away from the flight line.

Zack rolled up a magazine and swatted at the lizard running across the BOQ room. "I hate those creepy-crawlies. Everything over here slithers, crawls or squirms."

"Get used to 'em. They're harmless."

"Harmless, my ass. If I wake up in the night with one of those things doing a jig across me, I'll croak right there." He chuckled. "Can't you see the clipping in the paper back at Pope—'Air Force Lieutenant becomes the first combat casualty in the Composite Group—died of fright in his sack.'"

"You might die of fright before you get back, but it won't be caused by any damn lizard."

The shower felt great as the warm water tumbled down my body. Plans were already surging through my head. *Hit the bar for a few slow-sipping bourbons, later to the dining room for one great meal.*

Clark Air Base had a notable reputation for their amenities, service and great food during the Korean War. I hoped it maintained that image. Zack's shout broke my concentration. "Hey, you're gonna soak up all the hot water? You'll look like a friggin' prune if you don't get outta there—hurry up."

I stepped through the door. "It's all yours. Of course you'll have to step over four green lizards in there waitin' to share it with you."

"Screw you—and your green slimeys." He eased his feet into the shower clogs on the floor, examining them closely as to their height above anything that might be crawling in the shower.

I pulled on a pair of tan slacks and grabbed a yellow shirt. "Hey, Zack, I'm headed for the barber shop. Meet you in the bar in about an hour." I heard an indistinct acknowledgment of my comment as I closed the door behind me and walked toward the Officers' Club.

The massive oaks cascaded over the sidewalk, shading the large old quarters along the street. Built prior to WW II, the buildings were surrounded by a screened-in porch on three sides. Inviting wicker chairs, lounges, and strategically placed bamboo screens were visible on the porches. The ceilings of these old houses were high, dissipating the heat of long afternoons, much like the houses of the south back home. It was obvious to me that these quarters were designed for gracious living and the entertaining of pre-war days in the Philippines. I looked at the new, low-roofed, brick structures, which had been built nearby as new officers' quarters. What the new quarters lacked in size, they surely made up in ugliness. The contrast was conclusive, indicating the way new military construction allocations defined "adequate" quarters. Not even the soft wash of dusk could help the appearance of squatted brick exteriors extending for several blocks. The stately old structures, now reserved for senior officers, reminded me of sentinels to another time and perspective.

Thunder boomed in the distance announcing late afternoon rain showers. Dark swirling clouds moved from the east. Increasing the size and pace of my steps, I hunched over attempting to dodge the few raindrops splattering against the concrete around me. Thinking of my previous trip to the Philippines, as I jogged, a terse explanation of the weather came to mind. "There are only two seasons in this country." The grizzled Sergeant described the local weather to a new Second Lieutenant, "The dry season is where it rains every afternoon, and the rainy season is where it rains all day." I laughed to myself as I broke into a run.

The Officers' Club appeared as I bounded around the corner. It was as massive as I remembered: alabaster white walls, with citron trim advantageously placed across the facade, and olive shutters framing the long windows. The dark green canopy stretched out a welcome as I dashed under its protection. I opened the door of the foyer, wiping my feet before walking across the electric blue carpet. Glancing to the right, I saw the immense dining room, with a section for a full orchestra in the rear. I stared at the opulence of the butter-yellow walls, heavy molding, with massive chandeliers spaced strategically. I admired the ballroom elegance, and placed it on a par with the clubs of the old Air Force Bases like Maxwell, Randolph and Langley. Except for the Army-Navy Club in Manila, this was the finest Officers' Club I had ever been in.

Even though the only available light streamed faintly through the floor length windows, I could see the tables already set with china, glasses, and floral arrangements in anticipation of the usual Friday night crowd. The smell of food wafted through the room, adding another dimension to my anticipation of the evening. The appealing aroma gave a hint of some unknown delicacy being prepared in the kitchen.

Chuck was sitting at the end of the bar. Further down were Tom, Mac MacPherson, and Carey Hulsey. The three navigators were in an animated and heated debate. *Probably over phases of the moon, or some other highly absorbing topic.* I pulled up a stool beside Chuck and waved toward the bartender. "Wild Turkey and Seven." Turning to Chuck, I asked, "This where you get off the merry-go-round?"

"Yep. I'll have to suffer through about three more days of this tough living before the C-130's come back through. Any messages for those back at Pope? Want me to call your wife?"

"Nope. Don't reckon so."

A caterwaul preceded the raucous air crews descending into the stag bar. In front of the entourage was Lt. Col. Norwood, loudly explaining a story to his sidekick, Captain Larry Hazelwood. Our astute Adjutant obviously needed some slight clarification; he looked questioningly at Colonel Norwood before he broke into raucous laughter. Immediately, following these two, also engaged in conversation, were our Flight Surgeon, Captain Garner, and Major Lynch. Norwood fleetingly looked in our direction as he passed, but making no acknowledgment of our presence, migrated toward a table in the far corner of the bar with his entourage.

Chuck smiled and touched my arm. "I don't envy you the next six months over there with that SOB. You do realize the kinda start you made with that guy?"

"Well, as the Marines say: 'You gotta expect losses in an operation this big'."

"You can make light of this if you want," Chuck continued, "but let me tell you about this guy – the story I didn't finish. He slugged down the rest of his beer, motioned to the bartender, then focused on me again. "I was told by a Captain in Wing Personnel that he saw Norwood pull a file from officer records and place a sheet in the officer's record jacket and return it to the file. Later he walked over, perused which folder was sticking up in the drawer, and pulled out the record jacket. It turned out to be a Major in the 76th Squadron. He looked at the sheet added on top of the record. It was a 'Letter of Caution' regarding alcohol abuse, indicating he could be placed on the 'Control Roster'. He read it again, wondering why the Special Actions Division Head hadn't placed it there. Norwood shouldn't be handling that himself. No one but the Chief of Special Actions adds those letters to personnel folders."

I peeked over my shoulder at the table, focusing on Norwood. Glancing back at Chuck, I asked, "Well, maybe he didn't actually put it there—maybe it was already in the jacket."

"That's exactly what my friend figured and let it go. Two months later the Major was passed over for Lieutenant Colonel. You can bet he made a beeline to personnel to review his records. My friend pulled the jacket, as asked, and was just about to show him the reason for his predicament. He stopped cold in his tracks. That letter was gone. It just up and disappeared, no longer in the jacket." Chuck gave me a knowing look. "It mysteriously disappeared right after the promotion board met."

"Well, did your friend explain the irregularity to the Major?"

"He saw Norwood standing there watching him, close enough to hear any conversation. He just handed the record jacket to the Major and walked away."

"What a gutless prick." "C'mon, David, he wasn't sure at that time that this wasn't actually some proper procedure he didn't know about. Later, after some careful checking, he found out there was something drastically wrong. It was too late. It was only going to be his word against Norwood's—and there was absolutely no evidence left."

"He should have gone straight to the Inspector General." I stated.

"He would've looked like a damn fool, David, making an unsubstantiated allegation against the Chief of Personnel—not to mention that Norwood would have his ass later." Chuck bent over closer and whispered, "Later, he did some digging, just to see where Norwood's path would have crossed with this Major. He found out – ."

"Who's this mysterious Major?"

"That's not important—you probably don't know the guy anyway. Listen to this." Chuck looked around to see who was in earshot. "The Major was Chief of the Standardization and Evaluation Division. He randomly—well, supposedly randomly—selected Norwood for his annual instrument flight check ride. Ole Norwood failed the instrument ride. And worst of all, the Wing Deputy of Operations immediately changed Norwood's assignment from becoming a Squadron Commander because of the downer on the check ride. He all of a sudden became Director of Wing Personnel. Even though the selections for check rides by 'Stan-Eval' are random, Norwood blamed the Major for him losing the squadron. Obviously, he's not one to forgive and forget."

"Christ almighty, did the stupid SOB ever figure he busted the check ride on his own?" I asked. "No doubt he deserved the downer on the ride, and I'm damn sure he should never be a Squadron Commander anyway."

"Well, old Sport, he's one now—yours." Chuck's grin extended ear to ear. "Think about that one for a while."

I sat there mulling over the last statement, slowly becoming aware of the implications for my immediate future. Looking over my shoulder again, I considered Norwood, wondering just how guys like him become regular officers in the United States Air Force, much less get promoted. My faith in the promotion system had been shaken before, but not to this extent. *What are we in for in Nam?*

"Whatcha up to?" Zack said as he pulled up a stool beside me. "You two don't look as if you're enjoying that good booze—or you've haven't sucked up a sufficient quantity yet."

"We were just talking about old times at Pope," Chuck said.

"Now that's a great subject to get me in a buoyant mood," said Zack. "Do you think we could possibly change the subject to something pleasant like dogs, cars, or women?"

"Zack, you don't have a dog, you already drive a Porche, and we could add very little to your exploits with the opposite sex," I said. "Now what other subject would you like to consider?"

My withering look registered with Zack. He shrugged and looked for the bartender. "Martini," he shouted above the noise, and then looked back. "I made a reservation for dinner tonight. I knew you guys wouldn't think that far ahead." He swung around in the seat. "Hey, what about a simple 'Thanks, Zack'?"

In unison, Chuck and I sang out, "Thank you, Zack."

"Captain Barfield." Major Lynch's raspy voice intruded into our conversation like fingers across a chalkboard. "Pass the word to your flight on the scheduled intelligence briefings at ten hundred tomorrow. Colonel Norwood wants everyone in their seats at building 246 by 0950."

"Roger, will do." I replied.

Zack stared at Major Lynch. Without breaking his line of vision, he whipped out his trusty Zippo. He placed a cigarette in his mouth and spun the wheel. The fumes circled upward, blending with the noxious smoke filling the room. Zack's stare followed Lynch to the next table where he leaned down telling another flight commander about the briefing. He shook his head as he continued to watch Major Lynch. "You know, if he had a zit on his butt, it'd be called a brain tumor."

At precisely 0950 building 246 filled with aircrew, moving robotically toward amply cushion seats. It was fascinated me to watch their faces as they maneuvered in the partially darkened room. Their expression gave no indication of the thoughts hidden beneath the outward appearances. Laughter, mingled with light conversation, conveyed the expected machismo as they waited impatiently for the briefings. If there was any curiosity about their immediate future, any apprehension, or even some regard for this phenomenon called war, it didn't show. We maintain the guise, definitely part of the pilot persona.

I fixed on a young-looking Sergeant. His tightly set jaw, the vacuous look in his eyes, and absence of communication told me he was unsure of this mission he had begun. I examined his face, thinking here was a man who knew this venture could contain risk. The unknowns concerned him, and he made no effort to hide it. I smiled. *You're certainly not alone, Sergeant.*

Flashing on the screen were slides of jungle growth, dark escape tunnels, sharpened punji sticks, land mines, grizzled-looking Viet Cong, black pajama-clad kids with weapons, and a long list of known hazards. The voice droned on about trusting no one who looks different from us, carefully pointing out their ingenious ways of killing. A screen suddenly popped up with a map of Vietnam and the voice beside the projector changed. The new voice slapped his pointer against shaded areas in various colors for emphasis. Red indicated areas controlled by the Vietcong, blue denoted the ARVN areas of control, and Special Forces locations. It was apparent that there was much more red than blue. Outside the major cities, it was either enemy-held territory or questionable. *There's no "Bomb Line" here, as in Korea, no conclusive demarcation of the enemy, no defining of your side and theirs.*

The next voice was animated; seemingly taking great pleasure in the message he was bringing us. The words on the screen listed the various poisonous reptilian inhabiting the same space we planned to use. These were quickly followed by individual slides of snakes of different size, shape, and color. His grin implied the pure delight he took in describing the hooded cobra. "These reptiles are abundant in Vietnam; they conceal themselves in cool places, like under tents." Zack squirmed in his seat as the speaker's voice explained how the venom worked on the central nervous system. "Ah, but the cobra is not the cause of the most deaths." He flicked to the next slide, grinned, and said, "This is the sea snake. Looks like a harmless eel, doesn't it? They're salt water snakes, living in all the tributaries and inlets. These snakes kill more Vietnamese than any other reptilian. If you swim in the bay around China Beach, watch out for these fellows."

"Shit," whispered Zack.

Next was a picture of a small green snake. "Now for the most dangerous booger of all. Back in the States, you guys knew little green garden snakes were harmless. Fellows, that's not the case in Nam. This little creature carries the most deadly venom of all snakes in the country. One drop will kill a cape buffalo. The reason there're not more deaths is due to the snake's small mouth—it's got to bite a toe or finger, somethin' small enough to get its mouth on. If you go to the latrine at night, don't go barefoot or slip on shower clogs. Wear your damn boots."

"Christ almighty," Zack yelled out. "Are there any creepy-crawlies over there that don't kill you—maybe just scare hell outta you?"

Laughter momentarily stopped the briefing as the instructor also enjoyed Zack's chagrin. "Everything in Nam'll either scare the hell out of you or kill you—and that includes the women."

Tom reached forward and punched Zack. "If the women over there are dangerous too, Zack, you're really in a world of shit."

"Pretty astute, Tom," I added.

Zack wheeled around, looking at me. "Now, there are two words that don't usually bump up against each other — *Tom* and *astute*."

"Sorry," said the instructor. "But we have to paint the worst case scenario for you guys — just to be on the safe side. You can forget some of this stuff when you leave the room. All of us here wish you luck. Go get 'em."


Music saturated the air as we entered the Officers' Club dining room. The Filipino orchestra, filling the back stage, was playing its renditions of Glen Miller arrangements. The hostess led us to a large table, lit the candle and smiled. "Your waitress will be here shortly to take your order." Chuck, Zack, Rusty Prosser, Larry Raburn, and I pulled up to the round table and grabbed the menus. Tom continued standing, craning his neck, taking in the ambience. "Lordy, this is some Officers' Club." He sat hurriedly. "I've never seen a club with a full orchestra playing."

Zack was still looking across the table at Tom. "Well now, there's ten seconds of my life, gone, I'll never get back."

"Zack, you lost most of last night and didn't miss it," Tom said. "I'm damn sure that ten seconds was negligible in the time you've been on this earth."

Tom had finally hit on the deft humor necessary to neutralize Zack's skilled attacks, and become one of the crew. I figured he could hold his own now. I looked across at Zack and winked. He smiled knowingly as he quickly placed the menu in front of his face.

"Who'd like to split a Chateaubriand for two?" Chuck looked around the table for an answer.

"If you eat it rare, I'll go with that." I said.

"Now just what do you think of as 'rare'?"

"If a good vet could still save him—that'd be about right."

Chuck scanned the others. "Anyone care for some cooked meat?"

"Sure, Chuck," Rusty said. "I'll go with medium—sounds great."

"Hey, David," Larry lowered his menu. "I'll split one with you. Back in Texas, we'd just knock off the hoofs and horns before we ate 'em. Order that sucker 'rare'."

The evening took my mind into another dimension. All of a sudden there were no thoughts of flying, Lt. Col. Norwood, Major

Lynch, Vietnam, or war. I was in another place, whisked there by the music. As the waitress took the dessert plate away and placed the coffee cup in front of me, I eased back in the chair and focused on the harmony. In a flash, it mesmerized me into another location, another year.


The vocalist in front of the band was singing "Blues Serenade". She was sitting there in the soft light of Putch's 210 restaurant, sipping a glass of white wine. We had only been stationed near Kansas City for three months and still reveled in the Christmas atmosphere of Country Club Plaza. She was radiant as she twirled her wine glass in front of her face. She playfully moved it to one side. "Happy anniversary." Her hand reached across the table for mine. "I want you in my life forever."

*Forever—Forever is just an arrogant phrase—few people grasp the concept.* I refocused on the Philippine vocalist singing "It's Wonderful", and reality promptly surrounded me.

Tom moved ahead of Zack and me in the Sunday brunch line beside the swimming pool. His plate was piled high with eggs and ham, three different sweet rolls, and bacon. He juggled a bowl of fresh pineapple in the other hand. "Hey, Tom," Zack yelled. "You figure on eating enough there to last till lunch?" Tom gave a withering glace but didn't respond. He sat at a nearby table, motioning us to join him.

"You reckon the folks stationed here appreciate what they've got?" I asked as I sat down. "This is the best Sunday brunch I've ever laid eyes on." I pointed to the line. "There's certainly nothing missing from that selection. I've never seen three kinds of meat, four kinds of sweet rolls, and – ."

"Hi, fellas." Phil Merc interrupted.

I looked up abruptly at the sound of his voice. "Hey, when did you guys get in?"

"About two hours ago. Took this long to close out the clearance, fill out the aircraft logs, and clear customs. The other guys are over checking into quarters."

"Glad to see that engine didn't swallow a valve." I said. "Sorry I couldn't help you on delaying the flight."

"It worked out okay." He leaned over. "I need to chat with you when you have a minute."

"Okay." I pushed back from the table.

"Naw, go ahead and finish eating. It'll wait. I'll talk to you later."

I pushed back from the table, dropping the napkin beside the untouched plate of food. Walking beside Phil, noticing his look of anxiety, I asked what was bothering him. He stopped beside a huge oleander bush, then turned to face me. "Major Lynch got our inbound and met the aircraft. He asked about the aircraft status and told us to check into quarters, chow down, and prepare for an 0700 take-off tomorrow." His jaw tensed, "David, we're dragging ass. We've had no break in trying to get here like the Colonel ordered. Gary, my co-pilot, is sick—stubborn SOB finally agreed to go check in with the medics. Frankly, he should be in the hospital." He moved closer, almost eye-to-eye. "Goddamnit, we need another day to get it together."

"Let's go talk to Colonel Norwood. He knows there's a limit—you guys have hit it."

I spotted Lt. Col. Norwood, Major Lynch, and Captain Hazelwood off to the side of the pool, laughing and enjoying brunch. "Okay, Phil, let's go see what we can do."

As we approached, Colonel Norwood smiled and turned to Phil. "Glad you caught up. Major Lynch told me you got here—great job, Lieutenant. I really appreciate your crews' efforts to push on and get here that quickly."

"We really had to hump it."

"Colonel, they've had a tough trip trying to make up the time for that engine change." I leaned closer to make eye contact. "They took minimum crew rest along the way and they're beat. Gary Piotrowski's down at medical now—Phil says he's very sick. I don't think there's any way they can make a 0700 take-off tomorrow." For Phil's sake, I made sure my request contained enough humility for the Colonel.

"One more day won't make that much difference, Sir, since we got all sixteen aircraft here—we're just six hours from DaNang. I'd like for them to get one more day here at Clark. They really need it."

Major Lynch looked over toward the pool as if he didn't care to be brought into the discussion. Colonel Norwood shifted in his chair, then looked back at Phil. "Lieutenant, I know you and your crew have been giving max effort. You all deserve a rest—you certainly do." He wiped his mouth with his napkin. "I'm truly concerned about Lieutenant Piotrowski. How sick is he?"

"Pretty damn sick, Colonel. His fever is a hundred and three—he had the chills for the last four hours before we landed. The augmented pilot, John Mullin, and I took most of the last leg."

"Well, let's see what the medics say before we make any decision." He turned to Major Lynch. "Frank, if Piotrowski has to stay a few days, why can't the augmented pilot take it on in to DaNang and come back out with the C-130's?"

"We could probably get that approved back at Wing—but I'll need to get a message off pretty quick to get approval," Major Lynch responded.

I leaned in closer. "Colonel, that still doesn't give the crew a rest. They deserve another day to get their feet back under them—and by then, Gary might be feeling better," I argued. "If they do that, there'd be no need taking an augmenter on to DaNang."

"I know you're concerned about 'em, Captain—I am too. But listen, Phil, let's do this: eat some of this good food, get some rest, make the take-off tomorrow—with or without Gary—and I'll make it up to you when we get to DaNang."

"Colonel, I don't think you realize how tired they are." Trying to keep my voice unemotional was difficult. "It's gettin' close to being a flying safety problem and –."

"No, Captain Barfield, we've come this far with all sixteen aircraft, and only one short leg to go. If we get all sixteen aircraft to DaNang in record time, it'll mean something to the whole squadron. There's never been a deployment like this before. I know we can make it to DaNang with all sixteen birds."

"Colonel, what I was about to add was . . ."

"I've made a decision, Captain." His forced smile disappeared and his eyes narrowed on me. I knew there was no further hope. He turned back to Phil. "Let me know about Gary as soon as possible."

Phil nodded as we turned and walked away. I took Phil's arm. "Look, if you think for one minute you're jeopardizing safety to go—I'll invoke the safety issue in a damn heartbeat. He can't overrule that one."

"David, you know we'd all catch immortal hell for the rest of this tour. It would probably be the end of your career. He means for all his aircraft to get to DaNang tomorrow. He wants to make 'Bird Colonel' from this mission. No—no, we'll make the goddamn take-off at 0700." His eyes met mine. "Thanks for trying. I appreciate that—really do."

"No sweat. That's my job."

"Hey, see you later.' Phil said. "I'm gonna check on Gary then get some sack time."

My appetite was gone.

# 6

## DaNang

Sultry hot air hit my face like a blast furnace as I jumped from the aircraft. Zack hit the tarmac right behind me. "God almighty," he exclaimed, wiping at his forehead with the back of his hand. "We just landed on the far side of hell." The sticky moist heat enveloped my body and touched my spirit, and sweat poured from of my skin while I ignored his remark. Wiping at the sweat, I pointed to the old hangar with the other hand.

"Yeah, I see it," Zack snapped.

We walked together toward the only permanent structure on the flight line, scanning the barren area around us. Zack hurried toward the shade of the old French hangar that stood alone on the flight line. Off to the left were six bulky black rubber bladders filled with aviation fuel. Along the flight line were six A-1's, four 01-B "Birddogs", and several Huey helicopters. To the right were three dirt encrusted tents with crude signs indicating Operations, Intelligence and Maintenance. Immediately behind the operations tent was a larger t-shaped structure. Smoke coursed up in a white stream from its gas operated stoves and dishwashing apparatus. The food odors wafted our way. In spite of the heat, the aromas of the mess tent, moving with the slight breeze, were inviting.

I tried to ignore the clammy wetness of my flight suit as I took in the panorama of DaNang, Vietnam. Further in the distance was a horizon of olive drab tents. Several trucks bounced sluggishly over the rutted dirt road separating the flight line from the quarter's area. The border for the road was clearly defined by an endless coil of razor sharp barbs.

We walked faster toward the wide hangar doors. Once inside the old structure, my eyes followed the light source on the floor up to the high arched ceiling. Sunlight streamed through holes in the roof, casting spotlight splashes of radiance on the concrete hangar floor. Pieces of rotted material dangled from the holes, holding tenaciously to a decaying roof.

My morale seemed to be in the same condition as the hangar. A feeling of despair, swept over me. Once again I'd been hurled into a hostile and unpleasant environment. This psychological incapacitation was no stranger, it had visited me before and I knew it had to be shaken quickly. It could only be fought on its own terms, by focusing my thinking on the essentials: the mission and survival. My other world would always be waiting, a shadowy image to be brought into fine focus in quiet times. I knew, that in those thoughts, I'd find the solace, the balance—the incentive to do what had to be done. It always had.

B-4 bags, footlockers, and duffle bags were being piled in one corner of the hangar as we moved methodically through lines formed in front of three field desks. Loud talk and laughter made us listen closely for tent assignments. "Captain Barfield you're in tent four." The staff sergeant only glanced up briefly to make sure I was listening. "If you want to grab your own bags, the crew bus is loading out to the right of the hangar." His hand moved in the general direction. "Footlockers will be delivered later—if you want to wait, your bags will be dropped off then also."

Then I saw Phil Merc, Doug Pittman, and Gary Piotrowski walking into the hangar. "Hey, Zack." I tugged at his sleeve. "I'll meet you over by that pile of bags in a few. Wanna see how Gary's feeling." Without waiting for a comment I walked directly toward the three. One look at Gary gave a good indication of how he was feeling. The hollowness around his eyes formed dark shadows underneath, and an ashen pallor had drained the color from his face. His gait was unsteady, his feet shuffling him toward me until we came face to face.

"How're you feeling, Gary?"

"I'm makin' it."

"Bull shit. He aint makin' it. I tried to get him to check in the hospital back at Clark, but he was havin' no part of that." Phil looked steadily at me as he spoke. "He was too damned determined to take it on in to DaNang with me." Phil glanced at Gary and back at me. "He's been sucking up those antibiotics the medics gave him, and he still can hardly stand." His hand moved toward Gary. "Hell, take a look—that's one sick puppy."

"Don't you think it's about time you got off my case?" Gary snarled.

"Get him on the crew bus," I said. "I'll get your tent assignment and somebody to get your gear to you later." I pulled Phil closer. "Our Flight Surgeon got in early on the first C-130. Why don't you get him over to the Dispensary?"

"Listen, you two," Gary straightened slightly. "I don't need the damn Doc. Soon as I get to the tent and get something to drink and lie down, I'll be okay."

"Sure, Hercules," said Phil. "You're the picture of health." He took Gary's arm. "Just get your butt on the bus. You and I are gonna see a medic right now."

"I'll check with you later," I said but when I looked back over my shoulder, I saw Gary stumble against the hangar door and almost sink to his knees. I started toward him, but Phil already had him back up and moving through the door. He looked back and gave me a thumbs up as they disappeared into the bright sun. Zack moved beside me, watching the two going out the door. "Gary looks worse than dog shit. But reckon Norwood's happy now that all sixteen of his birds made it here in record time. To hell with the cost."

"Yeah," I whispered.

Zack pushed me from the rear as we boarded the crew bus. "Get it movin', Coach. We gotta go see what great quarters they have waitin' for us."

"Reckon those tents have central air?"

"Sure. You know Norwood looks out for his troops." Zack's laugh resounded throughout the bus, as others glanced swiftly in his direction.

I hit my hand against the heavy metal screen that was stretched and welded across the window. *Nice to see they've provided a little precaution against a grenade being tossed in. Sure makes me feel secure.* My attention turned to the outside. Rutted roads cut through the complex in irregular patterns, one angled off toward the east, leading to a Marine helicopter pad. The sun blazed down on palms and low bushes and greenish-barked trees. In the distance, just below the cloud height, I could make out the faint outline of Monkey Mountain. Its brown peaks stood erect, like dark green fingers thrust up through the jungle. It ended sharply as it fell abruptly into the sea.

The bus jostled to a stop, and two guards boarded through the front door. They held their AR-15's at the port arms position, moving slowly down the aisle. "Gentlemen, please hold out your ID," said the sergeant in front, bull-necked and sharp-featured, he had a deep booming voice. "We're required to check anyone who enters the compound." He glanced side to side as he moved steadily through the bus.

"Hey, Sergeant," Rick Haffenbrack yelled out, "I'm really a spy. You'd better send me back to the States for interrogation." The Sergeant showed only a faint smile as he strode back up the aisle of the bus, looking intently at pictures thrust up toward him. "Okay," he shouted as he jumped down, waving the driver through.

The bus moved about a hundred yards into the compound before stopping beside row after row of tents, melting into a sea of olive-drab canvas. There was a graveled walk between the first row of tents, fronting each other, about fifteen feet separating them. Another path led off to a long building with screened sides. A miniature water tower stood beside the long structure. Running out from the water tank on the bottom was a twenty-foot long gutter drain. We were to learn later this was the shower and the long building beside it was the latrine. The water tank, perched upon the rickety tower, was filled each morning for the Vietnamese sun to warm it. Later, several guys at a time would stand in the enclosure and pull on a long chain, allowing water to run down the gutter drain. Perforations in the bottom let the water fall gently over dirty bodies. Further over to the right, on the other side of the road, were several permanent buildings, low, white stucco structures. These were the only permanent quarters, offices, and Officers' Club on the Air Base. Their contrast was quite stark compared to the tent area.

I stood in front of the small white sign with the black number 4, obviously stenciled hastily with little care. Opening the screen door warily, I moved inside the over-heated canvas. Scanning the bunks, I decided on one halfway down the left side. Looking past the edge of the foot, I could see there would be room for a footlocker, which would serve as my closet, personal effects stowage, and laundry bag. The B-4 bag hit the floor with a thud, as I flopped onto the unmade bunk, dropped my hat beside me, and took a quick look around at the space inside the tent. There were seven other bunks, three on each side and two at the end. Each had been set up with a t-shaped frame at both the head and foot to support the mosquito netting. I thought back to Korea and living in a metal Quonset hut with three other guys, we called a "hootch." Those accommodations were opulent compared to what I saw here. Zack threw his B-4 at the foot of his bunk at the front of the tent and dropped down beside it in a heap. His head rolled back onto the naked pillow. "Hey, Coach, you can go ahead and turn on the air conditioning anytime now." When he got no answer, he looked back over his pillow. "Okay, I'll settle for . . ."

"Excuse me, Sir." A young Corporal peered through the screened side, about two feet from my face. "We've got the footlockers for tent four." He leaned even closer. "Captain, if you show us where to place 'em, we'll bring 'em in."

"The one labeled 'Barfield' can go right here." I gestured to the foot of the bunk. "The dead-looking Lieutenant over there is

'Williams'. You can drop his there. As for the others, just place one at the end of each bunk. Wherever the footlocker lands, that'll be their sack when they get here." Zack moved his hat to one side and looked up momentarily, swatted a mosquito and lowered it again without comment.

Tom surged through the opening, the large black spring snapping the door back into place with a whack. Walking along the row of bunks, a momentary look in every direction, his head swiveled back and forth. He stopped abruptly as he grabbed the netting bar of the end bunk. "Drop the one marked 'Johnson' right here." He pointed precisely to the place he wanted his locker placed. He strolled back and forth again, assessing his new surroundings. "What the hell, this isn't too bad—it could be worse."

I unlocked the footlocker and pulled out a towel. My face dropped into its softness as the material absorbed the perspiration; I caught Zack looking at me with a frown. Dropping the towel into my lap, I turned to him. "Tom's right. I reckon it could be worse."

"I wasn't thinking about that, even though I'm one unhappy, uncomfortable, pissed off Lieutenant. I was thinking about Gary. He sure didn't look good."

"I'll make sure their gear got placed in tent five." I grabbed my hat, moving toward the entrance. "Soon as I check out their tent, I'm gonna run over to the dispensary." I stood to one side as Rusty Prosser shot past, followed by Larry Raburn, his co-pilot, and Mac MacPherson, his navigator. Ignoring their presence, I turned back to Zack. "I'll be back and give you a report. Make sure those guys don't steal my mosquito netting."

"You'd better worry more about the mosquitoes takin' it. Christ almighty, these suckers look like dragonflies."

At the dispensary I read the sign, "Flight Surgeon", then bounded up the three steps and opened the door. A lanky staff sergeant was sitting behind a field desk working diligently on an IV bottle. He placed the plastic bottle on the protruding hook of the stainless steel stand, and without acknowledging my presence, moved through the second door, pushing his recently constructed apparatus. I walked over to the shelves of bandages, tongue depressors, boxes of rubber gloves, and a row of medicine bottles. The labels were mostly hand-written, taped around large brown bottles. I walked closer. The first bottle read: *Panther Piss*. Beside it was another, called *Magic Elixir*. The next bottle caught my attention as I turned it to read the label; *Potent Potient*.

"Can I help ya', Captain?" The sergeant reappeared. I swung around, still amazed by the shelf of bottles. "Sergeant, I believe they brought in Lieutenant Piotrowski a few minutes ago. I'm his flight commander and thought I'd see how he's doing." I looked at the sergeant for some reaction as I continued. "He seemed pretty sick when he got off the aircraft." Still no sign of hearing my comments. "Goddamnit, Sergeant, did you hear what I asked?"

"Sorry, Captain. I was thinking about something else."

"Where's the Flight Surgeon?"

"Doctor Singleton's busy right now." He pointed toward the door into the back. "He's back there with the lieutenant, whoever it was you asked about."

Ignoring the busy sergeant, I moved toward the door, my hand pushing it open. There on the table was Gary, fluids flowing into his left arm from an IV bottle. Phil was leaning against the wall, hands behind his head, watching intently. The captain in the jungle fatigues, unbuttoned to the waist, a stethoscope drooped across his neck, turned in my direction. "Well, hell, I should be selling tickets to my medical marvels today. Come on in, pull up a stool and join the party."

"I was worried about Gary. How's he doing?"

"I'm doin' fine." Gary chimed in.

"I wasn't asking you." I said.

Doctor Singleton ignored our comments. "I'll give you a quick medical update on our patient here." He touched Gary's arm. "He's dehydrated, elevated blood pressure, fever one-oh three point two, possibly some renal failure, and listening to him—slightly delirious. Other than that, he's doing fine."

"Hey, Phil," Gary half-whispered, "I want a second opinion."

Phil gave a quick look in my direction, shaking his head. "The Doc thinks he's got some severe kidney problem that's almost gotten outta hand. He's doing his best to get him some fluids for the dehydration."

Doctor Singleton was a tall man of slight build, dusty brown hair falling across his forehead, and wide-set eyes that moved constantly. He stood close to Gary, rubbing the stethoscope and looking quizzically at his patient. Phil pulled me out of earshot of Gary and the doctor. "He's sicker than he owns up to. We tried to catch our flight surgeon on the C-130 that diverted to Saigon. So, I figured he could authorize them to come back to DaNang for Gary before going to Clark." He shook his head. "I was too late."

"I thought our flight surgeon was staying here with us." "According to Major Lynch, he was only along for the deployment. He's on his way back to Pope right now."

I pulled Phil out to the front part of the building and pointed up to the shelves of medicine bottles. "This guy's nuts."

"Naw. Not really. He's just got a warped since of humor. I think he's pretty sharp under that zany exterior."

"Some sense of humor." I reached for the bottle marked "Panther Piss", pulled it from the shelf and turned it over in my hand. There on the back was printed "Pepto Bismol". Holding it toward Phil, he looked at the label.

"Well, I'll be damned," He said.

"Hey, how's Lieutenant Piotrowski?" Lt. Col. Norwood's unmistakable voice penetrated the room. Without waiting for an answer, he walked toward the door. "Is he back there?" His hand was already turning the knob.

"Yes, sir." Phil snapped. "He's back there with the Doc gettin' some IV fluids."

I watched the two disappear into the next room then heard muffled conversation as I walked out into the hot sun. The heat startled me. I had been standing in air conditioning without realizing how comfortable it was, my whole body mollified by the sensation, attuned subconsciously to what it had come to expect as normal. It reminded me of a Saturday matinee on a scorching hot July day in

Louisiana when I was a kid. I never realized how cool it was in the movie until I stepped out into the furnace-like blast of afternoon sun. The similarity here was startling.

By the time I got back to the tent, Doug Pitman, Phil's navigator, and Carey Hulsey, navigator from Rick Hafenbrack's crew had settled in the bunks on the right side. The *DaNang Hilton* was full. Footlockers were banging open and shut as eight officers arranged their personal effects, and prepared their new home for living. Cursing, laughter, and conversation blended with the sound of Mac singing *Puff, the Magic Dragon.* I unzipped the sticky flight suit and fell across the bunk. Instantly, I began to swat at stinging bites. Zack stood up, laughing and reaching for the nearby can of mosquito spray. "Here, try this and, for God's sake, pull down the netting." He tossed the can of spray at me. "These suckers'll eat your carcass as fast as a school of piranha." He waited to see the results of my spraying. "Well, what's the low-down on our patient?"

"Well, I reckon' he's gettin' some medical attention, but he should've been flown outta here with the C-130's." I rolled up on one arm, still spraying the area around me. "That Flight Surgeon's a couple bricks shy of a load."

"Meaning?"

"I mean he's a very strange dude indeed. You're not gonna see another flight surgeon like this one."

The bug spray began to work, and I eased back and waited for a breeze to glide over me. Instead, the heat sucked the air from my body. It was apparent that sleeping during the day would be close to impossible. I lay there, perspiration beading up, trying to transport my mind to another time and place. As I closed my eyes, Phil leaned over, his face pushed against the netting. "Colonel Norwood called Seventh Air Force headquarters and talked with the Deputy." He smiled broadly as he continued. "They're diverting a C-124 here to pick up Gary. He'll be in the Clark hospital in a few hours. Norwood had to go al the way to the Air Division CO to get it done. The Doc says some intravenous antibiotics might make the difference."

I sat up instantly. "Well, I'll be damned. Norwood came through."

"He sure did," Phil said. "Maybe you had him all wrong."


The night air cooled to a still stifling 102 degrees, but the heat was still noticeable as we settled in the movie tent. "Hey, guys, be a little patient," the corporal yelled out. "The damn projector just cut the film — ah, shit — well, Gentlemen, we'll miss the first two minutes of the movie." He bent over the machine, pulling film though the slot in an engrossed effort to start the movie. Muffled talking and clinking cans of drinks provided a noisy background as the movie was being readied. The operations tent provided the setting for this ritual evening showing of movies. The sergeant looked up from his work. "Saigon sent us one worth watching for a change." He smiled at his audience. "Tonight we've got "Home From The Hill". It's got Robert Mitchum, Eleanor Parker, George Hamilton, and George Peppard."

As we waited in the semi-darkness, muffled shades of light illuminated the sky in the distance, indicating lightning from thunderstorms. The flashes on the horizon, however, appeared more frequently than just a few moving thunderstorms. I leaned toward Zack, and pointed to the horizon past the screen. "Maybe that lightening means we'll get some cooling rain movin' this way."

"Don't hold your breath." The voice came from the seat behind us. We turned to face the sun-browned face of a lieutenant. "That's not lightening. Those are mortar rounds from the Special Forces camp about twenty-five clicks away." His demeanor was indifferent, even blasé, about shells exploding a few miles away. "They're takin' a few incoming from the VC, but they'll lay on a barrage of their own in a couple minutes. We have our A-one fighters in the air and I'm sure they'll call 'em in for an air strike. Wait a minute or two, and you'll see the sky light up." Zack looked at me and shrugged.

"Okay, here we go," the sergeant said as the lights went out. The screen flickered to life with a beautiful young girl blowing a truck's horn to get George Hamilton's attention. Just past the screen, the horizon lit up like a Fourth of July celebration. The almost continuous bursts of light from exploding artillery and napalm cast a glow like an early dawn.

"See what I mean?" The voice from the rear half whispered. "Right on time. That'll give 'Charlie' something to chew on." We nodded understanding without looking away from the gorgeous blonde making a move on George Hamilton. George was displaying his cool rebuff of the blonde's attentions when the tent light unexpectedly came on. The projector whined to a stop among groans and cursing. "Christ, not again," the voice from behind yelled.

"I'll just take a minute, then you can get on with the movie." Major Lynch looked embarrassed as he stepped to the front, shuffling a paper in front of him. "I hate to interrupt the flick, but we need to get this word out. There'll be a briefing for all aircrew of the Composite Squadron at 0700 tomorrow. Seventh Air Force just sent us frag orders for missions starting tomorrow morning. See you then." He looked back toward the sergeant. "It's all yours."


The voice from the rear started again. "Well, they sure didn't waste any time gettin' you guys into this thing." His laugh was sardonic as the movie started again. Zack and I both looked back at him as the Lieutenant leaned back against his chair. "Believe me, your CO had to volunteer you guys—even those weeneys at Seventh Air Force aren't that friggin' callous."

"Shh!" A voice bellowed from the right as we immediately turned back to the blonde in the truck still making obvious overtures of availability to George Hamilton. The muffled sound and diffused bursts of light surrounding the screen appeared scripted as background music for the human emotions being played out. Over the next hour, the shell bursts in the distance slowly diminished. The final scene evolved as the horizon became peacefully quiet again. Instantly the lights came on.

# 7

## Missions

Inside the mess tent, the early morning coolness disappeared. The smell of bacon simmering on the grill drew me toward the serving line. I grabbed a metal tray and fell into line behind Mac MacPherson. He was still humming *Puff, The Magic Dragon* as I peeked over his shoulder at the food line. A sweaty cook, his stomach straining against his wet tee shirt, was taking orders for eggs. "I'll take three scrambled medium," Mac announced. The cook's large hands broke three eggs onto the hot grill as he glanced at me. "Two over easy, please," I requested, while dragging three limp pieces of bacon onto a pile of hash browns. Automatically two eggs plopped onto the surface of the grill, making an instant sizzling sound. The coffee smelled delicious as I filled the ceramic mug and balanced it on the edge of the tray. Breakfast in hand, I moved toward the table near the back. Phil Merc was waving me in as he pointed to an empty spot at the table. I maneuvered my way down the rows of tables and slid in opposite Phil. "You look worried—what's the matter?"

"Gary's not doing too well. He's scheduled for a bunch of tests. They think it may be complete renal failure."

"How'd you find out?"

"Colonel Norwood caught me on the way to chow and told me he'd checked with the hospital this morning. He seemed pretty upset."

"Upset my ass," I said. "I wouldn't believe that SOB if his tongue was notarized. Gary might be better if he'd hadn't been pushed to leave Clark in the first place."

"You're being the ass," Phil said. "I know how you feel about Norwood, but Gary's damn stubborn streak was to blame for him being here. He was told he could stay at Clark and let the augmented pilot bring it on in with me. You need to get off Norwood's butt on this one. "

I looked hard at Phil, ready to jump him. Instead, I concentrated on the tray in front of me. "Yeah, you're right. I buy what you're saying." I slapped his arm. We'll have to shift co-pilots around for a while, so don't plan on a mission today."

"Hell, I don't mind takin' the right seat if it gets the mission done—I'm not proud."

I looked straight at Phil, conveying my amazement at his statement. A broad grin stretched across his face. "I deserved that mystified look you just gave me. I was a little testy with you that first day back at Pope."

"Testy? I'd say you were cantankerous as hell. You told me, in no uncertain terms, that you were the best damn C-123 pilot in this man's Air Force." I laughed. "The hell of it is, Phil, you might be."

"Well, now that you mention it . . ."

"Yeah, yeah. Finish that coffee and let's get over to Operations and see what the Old Man volunteered us for."

"Whatcha mean, 'volunteered'?"

"That's a long story. And as you said, let's give our CO the benefit of the doubt. Godamighty, I can't believe I just said that."

Zack dropped into the seat next to me as the Operations tent filled swiftly. He scrunched down in the chair, hands crossed on his lap, chin resting on his chest. It was the typical Zack pose for "Get on with this crap so I can go do my job." I nudged him. "You didn't make it to breakfast?"

"It's too friggin' hot to eat. Besides, it meant another thirty minutes of sleep." He groaned. "It must've been two in the morning before I even dozed off." He cut his eyes toward me, his head barely moving.

"I kept thinking about our CO, OPs officer, and Adjutant over there in that BOQ with those ceiling fans cooling their sorry-ass hide."

"There were only two rooms available in the 'Q'. Now think about it—which guys from all our aircrew would you pick to get 'em?"

"I see your point." Zack bit off the words. His eyes went back to the front of the room without comment. Tom dropped into the chair beside him and Zack didn't even cut his eyes in his direction. "Good morning, guys," Tom said, almost in Zack's ear.

I leaned across and placed my finger to my lips. "Shh. The lieutenant here didn't have a good night."

"That, Tom," Zack said, "means smile broadly and say absolutely nothing."

Tom stared at Zack for a few seconds. "Talkin' to you Zack is like walking into that jungle out there. You never know what to expect – none of it good."

Any response from Zack was cut short by the voice of the Sergeant standing near the side entrance. "TEN HUT".

Colonel Norwood strode to the front with a pleased look wiped across his face. Major Lynch followed closely and Captain Hazelwood stopped over to their right side.

"Take your seats, Gentlemen," Norwood said. "The first thing I want to tell you guys is how damn proud I am to be your Commanding Officer. There's no doubt this is the sharpest group of men in the Tactical Air Command. This unit deployed sixteen aircraft from the east coast, flew half-way around the world, arrived at DaNang with all sixteen aircraft, in record time—and think about it—flying missions the next day." His eyes searched the room, his face showing his elation. "The Three Fifteen Air Commando Group should be damn proud to have you assigned to it. In fact, starting this morning we'll be gettin' missions assigned by Special Operations at Bien Hoa. Now let's show 'em how professionals get the job done." With a fleeting look to his left, he said, "It's all yours, Major."

Major Lynch rustled some frag orders in front of him as he read off the assigned missions. He stopped momentarily and looked at me. "Captain Barfield, since you are short a pilot in your flight, I've assigned Lieutenant Merc to Lieutenant Hafenbrack's crew for today's missions. That'll put everyone in the air and give him a chance to learn the area and get a feel for the operations."

I gave him a thumbs up as I looked at Phil for his reaction. He was smiling.


Tactical loads, routes, and destinations were read off hurriedly, while Tom rushed up to get the frag order for our crew and started matching them up on his map of the I Corps area. I took a look at weather and got reassurance from the intelligence officer that there were no known heavy weapons in our target areas. Immediately, I thought of the armor plating placed under the pilot and co-pilot seats. They would stop thirty caliber and small arms—fifty caliber would be another story entirely.


We assembled at the aircraft and stood under the wing for shade. This was our first one, the gut buster, the one that breaks you in on where you are and what's expected of you. For only a second or two, I wondered if this was one war too many. *How long do you push Old Man Luck? Well, hell, it's not a matter of luck, or fate, or whatever else pilots conjure up. It's skill after all.* "The first part of today's mission is to get familiar with the terrain and major landmarks in the Central Highlands. We're going north to Hue, then directly west to Ashau Valley." I looked at Tom for emphasis. "We'll approach Ashau from the south, making a steep approach straight in to the runway," I continued. "Intelligence says they've had some activity there lately." I noticed Tom's frown, and then continued. "After Ashau, it's southeast to a drop zone called Hiep Duc. We'll make the drop at two hundred feet, and then a max climb to altitude. Last target is Gia Vuc. We'll shut engines there for an offload of the M-60, fifty caliber ammo, and the rations."

"How hot is Gia Vuc?" Tom asked.

"No intelligence available. That's probably a good sign." Tom nodded. "Check your emergency and survival gear, make sure everyone has his side arm on, and let's get on with the fun and games."

I pre-flighted the aircraft thoroughly, with Zack following closely behind. We both climbed aboard and began the checklists for engine starts. The heat was already cooking the aluminum skin of the aircraft at 0735. Getting to altitude would feel good. After a careful run up and tower clearance, we took the active runway behind a 01-B birddog. Zack pointed to the small aircraft roaring down the runway. "Wonder where he's off to, acting as a forward air controller?"

"I like seeing those guys hanging around," I said. "In fact, I wouldn't mind a flight of fighters on standby for providing air cover."

"If you see those guys coming in ahead of you, dropping napalm, you're probably in the wrong damn place at the right time." Zack said.

"Yeah—Starting number one."


At Monkey Mountain we turned slightly to the right, out to sea. Zack checked in with the radar controller on top of the mountain. "Oscar control, Delta 21 passing at your three o'clock position, enroute to Hue, then Ashau."

"Roger, Delta 21. Stay out over the water until opposite Hue, then make your turn inland. That'll keep you away from any of Charlie's ground fire."

"Roger that, Control."

The mountain cascaded down into an estuary of crevices and rocks. A misty film hung over the inlet, trees stretching up virgin and tall through the vapor. Further out, a few fishing craft off shore dotted the horizon. As we flew north, Tom's voice cut through the intercom, breaking the silence. "Left turn to two eight-five degrees, Hue in six minutes."

"Roger the new heading," I said, rolling into a left bank.

"Make that heading two six-two after passing Hue," Tom added. "That'll put us about ten miles south of Ashau for a right turn and a straight in to the runway."

"Roger," I acknowledged.

As we flew west, the green-crested jungle rose majestically in every direction. Some canyon walls were steep, others sloping gently into yet another valley. In places, it was easy to see the layers of growth that formed the jungle canopy. Giant trees, fifty to sixty feet tall, formed the upper cover, the second layer consisted of a thicket of smaller trees, and the lowest layer was thick twisted growth of vines and shrubs. Looking down at the predatory jungle it was apparent that a man would have a difficult time walking out.

"In four minutes, turn three five-nine degrees, that'll put us right up the valley to Ashau," Tom said.

"Well, here goes the first of many intriguing approaches." With a fleeting look toward me, Zack said, "Let's hope no one is terribly mad at each other this morning. I like things quiet on an empty stomach."

"We'll keep a thousand feet AGL until the last minute." I punched Zack. "I reckon next time you'll eat something. Let's get the before-landing check out of the way, but hold the gear and flaps until one mile out."

"You got it, Coach." Zack flipped the radio frequency to 132.5 MHz. "Ashau control, Delta two-one, five out for landing. Do you have any advisory on traffic or hostile fire?"

There was a long silence as Zack waited for an answer. I looked over to see him hunch his shoulders as if he had no suggestions. He keyed the mike again, ready to transmit a second time, as a clear voice broke through the headset. "Roger, Delta two-one. Read you loud and clear—come on down. There's no other traffic, no hostile fire, and we're lonely."

Laughter through the intercom signaled unanimous relief. This first mission into a Special Forces camp appeared to be a milk run after all. As we approached the one-mile point, I called for the gear and full flaps. As the large flaps extended, the nose suddenly dropped into a steep angle. There in front of us was a dirt strip of runway, a deep ditch running along the left side between the barbed wire and the landing strip. The scene was reminiscent of cowboys and Indians in an old western movie. There was the fort on one side and enemy on the other. The main gear hit the runway, as I dropped the nose gear onto the dirt, and pulled both engines into reverse. The aircraft shuddered to a stop amid the flying dust and gravel. I turned the aircraft 180 degrees, facing back down the runway. *No use being surprised while on the ground.*

With both engines at idle, Jocko lowered the rear ramp and unstrapped part of the cargo. A truck left the compound, speeding toward us in a cloud of dust. It maneuvered close to the rear, as three men in jungle utilities, green berets, and M-16's slung over their shoulders, began unloading the ammo and rations. A short, well-muscled Master Sergeant moved up toward the cockpit. "Hey, why don't you shut engines and stay awhile?" He shouted over the noise of the engines.

"We're on a short stay here—got two more to make," I shouted back. "Besides, you just had some heavy enemy activity here a couple days ago."

"Yeah, they bit off more than they could chew. Our patrols tell us they've retreated back into the hills for a while."

Zack leaned around. "Hey, Sergeant, what's all those things sticking up along the bank of that ditch?"

"Sharpened 'punji' sticks. That, a few land mines, and lotsa concertina wire keeps the VC away." Zack looked puzzled, so the Sergeant continued. "The little bastards sneak up at night, or in an all-out charge, to try to penetrate our perimeter. We nail most of 'em—sometimes a few get inside—then it's hand-to-hand."

The Master Sergeant gave a wave as he took the passenger seat in the truck. It moved off, once again, in a cloud of dust. I looked over at Zack. "They sure as hell didn't build any long runways over here. That thing looks even shorter than when we landed."

"Hell, I could snatch it off in half that," Zack said. "Ever hear of max performance take-offs?"

"Okay, Hot Stuff, it's all yours. Let's see a real max performance takeoff." I said.

The checklists were completed swiftly and Zack brought both throttles to sixty-two inches manifold pressure, hit water injection and inched the throttles to sixty-three inches. The C-123 shook violently as Zack stood on the brakes. He released the brakes and the aircraft leaped forward. I followed his hand up on the throttles and used the nose wheel steering until I knew his rudder was effective. I shot a quick look at the airspeed indicator as it moved to seventy knots. Zack sucked back on the control column. The C-123 was still too heavy as it skipped back onto the runway. Zack yanked harder on the control yolk and the wheels left the ground with the stall warning horn blaring its message. I looked out the left side and saw almost half the runway remaining. "Not bad, Sport. But I'd rather have some more airspeed before you try to make it fly."

He smiled. "It's flying, isn't it?"

"Would you two stop playing games up there," Tom yelped into the intercom.

"Unclench your butt, Tom," Zack said. "The scary part's over."


Twenty minutes later, we were moving down a deep valley, over a sodden corpse of decaying jungle. The lush green had been defoliated by "Operation Ranch Hand" C-123's spraying Agent Orange. Barren trees and brown terrain were testimony to the results of the defoliant. Further down the valley were areas scorched by napalm and pot-marked by bombs, mute confirmation to the battle fought here. "Hiep Duc eight miles ahead," Tom announced.

"Roger. Jocko, lower the ramp and stand by for a green light."

"Ready, Captain."

"Jocko, that drop area is damn small. I was told the drop better hit inside the circle—otherwise the VC'll get it first. Kick out both bundles on this pass. We don't want to make a second pass after we've lost the element of surprise."

"Roger that, Captain. Just give me the green light."

We skimmed in low, beside the compound, just above treetops. Hiep Duc's DZ was in a bowl-shaped valley with higher terrain on all sides. Turbulence bounced us sideways, the surface winds gusty and unpredictable. "Jocko, I'm gonna drop it down to a hundred feet to compensate for this damn wind."

"Roger."

My finger was fixed to the jump light switch, as the aircraft bounced harder.

"Three degrees right will do it," Tom crackled into the headset.

"Roger that—got it dead ahead." There in front of us was a faint circle with an "X" painted in the middle. My finger flipped the switch. The green light blinked its message to Jocko. The aircraft lurched slightly as the load dropped.

"Load's gone. Both chutes deployed," Jocko said.

I banked hard left, advanced the throttles to climb power and looked back to see an open chute floating to the ground, the other one lay drooped over the pallet on the ground. "Looks like a good one, Jocko," I said. "Now let's get some altitude and cool air."

"I'm having trouble with the landmarks, David," Tom said. "And we're outta range of VOR stations."

"Keep at it. We're too low and too far out for radar to give us a vector."

"These mountains and jungle all look the same," Tom said. "If I could just find that river—David, I think we'll have to abort this one."

"Negative on the abort. We're gonna get into Gia Vuc. So keep looking."

"Hey, Tom, look at our ten o'clock position," Zack directed. "Is that the river?"

Tom's head shot between us. "Yeah, I believe that's it." Tom scanned the area. "We're a little off course. Turn right to two-five-two degrees."

I rolled hard right and looked into the sea of green, trying to spot the elusive Special Forces Camp. "Got it." I stated. "We're not gonna be able to make a straight-in approach now. I'll fly a left-hand traffic pattern." I hesitated a minute. "Before landing check list". Zack called out items as my hands moved swiftly around the cockpit. Zack's eyes followed my movements, making sure my response and actions were accurate. "Gear," I shouted.

"Gear comin' down." Zack answered. "Gear locked, three in the green, pressure up."

Just as I was ready to ask for full flaps, I heard muffled backfiring from number two engine. The staccato popping sounds were indication of something seriously wrong on the right side. I glanced at Zack, who strained forward to check the sound. "Full flaps," I asked. "That damn engine's cutting up pretty good. We'll check that sucker out before take-off."

"Roger that. Flaps set—full."

The gear hit the sod runway with a slight bounce. My feet pushed hard on the brakes as the throttles were brought into reverse thrust. The aircraft vibrated to a stop. A stocky Major hobbled toward the left side as the engines whined to a stop. He walked like an old man, rocking side to side, favoring his right foot. Two other officers were walking beside him but provided no assistance. I swung out the side door as Jocko was releasing cargo tie-downs. I saluted the major as he came closer. It was then I noticed the makeshift cane he was using for support. He was a handsome officer, dark brown hair sticking out from under the Green Beret, ramrod straight, with sparkling sharpness in his eyes. I was ready to ask about his noticeable limp, when he began speaking. "They really cut down on you out there on final approach."

"What're you saying, Major?"

"They opened up with everything they had, as you lined up with the runway on final." He frowned. "By making that long pattern, you almost gave 'em time to adjust fire. We thought for a minute there, they had you."

My heartbeat increased as I tried to look nonchalant. "I thought the right engine was backfiring on final." I looked over at the aircraft, hastily out into the jungle, then back at the major. "I've flown missions in combat before—but that's the first time I ever heard somebody shootin' at me."

"Get used to it," The major said.

"Hey, Captain." Sergeant Picardo shouted, while waving me over to the tail of the C-123. Tom, and Zack were already examining the horizontal stabilizer. Jocko was busy with the cargo. I walked over to the assembled group as the major and entourage followed closely. Underneath the tail section, I could see five irregularly shaped holes in the horizontal stabilizer, and two in the rudder.

The major began to laugh as he turned to the other officers. "The VC still can't figure out how much to lead an aircraft." He pointed to the holes in the tail. "But they're gettin' better."

I turned back toward the major. "What's wrong with your foot?"

"Stepped on a damn punji stick in the bush last night. Shoulda' been more careful."

I could see the encrusted blood that had oozed out of the canvas portion of his right boot. Blood, turned a deep scarlet as it mixed with dirt, covered the right side of his boot. "Why don't you hop on board and we'll take you back to DaNang for treatment. I hear those things are dipped in all kinds of stuff. They can be deadly."

"Naw, my medic treated it." He looked down at his right foot. "Tonight we're gonna go out and get a few of those Charlies who fired on you."

"Lotsa' luck." I shook his hand and started back to the aircraft. My mind abruptly locked onto the need to get back into the air, to get to that familiar place next to clouds and blue sky, a niche I knew so well. I didn't want to think about the holes in the tail section, VC gunners, bloodied Green Beret majors, or jungle heat. I wanted to get into the cool air, far above the jungle, and let my mind dwell on anything pleasant.

With the engines set at cruise power, we flew east toward the coast, then north back to DaNang.


The mosquito netting was tucked in tight around me as I sat with legs folded, and paper balanced awkwardly on a writing board. I tried to get as comfortable as possible in that awkward Buddha position, then began writing.

*DaNang*
*April 4, 1963*

*Dear Leslie:*

The pen stopped moving as my thoughts unexpectedly became difficult to express. Not knowing her feelings at the moment made the task more difficult. My hand moved the pen across the page again.

> *We're settled into tent city here on the edge of the compound at DaNang. We arrived yesterday and began our missions today. No rest for the wicked. Eight of us here in the DaNang Hilton is not conducive to much privacy, but we do have a cohesive group. There's always noise going on—especially Mac's constant singing of "Puff The Magic Dragon". Add a daily temp of about 115 degrees and you look forward to flying to keep cool, then night to bring the temp down to a bearable level. We laugh and say constantly, "It could be worse." But you know the old cliche' that goes with that line—"then it got worse." At least no one has attempted murder yet. I came pretty damn close after Mac's hundredth rendition of "Puff", but he explained that was the song he sung to his little girl every night. I reckon we can put up with it.*

> *Hope all is well with you. Wish I could be there to help with selling the house. I left you with too blasted much responsibility—but we had little choice in the matter. You have that unique ability to accomplish the impossible, so I know you'll handle this one the same way. As for other decisions and papers, just send them over and I'll sign whatever is required.*

> *No need to tell you I miss you. That's a given. Maybe our thinking will change by the time we get back. Who knows? I know it would be good for us to get away for a long*

*trip—maybe just lying around some isolated beach. We need some time alone, away from all the stress. Life, the Air Force, deployments, and Vietnam were piled on top of other things. Think about the offer—it has possibilities.*

*Use the address on the envelope for all mail. Give my love to Miss Ellen and keep a little for yourself.*

*Love,*
*David*

"Hey, anybody not ready for lights out?" Mac shouted.

"Flip 'em off. Maybe that'll lower the temp about two degrees," Zack yelled back.

Instantly the tent became dark. I lay back on the damp sheet, perspiration gently rolling into my hair, waiting for sleep to end this day. Thoughts of the first missions, the new house back at Fayetteville, and Leslie floated around in the dark tent. The panoramas faded gently into one scene—Leslie standing beside the car, looking beautiful. It brought on sleep.

# 8

## Jungle Utilities

Even though it would sear the body later, the sun's gentle announcement of dawn soothed the spirit. This was a pleasant time for me as the cooler night, having mitigated the heat and sultry humidity, was ending quietly. I relished the serenity of daybreak, watching the almost imperceptible pale glow on the horizon turn slowly into the first sight of the morning sun.

I pulled on my flight suit, as I watched the activity around the bulletin board area just outside the tent. The First Sergeant was busy posting his morning communications for the unit. The thatch-covered bulletin board had been closely supervised by the First Sergeant, and as soon as it was finished, he ceremoniously added a large blue box with a slit on top to receive mail.

As he pushed in the last thumbtack and stood back admiring his work like an artist, I eased up beside him. "What's the latest scoop today, Sergeant?"

"It's a new Standard Operating Procedure for the squadron. The Colonel wanted it posted right away." He adjusted another thumbtack, and then swung around to face me. "He had the clerk type it up last night."

"Well, reckon I'd better read this new hot poop from the orderly room tent. It probably contains all the latest world news and baseball scores—right, Sergeant?"

He frowned. "Captain, you should tell all in your flight that the Colonel has placed maximum importance on this." He abruptly strode off toward the orderly room tent.

I moved closer to the official notice and shook my head as I read the words hurriedly.

*Hdq. 315ᵗʰ Air Commando Gp., 309ᵗʰ Air Commando Sqdn.*
*18 April 1963*
*SOP No: 6*

*The following Standard Operating Procedure will be initiated as of today:*

*All members of the 309ᵗʰ Air Commando Squadron will wear the jungle utility uniform at all times. This applies to flight duties as well as those on the ground. The Air Commando Bush hat will be worn with this uniform instead of the flight cap. The use of the Air Commando swatch as well as the Vietnamese rank insignia may be used on either side of the bush hat to keep the sides turned up. Pants will be bloused over the boots, as is customary for other Special Forces Units. The Air Commando patch will be worn over the right breast pocket vice the Tactical Air Command Patch.*

*Signed*
*Douglas P. Norwood, Lt. Col., USAF*
*Commanding Officer*

My eyes moved down the page again to make sure I understood the posted SOP. Looking over at the orderly room tent, I weighed my decision carefully. The last two weeks had placed Major Lynch and me at odds twice on scheduling my flight; no doubt these discussions had been brought to the Squadron Commander's attention. It didn't matter; this had to be addressed now. *Maybe he'll be reasonable, but that would be a first.* By then I was already opening the orderly room's squeaky screened door, moving in front of the three field desks. The clerks were deep into their paperwork. Dead ahead was the First Sergeant's desk, standing sentinel duty to the metal divider that separated the Colonel's area. Off to the right was Captain Hazelwood, his head buried in papers scattered over the desk top. He didn't look up.

"Sergeant, I'd like to talk to Colonel Norwood—if he's got a minute."

"Just a minute, Sir, I'll see if he's busy. Could I tell him the nature of your business?"

"It's sorta personal."

The inaudible voices behind the partition gave no indication of how busy the Colonel might be. There was a pause, more mumbling, and then the Sergeant stood at the opening. "The Colonel says to come right in, Captain."

I walked to the desk, saluted and was greeted with a broad smile. "Have a seat, Captain Barfield. What's on your mind so early this morning?"

"First thing, Colonel is the status of our request for automatic weapons for the crews."

He rocked back, still smiling, but not as much as before. "I've talked to the Air Police unit and they state flatly that M—16's are issued only to those on guard duty. Frankly . . ."

"Excuse me, Colonel that jungle out there is not the sort of country you want to bail out in. My flight's decided that the best hope of survival is to put down in a river bed or rice paddy. If the crew survives and has automatic weapons, we'd have a damn good chance of holding out at the crash site until SAR arrives."

"I see your point—really do—but the Air Police have control over all automatic weapons at DaNang. Nothing else need be said on that subject." *Obviously, discussion on this subject is over.*

"The other thing, Colonel"—time to approach the hot topic—"the SOP just posted could be a real hardship for the aircrews. Jungle utilities are just too hot and uncomfortable for flying in this heat. We all wear our Bush hats and have the Air Commando 'ZAP' patch on our flight suits. That's what other Special OPs people wear."

"We're damn professionals in the 309th," he said, "and I intend for us to set the pace—not just follow."

"Colonel, this could be a safety issue as well . . ."

"Captain," he interrupted, "I don't post SOP's with no thought to the consequences." His flashing blue eyes bore into me. His open features, expressing good humor, contradicted his hasty temper. That fiery disposition was probably held in check by a very thin thread. His face contorted just enough for me to see his benevolent malice. "I intend for this squadron to wear jungle utilities for the rest of this operation." His eyes still fixed to mine. "That's about as clear as I can make it."

"Yes, Sir."

As I was getting dressed again in my jungle utilities, Zack bounced through the door with a towel draped around his neck, carrying his shaving kit. He stopped suddenly, still wiping his face with the towel. "What the devil are you puttin' . . ."

BLAM, BLAM, BLAM—BLAM rang out from the next tent. I instinctively rolled onto the floor, clasping my hands over my head. Zack hit the floor with a thud, his shaving kit bouncing against the footlocker. His mumbling was incoherent with his face against the wood. Tom banged headfirst into his footlocker trying to get as low as possible, while Mac never moved from his bunk.

I rose slowly, searching for the source of the shots. Laughter was gushing from the next tent as Zack's hand fished around for various articles from his kit. Tom, rubbing his head was sitting on his bunk. I walked to the tent door and yelled, "What the hell was that?"

Still laughing, Frank Wiggans stumbled out the screen door. "Guy saw a cobra slither under the tent floor and he was blasting away at the damn thing. It's a wonder he didn't blow off a toe the way he was dancing around our floor with that forty-five."

"Godamighty, Frank, we thought the VC were firing into the tents."

"The friggin' VC probably aren't as dangerous as Guy." He started laughing again.

"Not too damn funny to me," Tom yelled. Cautiously, he moved closer. "Did he kill the thing?"

"Yeah, I think he got it—look, they're fishin' it out now."

I turned away from the limp brown serpent draped over a broom handle and went back into the tent. Zack was staring at the dispatched snake as if hypnotized. He slowly looked toward me. "This whole friggin country is full of creepy crawly things."

"Get dressed in utilities and let's get some chow before we hit operations."

"What's with these utilities?"

"New SOP—just pull 'em on and let's go." I shot a glance at Tom. "You too."

"You gotta be kiddin?" Zack asked.

"That's the word from the CO."

"Damn," Zack said, as he kicked the footlocker.


Tom, Zack, and I ambled down the narrow gravel path that led from the mess tent to operations. Zack bent low over the lighter and sucked in a long draw on the cigarette. Each was in his own world, thoughts privately held and viewed as we walked toward the mission for this new day. I wondered if Zack was mulling over the missions as I was. By now, he must realize flying into these LZ's and DZ's with high gross weights, low visibility, mixed with ground fire, were a sure test of flying ability. We both knew even the best of us were on the edge of our capabilities when faced with runways too short, an 800-foot looming gorge beside the Khe Sanh runway, the shearing mountain winds at Diep Duc, and dropping in, straight down over the ridge, at Kham Duc—and always listening for that tell-tale slap of metal against metal from a "hit". *The hazards lurking in every mission are a constant challenge, but an exhilarating sense of accomplishment accompanies beating the odds. Every mission is the usual gamble: the perpetual bet is that the critical, unforgiving mistake won't be made on this one. That's how combat flying has always been. Suck it up — the game has to be played.* My thoughts snapped back to the operations tent up ahead.

Zack headed back from the front to the seat beside me, waving a frag order for Ashau. Major Lynch was still handing out the missions of the day at the front of the tent. He wiped the sweat on his forehead, looking up quickly at the faces near him, dealing out missions as if they were tickets to a social affair.

"Let me have your attention," Major Lynch raised his voice to make sure he was heard. "One new requirement starts today." He looked up to see that every eye was looking at him. He cleared his throat. "As of today, you'll file a flight plan at each landing zone—just like you would stateside."

"You aren't serious, Major?" I asked.

"Damn right, I am."

Phil stood. "Just where the hell do you file a flight plan?—there're no operations at these LZ's."

"Then put it under a rock, Lieutenant," Lynch said.

Zack leaned over close and whispered, "If he's here, who's running Hell?"

I pushed Zack back from my ear. "Major, where the hell did this come from? Is this from the three fifteenth?"

"It doesn't matter where it originated, Captain. That's the requirement."

Phil stormed through the tent opening, and then spotted Zack, Tom, and me huddled over our map. He walked up briskly and hesitated, we automatically looked up. "Gary died this morning," Phil said, his jaw quivering. "They did everything possible, but the renal failure had progressed too far."

"Goddamn Norwood," I shouted. "He had to get his sixteen aircraft here on time. Just had to make his fucking career move regardless of Gary."

"Norwood didn't give Gary the disease—it was probably hereditary—Gary was too stubborn to stay at Clark and check into the hospital," Phil said. "I told you once, this isn't Norwood's fault."

"Bull shit." I leaped up and left the operations tent.

We flew west toward Ashau, sweating more than usual in our jungle utilities, my mind locked onto the latest turn of events making missions, and life in general, more difficult. Morale in—flight was hitting a low ebb; I figured the whole squadron's morale was hovering there. Wh*at's their motivation for these ridiculous requirements? How much was the Colonel responsible for Gary's death? What's the damn secret between Zack and Norwood?* There were more questions than answers spiraling through my mind. At that moment, I knew that the morale was the most important thing right now. I had to do something to turn it around—at least in—flight. I had to do something.

"Zack, give Ashau control a call and tell 'em we're ten out for landing."

"Roger." He flipped the radio frequency dials. "Ashau Control, Tango three two, ten out for landing. Got any advisory on enemy action?"

"Negative action, Tango. I do have a message for you, relayed through our Battalion—ready to copy?"

"Roger, Ashau." Zack took his pencil from his sleeve pocket.

"Three fifteenth directs you make a quick turn around at Ashau and proceed directly to Khe Sangh. Aircraft down due to ground fire. Extract crew as soon as practical. Expect enemy action at the site."

"Roger. Got that. Now two out for landing."

Zack and I passed quick glances. If there was one name that struck fear in the hearts of aircrew in the I corps area, it was Khe Sangh. That name on a mission frag order put an aircrew in a more somber mood. Charlie had a fist-like grip on the surrounding valley, placing weapons in camouflaged positions ready to lay on heavy fire on the approach end of the runway. That was unimportant now. We couldn't leave our crew there overnight, that was unheard of. It might seem like accepting an insupportable mission risk, but it was an unwritten assumption we have a God-given right to a shower and a drink at the end of a day. That's why we all knew someone would be coming for us.

"Go ahead and get the before landing checklist expedited—we'll make a fast approach and swing around ready for take-off." I said.

I heard the gear hit the down position and watched Zack methodically check items, move switches, push levers, adjust settings, and then twist toward me. "Checklist complete. Call flaps when you're ready."

"Give me full flaps now."

We skimmed in over the edge of the runway, as I pulled off power and waited for contact with the pierced steel planking. Recent rains caused mud to seep through the holes in the steel, making it an oozing slick surface. The aircraft skidded as brakes were applied. I took pressure off the brakes and almost bent the throttles in the reverse position. The engines worked against the wind as we slithered down the runway. The C-123 groaned to a stop at the end of the runway. I turned the nose wheel steering hard right and advanced the left throttle nursing it into a 180-degree turn back down the slick surface. Without my asking, Zack threw off his headset, bounded down the ladder and met the Special Forces Sergeant at the door. I couldn't hear the conversation but could tell Zack's message was received. It took exactly nine minutes before we were lined up ready for take-off.

"Take one niner-two degrees. Estimate Khe Sangh in twenty-seven minutes," Tom said.

"Roger, one niner-two," I said. Zack looked at me, obviously wanting to talk about Khe Sangh. I had questions too, but knew we first had to get to altitude to be able to contact Parrot Control. The air was turbulent with heated updrafts bouncing us side to side. Cumulus clouds were boiling in front of us, forming the bases for afternoon thunderheads. There was beauty in the shifting white and gray shapes rising in an undulating column of darkening moisture.

The altimeter was steady at nine thousand feet. I nodded toward the instrument, "Give Parrot a call and get all the info they have."

Zack keyed the mike. "Parrot Control, Tango three two."

Silence.

"Parrot Control, Tango three two."

Zack looked at me and shrugged. I moved the prop controls to 2000 RPM, mixture auto rich, and eased the throttles up to forty inches manifold pressure. "We'll try at ten thousand—we need some info before we blow in there cold."

I set cruise power once more. "Parrot Control, Tango three two." Zack's voice was louder in the radio.

"Roger, three two, Parrot Control, we've been reading you but you obviously couldn't receive."

"Tango three two inbound Khe Sangh to extricate a downed crew. Do you have any further info to pass to us?"

"Tango three two, the only info available is that a C-123 is down due to ground fire. Be advised Khe Sangh may be under attack. Three Fifteenth Group doesn't want to leave the crew there overnight. You can probably expect enemy fire going in."

"Roger that, Parrot. Any status on the crew?"

"Negative. Group advises you make a steep turning approach to avoid some of the ground fire."

"Damn straight, Parrot—we ain't stupid," Zack snapped.

"Target dead ahead eight miles," Tom announced.

I turned the aircraft hard left, off-setting the runway three miles to the right. I figured it would help if we could sneak in, making a steep circling turn, almost diving toward the runway. It all depended on the element of surprise. The old feelings of flying a fighter in combat came back. The adrenalin flowed readily and my total concentration was focused on the mission, no thought of the other consequences.

"Khe Sangh, Tango two-three will be turning final in two miles," Zack said. "This'll be a steep approach."

"Tango aircraft, read you loud and clear. Be advised we've got some incoming—some impacting near the runway. Use caution with the crashed aircraft still sticking out over the runway."

"Damn, Control, we're on final now. How much of that aircraft's on the runway?"

"Keep as far right as possible—you should clear it."

"Goddammit," Zack whispered.

"Zack, you get all the checklist items again while I fly this thing. We're gonna make a very tight descending left turn onto the runway.

Initial flap setting will be full—we need a barn door out there to get us down this fast."

"Roger," Zack said. He was all business in a crunch situation. No jocularity or humorous sarcasm. Zack glanced back quickly, his hand resting on the flap handle. "Before landing checklist complete. Call flaps."

"Khe Sangh," Zack called into the mike. "We . . ."

There was a loud explosion in the rear, freezing Zack's transmission in mid-sentence. Tom was laying flat on the floor, where he dove at hearing the noise. Additional hits reverberated throughout the fuselage, but the loud explosion caused Zack and me to stare at each other, expecting the worse. "What's the damage, Sergeant?" I asked.

"That round came up through the belly and hit a tie down ring—when it flopped over hard, it made the loud noise. Damn." He was looking at light through two holes that appeared right beside his right boot. "They're hittin' us pretty good."

By then we were almost vertical, coming in to the runway. I hauled back on the control column as I heard popping metal sounds in the rear.

"We just got whacked again—damn." Sergeant Picardo yelled into the intercom.

The aircraft slammed onto the PSP runway. This was no time to try a grease job. *Just get it down.* The aircraft bounced hard. *Stay down you sonofabitch.* Immediately, I saw the tail of the crashed C-123 extending over one third of the runway. Slapping hard on the right brake, I yanked both throttles into full reverse power. The tail of the crashed aircraft slid by only a few feet from the left wing. A mortar round hit twenty yards to the right front. The C-123 lumbered to a stop and I grabbed both mixtures, slamming them to the off position. "To hell with checklists. Get the hell out and head for cover—no use waitin' for a mortar round to land right on top of us."

Sergeant Picardo leaped from the door, running hard toward a trench between the gorge and the runway. Jocko hit the ground, but stumbled twice trying to run to the protection of a ditch. Tom grabbed him and pulled him forward. Zack and I were right behind them. We hit the ditch face down, motivated by instinct, as other mortar rounds exploded inside the compound, sending dust and debris towering into the air. All of a sudden, the sound was deafening as fifty-five millimeter guns opened up with a barrage into the jungle. The mortars added their distinctive voice to the crescendo, providing that little "thrump" as round after round left their barrels. Our bodies burrowed as low into the reddish dirt as possible. We lay there for close to ten minutes. Just as the chaos began, immediately there was silence. A bird chirped down the gorge. We rose slowly from the ditch; smoke and flames rose around us. A few columns of smoke mounted perpendicularly into the stagnant air and were lost. I glanced down at Jocko, who was rubbing the back of his left leg.

"Roll over, Jocko, let's take a look," Zack yelled.

He rolled over slowly, face into the dirt again. Blood covered the back of his utilities, running into his boot. Zack snatched out his knife and cut the cloth right up the back of Jocko's leg. Tom ran back to the aircraft and returned with a first aid kit. When Zack and Tom began wiping blood away they saw a small hole directly behind the left kneecap. Blood continued to ooze through the opening but was trying to coagulate. "You must've picked up a round during our approach," Zack said, as he dabbed at the wound. "Hell, you aint hurt, Jocko. Just a small hole in the back of your knee."

"It ain't your knee, Lieutenant."

"True indeed."

Two jeeps bounced down the side of the runway and slid to a crunching stop. The corporal driving the first one kept looking around as if looking for the next barrage. A lanky major strode over and squatted beside us. "Better get your ass outta that ditch before the next incoming. Never know how long these lulls will last."

Zack and Tom gave Jocko support as we scrambled aboard the two jeeps. The driver spun the tires as we raced back down the runway and into the fortified compound. I yelled above the sound of the engine, leaning close to the Major. "How's the crew we came for—are they okay?"

"Damn lucky, if you ask me. They caught a real ration of small arms fire and possibly fifty caliber on their approach. Charlie knocked the shit outta their aircraft, but they came through it pretty good—just beat up a little. Our medics patched 'em up."

We stooped to enter the low door of the bunker housing Khe Sangh's medical team. A heavy smell of alcohol, stale bandages, and antiseptics hung in the air like a foul vapor. Three medics were busy attending to three soldiers on stretchers, one adjusting a bottle of IV fluid above a red-headed private with a bandage covering his right eye and half his face. His left arm was covered in a blood-soaked bandage. Another medic was bent over a writhing figure with a large dark red stain covering his entire mid-section. The harried medic was trying to hold the soldier's arm still long enough to administer an injection. The third, turned abruptly from his bandaged patient, to analyze the hobbling Jocko. He patted a large examining table and motioned to Jocko. Once he uncovered the bloody leg, he began probing the small hole that still oozed blood. I turned away hastily, as a queasy feeling hit my gut. It was stifling hot in the bunker, with no noticeable circulation in the stale atmosphere. I walked to the door and sucked in some good air. It tasted of burned wood and smoke—but it was fresh.

I looked back over my shoulder at the five exhausted individuals leaning against the wall of the medical bunker. They were dirty, bloody, and bandaged. Gene Budnik, the pilot, stood quickly and moved toward me. A wide strip of tape across the bridge of his nose highlighted the swelling and gauze was stuck up both nostrils. I almost laughed at this Halloween face. "Damn glad to see you guys." His nasality was noticeable as he continued, "We figured we might just be here for a while. Did you catch any ground fire on approach?"

"Damn right," Zack cut in. "Do you guys really think you're worth it?"

"What didja' expect—a kiss?" Gene said.

"It'll take a lot more than that," Zack said. "You guys are buying tonight.

"We aren't out of here yet," Gene retorted.

I scanned the other crewmembers. Harold Stubbs, the co-pilot, showed no signs of injury; Jim Keel, the navigator, had a large bandage on his forehead; Staff Sergeant Jim Broussard, the engineer, had his left arm in a sling; and Airman Marshal Norris, the Loadmaster, had his shirt off and his left side taped from his armpit to his waist. The gist of the stories showed they obviously had no notice that Khe Sangh was under attack as they made a straight-in approach. Ground fire knocked out the hydraulic system, the left main gear, and shot the cowling off the left engine. Luckily not one on the crew was hit.

Harold picked it up from there. "Gene barely got it on the runway when we lost the left engine. They blew the cowling slap off that damn engine, not to mention a couple of jugs." He sucked in a breath then said, "Christ, pieces of aircraft were flying everywhere. As soon as we hit, the nose gear folded, the left wing caught a small mound of dirt and we swung off the left side of the runway." He started to laugh. "When that sonofabitch finally stopped, Gene went through the small window on the pilot's side—chute and all." He laughed harder as others began to laugh along with him. "The dust hadn't cleared as he dove outta' that damn small window. That's how he broke his friggin' nose—he dove head-first out on the ground."

Zack looked the 180-pounder over carefully, shaking his head. "No way could he get through the pilot window, even without a chute."

"The hell you say," Jim Keel spoke up. "He went through that sucker, chute and all. We were shakin' the cobwebs loose, waving the dust outta our faces, as he snatched open the door to get us out of the back. His nose was flat, with blood runnin' all over his face. Lord, that was one ugly lookin' sight."

I looked at the five again. "You guys were lucky as hell. A few more yards and you'd have been at the bottom of that gorge."


"Hey, you'd better make a damn quick departure," barked the major, who was hunched in the doorway again, both hands braced on the upright timbers. "We laid down a heavy barrage where we saw the muzzle flashes that were shootin' at you. A few fifty-five howitzer rounds and some sixty millimeter mortar may have caused them to move their position." He squinted into the sun, forming dirt-encrusted lines around his eyes. "Shifty little bastards." He shielded his eyes. "You'd best get that thing out of here before they open up from another position."

"We'll take-off as soon as Jocko's patched up and we load these sorry lookin' individuals on board." I pointed to the five along the wall, and Gene flipped one off toward me. The major smiled, nodded, and ducked back out into the bright afternoon sun. I turned to the medic sticking a long needle into Jocko's leg. "What's the verdict?"

"He didn't take a full round in that small hole. If he had, he'd still be lookin' for his kneecap. I think he got a piece of a round that ricocheted off somethin'." He mashed the wound again. "I'm gonna take a couple of stitches, bandage the thing, then they can take care of it back at DaNang."

Sergeant Picardo leaned over Jocko, looking at the wound. "I bet he took a small piece of the round that hit the tie down ring."

"Probably," I stated. "Hurry with the stitchin'—we need to get th' hell out of here while Charlie's on the move."

The Major reappeared in the doorway. "Can you take our three wounded on the stretchers? They need a hospital."

"Sure."

He smiled and gave a thumbs up. The medics started preparing the three stretcher cases to go with us. I turned back to Zack as he watched intently. I had no way of knowing what he was thinking as he watched the medics adjust bandages and talk to the patients. His eyes were fixed on the pain-killing shots being administered hastily. His mouth drew tight. He turned slowly toward the major. "No medic going with 'em?"

"We need 'em here," said the major.

Four jeeps scooted across the runway to our aircraft. Zack and I jumped from the first jeep as Sergeant Picardo helped Jocko in the aircraft. Four Green Berets assisted with the stretchers. I waved my arm toward the dust covered C-123. "Get movin', guys. We've gotta get this thing in the air quick-like."

The Major looked out over the jungle hills rising along each side of our departure route. "I'd recommend you make your turn right over the same route you came in."

"Godamighty, Major, that's where we caught the most fire."

He smiled as his eyes squinted. "Charlie's smart. They moved to the other side, knowing you'd fly away from the last ground fire. Go right back out the same way—we'll lay down a barrage just before you release brakes. That'll keep their heads down for a few minutes. Good luck."

"Thanks."

I turned and jumped aboard, bounding up the ladder and into the left seat. Zack had the checklist complete and slapped my shoulder as I buckled up. "Clear to start number one, Coach."

"Roger."

"By the way," a smile crept across his face, "which rock did you file our flight plan under?"

We both laughed as the left engine belched, coughed and roared to life. The second engine started and we quickly taxied into position facing the green jungle that extended in front of us. "Let's make an abbreviated run up while we get ready to roll."

"Sergeant Picardo, is everyone strapped in back there?"

"Roger, Captain," he answered. "Airman Norris is lying down next to the stretcher cases. Says he can't sit up with his broken ribs."

"Tell him to hang on—this could be bumpy."

Zack flipped on boost pumps, moved the mixtures to auto rich, pushed the prop controls full increase RPM, and adjusted the cowl flaps to full open as I ran the engines up checking rapidly for a mag drop on either engine. Guns on both sides of us boomed their accompaniment to the straining engines. Zack pointed to puffs in the jungle about two clicks away. The barrage had begun. Green jungle erupted into the air with shell after shell impacting the ghost-like enemy.

"Rolling." I released the brakes, my knuckles white from holding the throttles forward. The aircraft lumbered down the strip. *God, I hope the Major was right. If they maintained their position, it's gonna be a rough one.*

Zack looked straight ahead. His determined gaze into the jungle was either one of wonderment or serious concern for our future. "Gear up," I called. Zack flipped the gear handle to the up position, still focused on the terrain ahead. I banked hard right, the wing almost touching the ground. "Milk the flaps up slowly—I'm climbing at minimum airspeed." Zack moved the flap handle in measured increments to keep the aircraft climbing on the verge of a stall. He said nothing, still staring straight ahead. It was unlike Zack not to verbally confirm commands. Abruptly, the stall warning horn blared its message. The controls were sluggish at this speed, but I forced the aircraft to climb at 1,200 feet per minute. I tensed, waiting for the first rounds to hit. The altimeter indicated 1,500 feet, approaching an altitude safe from small arms fire. I knew the engines were laboring with maximum power, but dared not throttle back to climb power. *I hope we don't blow an engine with this much being asked of them.* It was a trade-off I had to make. The altimeter read 2,000 feet as I rolled the wings level, still maintaining maximum climb.

Zack broke his trance. "The goddamn engines won't take max power forever. Reduce to climb power while we're still flying. Number one just detonated a second time."

"Goddammit, I'll call for climb power when I'm ready."

His withering look was similar to our outbreak on the flight over. It felt like he was looking into my soul. Fire danced in his eyes. *Blam.* The distinctive sound of a hit froze my hands on the throttle. *Blam,* in almost overlapping racket, caused us to look out the right side. Two holes tore into the wing root next to the right engine nacelle. I kept climbing, the nose pointed toward the white puffs above us.

"We've blown a jug on number one – it's gone, Zack said."

"I'm holding max power if the damn thing falls off."

"And that's just about to happen," Zack said.

The aircraft trembled the tell-tale sign of a rough engine, the control column vibrating in my hands. I lowered the nose slightly and the increase in airspeed helped the effectiveness of the controls. The left engine still shuddered; ready to blow a jug at any instant.

I called for climb power at 3,500 feet. "Roger, climb power set." Zack grabbed my shoulder. "If you'd leveled off when I asked you to, they could've knocked our ass outta the sky." He pointed to the right wing. "Fifty caliber made those damn holes. Reckon I was spooked back there – sorry ."

I shouted back over my shoulder. "Everyone okay back there, Sergeant?"

"Roger, Captain."

I turned to Zack. "I was puckerin' myself. Sure gets the friggin' adrenalin flowing." We both started laughing, but more in relief than camaraderie. "Hey, don't sweat it, Zack. My butt puckered a bit too."


At 9,000 feet the air was cool inside the cockpit as we cruised through the iridescent blue sky, barely beneath the white cumulus cloud bases. With reduced power, the left engine settled down and purred its approval. There was no use to feather it as long as it gave us some power. The tension that had built up in the past few minutes seemed to flow magically from my body, as a calm feeling overtook me. Cheating the odds was exhilarating, like electrical impulses surging through my body. The stimulation was like an automatic spell that boosted my faculties to meet the challenge when circumstances called for all within me. Later, when the adrenalin stops, and the calm sets in, reality takes over. Invariably, there's a somber analysis of why the odds were in our favor again. It didn't pay to dwell on those questions too long.

I thought of Leslie. That was always motivation enough to beat any odds. I could see her standing there that last morning. Her beauty was intoxicating. I glanced over my shoulder at the others and wondered what incentives propelled their passions. *Reckon it's just to beat the odds.*

As requested, three ambulances from the hospital near China Beach were waiting as we landed. They pulled alongside the beat-up aircraft as the engines whined slowly to a stop. Carefully they transferred the stretcher patients to their gurneys and leaned the canvas stretchers upright against the concertina wire. I looked at the blood-soaked stretchers; their ugly dark stains drying in the hot Vietnamese sun. The soldiers being loaded into the waiting ambulances reinforced the grotesque cost of this damn war. There were times like these when I had to search my soul for the meaning of: "duty, honor, country".

I shook the image of the stretchers and glanced at the last patients entering the ambulances. Jocko was laughing as he sat in the back of the ambulance holding his leg straight out. Zack leaned in close to the patient. "Jocko, if you think that's the magic wound to send you back to the States—forget it. A band-aid, two aspirins, and you'll be back tomorrow."

"Don't count on it, Lieutenant."

Several crew chiefs from maintenance were walking around the aircraft, pointing, and examining the bullet holes. A short stocky Master Sergeant turned back to me. "This damn thing'll have so many sheet metal squares riveted over these holes, we might as well name it 'Patches'."

"While you're patchin' holes, make sure those two in the wing didn't damage a spar. Those fifty caliber go through spars like butter. And you might need an engine change on number one – I over-boosted the hell out of it"

"No sweat, Captain, we'll check her good before she goes up again."

The three of us walked into the tent, wanting to shower, eat, and hit the bar at the club. This day needed to be washed away. Towels around our necks, we shuffled to the make-shift drain chute we called a shower. There was no conversation as we let the water run down our bodies. The warmth cascaded over me as I turned my face into the steady stream. I closed my eyes and let it beat directly on my face – but all I could think about were those blood-soaked stretchers drying in the sun. The murky stains on the stretchers formed irregular patterns like a surrealist painting. The picture was not easily shaken from my conscious thoughts.

Tom, Zack and I leaned on the bar pacing ourselves for another round. We'd already thrown back that first drink, while exchanging reports about other missions. The blond Lieutenant, who we met the first night at the movie tent edged between us. We had seen him several times since watching "Home From the Hills", but now we were able to put a name to one of the club regulars. His name was Martin Baker, Marty to all at the bar. Marty was an A-1 pilot, from Bakersfield, California, assigned to the First Air Commando's Detachment 3A. Their missions were usually night sorties against known Viet Cong bases and in defense of Special Forces camps under attack. Marty and his friends made the bar their first stop after every night mission, a good luck ritual. Marty was smiling as he ordered his bourbon on the rocks. He took a long slug and turned to me. "I figure you guys are just about special ops indoctrinated after today. Hear you had a real jolly time of it."

"Just another day at the office." I grinned.

"Yeah, right." He laughed and swallowed more bourbon. "Some in the Detachment resented you guys wearing the Air Commando patch." He tapped the patch on my right pocket. "You're entitled."

A short, square-jawed Lieutenant meandered up to the bar. He was wearing a flight suit with his name just under his wings. As I strained to see it, he saw my curiosity.

"It says Lieutenant B. L. Connors," he said, slapping his nametag.

"Sorry, if I was too obvious," I said.

"No sweat. Know where I could find a Lieutenant Merc?"

"Right down there," Zack said, pointing down the bar. "He's the ugly one." Zack leaned back on the bar stool as far as it would go, watching the newcomer. "By the way, what does "B.L." stand for?"

The new lieutenant stopped and spun around. "Just B.L."

Later, Phil ambled over and introduced B.L. to Zack and me. "He's been reassigned to us from Operation Ranch Hand, in Saigon, Phil said. "Obviously a replacement for Gary."

"Glad to be here," said B.L. "Spraying Agent Orange at tree-top level was no fun when Charlie didn't want to be sprayed."

"Well, you came to just the right place, B.L.," Zack said, "we've got nothing but 'milk runs' up here, the best chow known to the Air Force, great quarters, and an absolute Prince of a guy for CO. Yep, you sure came to the right place."

"Just like Zack said, this is as good as it gets," I added. "Sure glad we didn't have to go to Saigon and stay in some air conditioned hotel down there." I stared at B.L. "Is traffic really bad downtown?"

He stared back. The point obviously made.

I took my drink and moved further down the bar. Zack slid up on the stool next to me. "I take it you don't care much for 'ole B.L.—that right?"

"I didn't care for the way he came on about how tough it was with 'Operation Ranch Hand'."

"He's a member of your flight, you know? I know how you feel about Gary, but you're lettin' it get to you way too much. That ain't good."

"Sorry." I turned to face him, ready to make some retort, when I suddenly realized how right Zack was. "Gary's death did get to me." I looked at B.L. and thought how Gary was so casually replaced— like he never really mattered, just a body, another pilot. "I reckon Gary was expendable."

"We all are—expendable, that is." He smiled. "Have another drink, Coach."

"Okay, Butt Head, I'll go apologize after this drink."

There was loud talk, some singing of ribald songs, and more drinks being consumed. The day was improving with each drink. Thoughts of the mission were temporarily buried in the camaraderie and jokes. I glanced around the smoky room and realized how many missions had been washed away at some bar, in some club, in some war. I smiled at the revelation.

Joining in the evening's festivities were Gene Butnik, Harold Stubbs and Jim Keel. They had just left the hospital after checking on the rest of their crew. Gene's eyes were a deep purple with red forming a border between the dark indigo and the rest of his face. His nose was twice its normal size.

Zack wheeled on them as they approached. "Godamighty, I'm drinkin' free the rest of this night. I told you, you were buying." Zack kept looking at Gene's face. "You look worse'en horse shit."

"Zack, your face didn't come in contact with anything today—and you look about that bad to me." He laughed, then slapped Zack on the back. "Thanks, you guys. The rest of the crew said 'Thanks' for them too. Drink up."


Four bourbons into the evening, being there with my fellow aircrew, and bonded by a common denominator, made it a pretty good day after all. The bloodstained stretchers had been washed away—at least for this night. Gary never would.

# 9

## Casualties

Brilliant orange, red, and yellow radiated with flickering intensity against the clouds. Beneath us, along with the flashes of gunfire, the jungle became an eerie verdant, creating a ghostly pallor on the vegetation. Our last three flares floated slowly to earth, still providing light for Diep Duc to lay in a fusillade of fire toward their usually unseen enemy. We had completed our mission, keeping the sky ablaze with well-spaced drops. A few tracers curved up in our direction, attempting to discourage the illumination we provided the battle below, but no hits. Now that we had exhausted our last flare, we turned east. The inbound C-123, called at the initial checkpoint, relieving us from this mission. The night flare drop kept us keyed to a high pitch. The three night flare drops had gone off smoothly. Luck had been with us – or maybe it was skill after all.

As we reached altitude and headed north on our way back, Zack flipped on the navigational lights and the rotating beacon. It was safe all the way up the coast to DaNang. Tension drained from my body as we darted among rain showers. The needle of the radio compass pointed dead ahead to the Base TACAN station. *Fifteen more minutes and sleep.* Zack cranked back and flipped a Marlboro from his sleeve pocket, rotated his zippo, and sucked in a long draw. This was the part of a mission where we relaxed. Zack started his usual banter and joke telling. The crew tolerated his jokes, occasionally laughing hysterically. He never seemed to run out of new material.

"Hey, let me tell you about some of the good, the bad, and the ugly." The intercom was quiet, anticipating his latest. "The good: Your wife's pregnant; the bad: It's triplets; the ugly: You had a vasectomy five years ago." Groans were heard immediately, but the verbal rebuff didn't deter Zack. "The good: You give the 'birds and bees' talk to your daughter; the bad: She keeps interrupting; The ugly: With corrections."

"Save some for the bar," I said.


The screen tent door banged shut behind us and Zack stopped short, seeing two letters on his bunk. I made a fleeting look at mine – a tell-tale blue envelope. Tom also had two. Mac stuck his head around his mosquito netting. "Thought you guys would like to have your mail when you got back. If I didn't pick it up, you'd have to wait till tomorrow."

"Thanks, Mac," said Zack.

We dropped onto the bunks in our sweaty utilities, eagerly opening, but teasing the contents out, making each last as long as possible. Even if the envelope color didn't give it away, it was definitely Leslie's handwriting. I slipped out the two pages and unfolded it gently.


*Sunday night*

*Dearest David:*

> *I've never figured out why Sunday is absolutely the loneliest day of the week. The weeks grow longer too, waiting for your return. You've been gone ten weeks now, and each of those Sundays were horrible. We always filled those days with fun things to do, sometimes we just relaxed. Maybe it was the company we kept – reckon?*

*The real estate lady called again yesterday, telling me she had someone interested in the house. I had already told her I was waiting until you got back before doing anything. She is so blasted persistent. I explained, politely of course, but the house is off the market for now. Maybe for good. But that's another story.*

*We do have lots to talk about. These weeks have given both of us time to think, take stock of our lives. Maybe we could go to New Orleans for a few days when you get home. The future is always a question—there is no certainty in life. Things we were so adamant about at one time, seem so inconsequential now. We never know what the future holds, but I know we'll make the right decisions.*

*Several of us "girls" are going for several days to the beach next week. Betty Hafenbrack, Linda Raburn, Zoe Sheridan, and I have rented a cottage in the Outer Banks. Zoe is new, her husband was just assigned here. She and Linda were good friends at Vance. It's a darling three-bedroom cottage with a sleeping porch—plenty of room. It'll be a week of relaxation.*

*I'll miss your letters while I'm gone, but I'll try to send you one every day or two. Keep safe.*

*Love,*
*Leslie*

I carefully folded the letter and slipped it back into the envelope. Lying there in my own sweat, I was in no hurry to shower. I wanted to digest Leslie's suggestion. Closing my eyes brought back happy days and nights in New Orleans, walking down Bourbon Street and browsing through the little shops in the French Quarter. I saw her hair blowing in the open streetcar as it rocked along the tracks of the Garden District. I recalled how much she was captivated by the music from Pete Fountain, making his clarinet virtually talk. I laughed, as I remembered her eyes riveted on the spinning wheels of the slot machine, her mouth set in fixed determination, oblivious to the movement of the riverboat. The images of intimate candlelight dinners at Louis XVI, Antoine's, and breakfast at Brennan's flashed in my head. *Is it possible to capture those feelings again? Was time spent in New Orleans one of those transitional things, a baroque moment in time?*

Then I opened my eyes and looked around the hot musty tent. Rising up on one elbow, I called to Zack to see if he was ready to hit the shower. His head was lowered as he sat on the bunk, his hands crumpling a piece of paper. He never looked up. "Zack," I called out. "What the hell's the matter?"

His head turned slowly in my direction, a pallid look on his face, his eyes narrowed. He just shook his head and looked back at his letter. I stood beside him. "Is it bad news?"

Zack rose slowly from his bunk and headed straight for the door, motioning me to follow. I walked haltingly, staying a few feet behind him. He stopped at the thatched bulletin board and looked around to make sure we were alone. "Mom just wrote that my father has cancer—a pancreatic tumor. They gave him six months to live, about two months ago."

"Do you want to try for a humanitarian leave? The Red Cross can confirm it and you'd be on your way home in about a week."

"I don't know what I want. The reason he told her was to let me know there was very little time left for us to get things right between us." He grabbed my sleeve. "Why the hell did he wait till he was dying for his conscience to kick in? Did he really have to be dying to want to see me? My God, why now?"

"The big question is: how do you feel? Are you gonna wake up one day with a pile of regret riding on you if you don't see him?" I slapped him on the back. "Think about it."

He looked directly into my eyes, "David, I've been thinking about it for lotsa years."

"But you always knew there was time – now, you don't have that option."

"I was gonna take a shower and try to sleep in this damn humidity. Now, I think I'll go to the club and have a drink." A slight smile crossed his face. "Besides we've got two days off. Care to join me?"

I really didn't want to go. I was tired. "Yeah, why not?"

The bar crowd was thinning, only four of us in the room. It didn't matter that it was slow. Soon the A-1 types would roll through the door like thunder. Zack tossed down his second drink, looking more relaxed as we chatted with the other two at the bar, avoiding any further mention of his father.

Suddenly the door swung open with a burst that sent the doorknob into the sheet rock wall. All four of us turned toward the door as three pilots from Detachment 3A strode through the opening and sat around a table toward the back. They were in no hurry to come to the bar or to put in their usual order. Instead they lit a smoke and stared at each other. I leaned against the bar, my arms bracing me. "Rough night?"

The three looked my way and said nothing. I shrugged and turned back to the bar. Fighter pilots can be in a foul mood with very little encouragement. If they were, it was of no concern to me. Zack, on the other hand, pushed a little harder. He stood and started toward them. "Hey, where's Marty? He might get some life into this sullen group."

"Marty 'bought it' on his second pass tonight," said the auburn-haired lieutenant, never raising his eyes from the table.

Zack stumbled as he came to an abrupt halt. "Goddammit." He shook his head. "Goddammit." He turned back to his seat, his head slightly bowed.

"How?" I asked.

"He must've taken a direct hit, 'cause he never pulled out of the low pass. The aircraft went straight in."

"What're you guys drinking?" I asked.

All three glanced up, looking perplexed at the question. The same lieutenant that gave the description stuck his thumb in the air. "Sure. I'll have one of those San Miguels."

The other two quickly chimed in, "Me too—and thanks."

After a while, the three moved to the bar, their demeanor less morbid. They bought the next round, and talked about Marty. Their Detachment Commander approached the bar, having just been notified of the loss. There were ample stories of Marty's exploits on the ground as well as in the air.

There's a gamut of emotions one must work through when you lose a friend—a fellow airman. I had seen it too many times before. There's that stunned silence as you try to accept it happened. Even if you are an eyewitness, it is too incomprehensible to be believed in that grotesque instant. Your mind is numbed. The realization that there is mortality in this profession grips your thinking. At that point, you coldly analyze the event, knowing there must be some logical explanation, some mysterious actions that need to be put into perspective. Only when you fix the cause in your mind, can you understand why you won't make the same mistake. Your intuition demands to know this. Lastly, there is an urgency to talk about it with those who understand flying. It's camaraderie and catharsis that bring final acceptance.

They wanted to talk about Marty.

It took most of the morning to work through a headache of monumental proportions. Zack moaned lowingly, softly swearing he'd never touch alcohol for the rest of his life, then rolled back to a prone position. Tom showed little patience or understanding, even after being told that one of the A-1 pilots went down last night. Instead, he carefully explained the after effects of intemperate drinking. He left us in our misery to spend the morning at operations, on some project he'd dreamed up with Mac and Rusty.

By noon I felt like my stomach could tolerate food again, maybe even the chow offered in the mess tent. I pushed the tray away and took a long drink of grape kool-aid. It stayed put in my stomach, and for the first time in six hours, I figured I might survive.

The walk back to the tent under a blazing sun was enough to soak my utilities all the way though. The heat made me relive the sick feeling and drove me straight for my bunk. As I walked through the tent door, the scene in front of me didn't help my feelings. Rick Haffenbrack sat buck-naked on the edge of his bunk, legs spread apart, sprinkling powder on his private parts. Almost touching his legs was a 10-inch electric fan, running on high, he was sighing with relief. He looked up, with a full smile. "Godamighty, this is the first time I've had relief from this damn jock itch in six weeks."

"Where'd you get the fan?"

"I bought it from one of those 'weeneys' over on China Beach. Paid fifty bucks for it." The smile spread even further. "Worth every . . ."

"Hey, guys, take a look at this," Tom yelled. "He was struggling with a large bucket, shifting it from hand to hand he waddled into the tent. Mac and Rusty dashed through the door, holding their fingers to pursed lips. "Keep it down for God's sake, Tom. That damn bucket is top secret."

Zack appeared to rise from the dead to see what was going on. "Tom, you're a prime candidate for natural deselecting."

Tom dropped the heavy object, with a thud, and glared at Zack. "You don't get any."

All of us gathered around Tom, looking down into the unknown contents. There in his bucket was a huge piece of ice, surrounded by some water as it slowly melted. We stood in awe of the object. We had seen no ice, except for the closely guarded piece that floated in the Kool Aid. This was just short of a miracle. Tom grinned as he dipped a cup into the ice water, then savored every drop. Zack stood there slack-jawed at the sight. He pointed down at the prized liquid. "Where the hell did you get that?"

Tom passed the cup to Rusty. "Zack, you underestimate the true genius at work around you. We're creating these miracles while you lay around in a hung-over stupor."

"Seriously," I asked, "where did you come up with this block of ice?"

Rusty leaned closer and lowered his voice. "We swapped eight cases of beer to the Green Berets at Gia Vuc for a field morgue. That sucker makes ice like a regular freezer. We've got it hidden right under Major Lynch's nose, under canvas, at the back of operations."

Mac jumped in the conversation. "We'll damn well have ice-water the rest of this tour."

"It doesn't bother you there that several bodies might have been stored in that damn contraption?" Zack said, rubbing his stomach.

"Not a bit," Tom said. "Besides, the Green Beret types said it was new."

"Oh yeah, only driven on Sundays by a little gray-haired . . ."

"You gonna have more trouble than you can handle if the Major finds that thing," I interrupted Zack.

"Don't worry," said Zack. "He's so dense, light bends around him. But the Colonel will have your balls." Zack reached for the cup. "I apologize, Tom. I know I always accused you of being one neuron short of a synapse. But today, Buddy, you've just gained my total and undying admiration. You're a damn genius."

Tom slapped his hand away. "You gotta do better'n that."

"Aw, c'mon, Tom. I'm dying here."

"You gonna owe us for the duration—you got that, Zack?" Cautiously, Tom moved the cup toward Zack. "One swig to save your worthless hide from dehydration."

Zack drank slowly, undulating sounds of satisfaction emanated from him as the ice-cold liquid ran down his throat. Tom eyed his reaction with enjoyment. He loved the control he momentarily exercised over Zack.

We soothed our heated throats with the cold liquid and talked about Marty. Even though assigned to another unit, he'd become a regular at the bar, mingling with us like he was in our flight. "Marty was a distinct personality, Zack said. "He'd be missed from any group." He passed the cup back. "This one hit me right between the eyes. That bar'll never be the same to me."

"Excuse me." The First Sergeant was holding the screen door open. We all looked up, as Tom eased the bucket to one side, shielding it with his leg. "Lieutenant MacPherson, Colonel Norwood wants to see you, sir."

Mac rose quickly, glancing back at Tom and Rusty questioningly. There was quiet in the tent as Mac followed the First Sergeant. Once out of earshot, Zack handed the cup back to Tom. "Looks like you three are in a world of dung. The Colonel probably just discovered your ice plant." Now he could get even with Tom for making him squirm for the ice water.

Rusty looked at Tom, then me. "You reckon the Major found the thing that quick?"

"Christ, I don't know." I shook my head. "I wouldn't recognize one of those things if I stumbled on it. I doubt Lynch would either."

"Lynch may not be the sharpest knife in the drawer," Zack added, "but even he can figure out that ain't no regulation ice maker sitting there behind his operations."

"If they found it, I'll take the heat. It was my damn idea," Tom said.

"Don't be so damn noble," Rusty said. "It as my friggin' beer we traded. If they stumbled onto the thing, remember it was all three of us who pulled this off."

We took turns sipping the cold water, impatiently waiting for Mac's return. Rick handed the cup to Tom, sprinkled more powder on his crotch and adjusted the fan.

"Can't you at least put a towel over your balls – you aren't the only one in this damn tent," Tom said.

"Bite me." He draged a towel from the end of his bunk and placed it across his legs. "I don't want you to get too envious, Tom." He occasionally lifted the edge of the towel to capture the cooling currents, smiling at Tom's indignation.

"Keep that towel down flat, so I don't barf," Rusty stated.


Crunching footsteps on the gravel walk was the first clue that Mac, and then we heard the muted humming of *Puff The Magic Dragon*. Every head swirled toward the tent opening. Mac was all smiles as he plopped down next to Tom. We waited as he slammed his fist into his hand. "I nailed that bastard, but good. I enjoyed the look of bewilderment on his face – with nothing he could do about it."

"What the devil you talking about?" Rusty asked. "Did he know about the field morgue?"

"Christ, no. You guys remember I wrote a 'thank you' to Senator Montgomery for sponsoring the new GI Bill. When it passed, I decided to go back to law school. I told him what it will mean to us." He began laughing again. "Norwood called me into his cubicle and asked if I had any problems I wanted to discuss, was something really bothering me? I was puzzled until I saw my letter sitting in front of him, but I played dumb."

"Not too difficult," said Zack.

Mac cut his eyes at Zack, and then continued. "I asked, 'What exactly do you mean, Colonel?' He started to squirm as I turned the knife. Finally, when he couldn't get me to bring up any problems, he held up the letter. His face was red and his finger shook as he pointed it at me. "Why did you write to your Senator, Lieutenant?"

Tom moved in closer. "Then did you tell him why you wrote the letter?"

"Are you kidding? – that's when I nailed him. I looked at the envelope he was flapping at me, and said: 'Colonel, that letter was placed in the U. S. Mail. It might just be a blue box nailed to a bulletin board, but that constitutes a regulation mail drop. I figure you just illegally took a letter from the U. S. Mail. I would suggest, Sir, you get that letter back into the mail system as fast as you possibly can. Mail tampering is a felony.' That sucker's face turned beet red—I thought he'd explode. He told me to get the hell outta there. God, I loved it."

Zack and Rusty did the "happy monkey" dance around the tent like total fools. Everyone was chuckling and slapping Mac on the back. It was the first time the flight showed any spirit since we got here. They needed a victory, anything to boost morale. Mac gave them a small triumph and they savored it.

We were content to enjoy an occasional cup of cold water and not worry about when, and how, it would end. I knew there was no way to defend their actions and felt guilty that I was participating in this deception. Who gives a damn about the consequences? I stifled a laugh as I thought of the incongruity of a hidden field morgue, used as an ice plant. Hell, they needed this diversion.

There had been a buzz of conversation at the mess tent about Mac's encounter with the CO, each story better than the last, even though we all agreed that Lieutenant Colonel Douglas Patrick Norwood would retaliate – but where, when and how?

The wait was fairly short. We sat around after chow waiting to go have a drink at the club, when Major Walt Trimble, the Squadron Navigator, ducked into the tent. He walked over to Mac and patted him on the shoulder. "Lieutenant Mac Pherson, may I have a word with you in my tent? Everyone in my tent has night missions and we could go over a few things—privately."

"Sure." Mac grabbed his bush hat and followed Major Trimble out the door to his tent, about 40 feet down the gravel path.

We all strained to hear the conversation but could pick up the occasional word. There was an incoherent buzz of conversation, with only an occasional word being picked up. The voices became louder and more animated. Words, barely understood, suddenly became clear. The Major was talking about Mac's letter to the Senator and his encounter with the Colonel. Obviously he was making threats, not too thinly veiled, about Mac's career being affected by input from this unit to his Officer Fitness Report. Mac's voice rose to a crescendo, obviously for our benefit. "How damn stupid can you get, Major? You have the mindless audacity to threaten me with a goddamn fitness report. I'm sittin' here in a damn tent in 115 degree heat, with seven sweaty bodies, fightin' off mosquitoes, drawing one dollar a day per diem, and getting shot at about every day. I'd already resigned my commission before we left Pope." Suddenly it was quiet. "Now, Major, why would I give a happy damn about your idiotic report?"

Loud laughter ricocheted down the row of tents. Cheering went up immediately for Mac as he reentered the tent. Zack stuck his head in his pillow, rolling around on his bunk in laughter. Absolutely no sound came from the Major's tent. Mac had done what we'd all dreamed of doing since we formed this squadron. The Major dug himself a hole before he knew it and there was absolutely nothing he could do to Mac, short of a court martial for insubordination. Witnesses would be impossible to find. Mac had done it and gotten away with it. A second victory sent morale to the pinnacles of delight.

Rain lashed the operations tent as we sat waiting for Major Lynch to ration the mission frag orders. A hold had been placed on several missions because of the monsoon rains. Most mountains were covered with low-lying clouds. Scud slid down the slopes, filling the valleys. There was no way to get into several fire bases. Zack stared at the rain, and smoked a Marlboro, while I paced restlessly. The canvas billowed out and popped inwards with each gust of wind. I didn't ask Zack directly about his decision regarding his father. I wanted to get him to bring up the subject – he needed to talk about it. Zack would have to initiate the topic. "What do you hear from Jane?" I asked.

"A good question. I know you expect me to come out with some innocuous statement that all relationships with women are generic." He pulled on the cigarette. "This is different." His eyes narrowed and I knew he was serious. "I haven't come right out and asked her yet, Coach, but I'm gonna' marry that gal."

"Is this the Zack I've known all these months?"

"I've never had a relationship that transcended a good time and good sex. There was nothing there past those attractions. Jane's different. We communicate on a level I never knew possible. Don't get me wrong; she sure does fill out an angora sweater—it's snugger on her than the goat." He smiled, glancing suddenly back out at the rain. He flipped the butt out into the water and looked directly at me. "I'm a different person with Jane—she's my sanctuary."

"Those are the right words, old Buddy. Hope you mean 'em."

Zack's smile told me the answer. We stood there listening to the rain, not talking. He nervously lit another cigarette. "I'm sorry about you and Leslie."

"Who knows how that'll turn out? I've learned that if a relationship is over, and you experienced more smiles than tears, it wasn't a waste. We've had more smiles, Zack."

"One more thing," Zack said. "I'm gonna visit my Dad as soon as I get home."

"I don't think you'll regret it. You've got a lot of . . ."

"Listen up," Major Lynch shouted his interruption. We spun around to the sound of his voice. "Weather says it's clearing rapidly to the west, just some low hung stratus around the mountain tops." He shuffled a mission frag order. "We need a resupply drop at Firebase 9." He looked up and pointed to Rick. "You've got it, Lieutenant Hafenbrack."

"Oh well, let's go earn some flight pay." Rick motioned to Jeff and Carey. They started toward the opening when a second lieutenant dashed past the crew. He handed Major Lynch a hand-written note.

"Hold up a minute," Lynch shouted to Rick. "Intelligence says the Firebase is under attack from a reinforced battalion. We may scrub this one."

Colonel Norwood's entrance was not noticed as he approached Major Lynch. "Let's not be so hasty, Major. Let's not scrub the mission before we know all the intelligence." By now Colonel Norwood was standing in front of the second lieutenant who rocked back and forth, inching his way back from the colonel. "What's the source of this intelligence info, Lieutenant?"

"It was in the standard traffic. Since it's in our area, I rushed it over."

"When did the attack begin? How do you know that Charlie hasn't withdrawn?"

"Well, I figure it's still a hot area. It may be . . ."

"*You* figure. It *may* be. What you really mean, Lieutenant, is you don't have any damn idea." He turned back to Major Lynch. "We don't want a reputation of scrubbing missions arbitrarily, do we?"

Before Lynch could give his usual "okay" to any request by the CO, I stood quickly. "If there's any doubt, Colonel, Intelligence should follow up." I glanced at Major Lynch. "Was that original frag mission request coded 'essential'—or was it 'routine priority'?"

"Any damn mission in I Corps area is essential, Captain," said Colonel Norwood. He stood there, his eyes fixed on me, waiting for a reply.

"If it's routine, Colonel, there's no need to risk it until the firefight's over." I continued my argument before he could reply. "Those low clouds will force an aircraft right down the valley with no possibility of evasive action, and that could be right tough."

"Tell me something, Captain. Do you second guess every mission—or just those we've been assigned today?" Before I could reply, he handed the intelligence information back to Lynch, his eyes still on me. "The mission goes." Then he strode out of the tent.

"What the hell does it take to keep him from risking a crew unnecessarily?" I asked. Just what doesn't he understand about this goddamn operation, Major."

"That'll be enough, Captain." Said Major Lynch. "He's the CO. It's his decision."

"It's his decision – somebody else's butt."

Lynch moved closer, as everyone watched us. "It's my decision too." Lynch said. "The mission goes. There'll be no more discussion." Major Lynch stood there, back straight, hands on his hips, jaw set." Somewhat out of character, but he was definitely in command of the situation. "Here's the frag order, Lieutenant Hafenbrack. Let's go get it done."

I stepped closer. "We'll take the Firebase 9 mission."

Major Lynch looked at me, then at Rick. "You don't think you can handle this one, Lieutenant?"

Major Lynch knew damn well what response he was going to get. Rick bristled as he wheeled square around. "You assigned it to us, didn't you, Major?"

Lynch's hand shot out. Here's *your* mission, Captain – Gia Vuc.

While we got our gear together and planned the course, the Intelligence Lieutenant popped back in. "Here's a hot one, Major." He stuck the mission request in Lynch's face.

He read it rapidly and looked at Phil. "Get your crew together and get in the air ASAP." He began to talk faster. "Kham Duc is holding a VC officer. Go pick him up; two guards with will be with him." He continued to read. "This message says there's an aircraft leaving now for DaNang to take the prisoner back to Saigon for interrogation. They'll be on the ground here waiting, so expedite."

"Roger, that." Phil spun from his seat, with B.L. running right behind him.

We had a quick turn-around at Gia Vuc and were back on the ground at DaNang in less than an hour. As the engines spun down I rolled out of the seat and took the aircraft forms with me to the parking area where a C-130 stood poised to accept its prisoner. I leaned on the post nearby, completing the log and watching for Phil. Zack eased up beside me, pointing to a C-123 touching down. "There's Phil now. Let's see what a VC looks like up close."

"Yeah," I laughed. "It's nice to know who's so hell-bent on killing you."

Phil hit the brakes at the crew chief's signal and both engines coughed and died. The tail gate banged down even before the props stopped turning, and four Security police ran to the back of the aircraft. They had their M-16's pointed inside the opening as the loadmaster jumped down, followed by the engineer. The Saigon group lowered their weapons as they talked with loadmaster. Suddenly they turned and walked quickly back toward the C-130. Zack and I looked at each other, wondering where the prisoner was.

Phil and B.L. jumped down from the aircraft side door and walked toward operations. Zack and I ran to intercept them. Zack grabbed Phil's arm. "Where the hell's the VC?"

Phil turned to face Zack and me, looking somber. "When we got there . . ." His face was ashen. "When we got there, his head was stuck on top of a stake just outside the compound. The Montagards wouldn't wait. The American advisors said they couldn't do anything to stop them. They hate the VC so much –."

"Wouldn't *you* if they destroyed all your villages, killed your animals, and raped the women?" said Zack. "Those peaceful little people kept to themselves; they only had cross-bows to fight back with." His voice rose an octave. "Hell, I understand it."

Phil shook his head. "That image'll stay with me for a long damn time." He turned and walked away. B.L. slung his flak jacket over his shoulder and walked along with him.

Zack tugged at my sleeve, pulling me along to the mess tent. We walked together, neither saying a word. A repugnant and disgusting vision had been imbedded in our brains, one that would be forever difficult to understand, and more abominable to talk about it. There was no rational analysis of man's inhumanity to man.

I walked up to the large vat and pulled the handle. At noon it was orange Kool-aid, better than the strawberry at breakfast. I headed back to the wooden mess table and saw Captain Hazelwood, the Adjutant, leaning over talking Zack and Tom. I had seen many expressions on Zack's face, but this one was hauntingly strange. The feeling in my gut stopped me cold. I was not anxious to join them. Zack walked toward me, his look never changed. Larry Hazelwood followed him. Tom sat and watched, then looked away. Zack stood there in front of me, searching for words. "David, we have an aircraft down—it's Rick's crew."

"Go ahead, give it to me." I glanced past Zack, to Hazelwood. "He didn't look like it was good news."

"The Firebase sent a message; A C-123 was shot down half-mile short of the compound."

Hazelwood stepped closer. "There was heavy ground fire, some heavy caliber stuff thrown at 'em." He lowered his voice, almost to a whisper. "They sent a patrol out there even though there was heavy fighting in the area. There were no survivors, David."

I was numb. *Not Rick. God, not the whole crew.* "David. David." Zack was in my face. "Let's get outta here."

I had an overwhelming urge to confront Norwood and Lynch. There had to be some retribution for their sending five men to their death. Stupidity or arrogance, it was unimportant. The results were the same. I felt the blood rushing to my neck and face. My hands shook with pent up rage. As we approached the tent area, I veered off toward the Squadron orderly room. Zack jumped in front of me. "David, not now." When I pushed past him, he grabbed my shirt and yanked me around. "Goddamit, David, you'll gain nothing—absolutely nothing. Listen to me. I know this man."

I stopped and looked Zack in the eye. "What do you mean you know this guy?" Zack just stared at me. "Okay, not now. But so help me God . . ." I couldn't finish. I moved Zack aside and rushed through the screen door and ripped off the jungle utility uniform. I threw them as hard as possible at the footlocker and stared at Zack. "Enough of this shit too." *I'm damn well wearing a flight suit from now on.*

Lying on my bunk, I thought about the blue Air Force staff car driving up to the beach to tell Betty. Thank God Leslie and the others will be with her. Notification of downed pilots and crew has become rather routine and more sophisticated in an Air Force with a lot of practice. No matter how it's approached, nothing mitigates the loss.


Lying there, my mind churning aimlessly, I let it drift back a few years. There was a similar time in my life.

Filtered sunlight streamed through the large poplar tree in our yard back in Bogalusa. My old dog, Sadie, jumped up beside me on the bench. When my hand automatically fell onto her black and white coat, she looked up at me as I stroked her soft fur. Those ebony eyes told me she was content being here. She sensed I felt the same as she placed her muzzle on my leg. The cool wind raised her fur and the tinted leaves fell around us. This weathered bench had always been my retreat from the rest of the world—to think, to just be. And autumn was my favorite time of year in Bogalusa. The cooling of the air, a pallet of vivid colors washing across the horizon, and the sun hanging low across the Louisiana sky refreshed my soul. I retreated to this old bench to find elusive answers. This was where I came to process my father's death.

Now I sat here in disbelief at Rod Gattlin's death. His crash in a Marine fighter jet snuffed a young life and took away my friend. Emotions felt here were exclusive, concealed from the world. Shared only with Sadie. This was the first time a loss had hit so close to home. Rod and I had been friends for all of our twenty-six years. We shared boyhood intimacies, which are only confided in your best friend. We were close.

The moisture in my eyes gradually dried. Understanding the critical mistake he'd made in the aircraft gradually sank in. I patted Sadie, rose from the bench, and headed for Tyler's house. I needed to talk about Rod. Tyler and I could laugh about knowing our friend and find that final acceptance.

Now, the death of Rick's crew grabbed at my insides the same way. I knew tonight, at the bar, I would look for another final acceptance.

# 10

## Tent Rosters

The tinkling of glasses being arranged by the bartender, heavy breathing, and the occasional clunk of glass meeting wood was the only sound. We couldn't overcome the maudlin cloak that engulfed us, numbing our feelings. It was impossible to follow the natural progression of adjusting to such a loss. Rick and his crew's deaths were not easy to deal with on any level. Even though my guts were in a knot, I needed to celebrate the dynamic life of these men with the usual exuberance. But I couldn't. When you're in combat, usually a flyer's death can be attributed to luck of the draw. Aircraft accidents can usually be narrowed down to some critical mistake or material failure beyond any pilot's capability. This was not the case. Without verbalizing it, everyone around the bar knew the cause.

It took three drinks for me to even begin to loosen up. More for Zack. We began telling of hilarious times spent with Rick, Jeff, and Carey. The stories unfolded at the same rate of liquor consumption. Sobriety was not a goal this night. The stories centered on Rick, sometimes Jeff and Carey—but we really didn't know the two enlisted men. This bothered us. A squadron formed as quickly as this one prevented the usual camaraderie found in permanent units. All we could do was drink a toast to them.

Rusty recounted Rick's answer to his raging case of jock itch, with minute detail. Laughter shook the air as Rusty described the fan, situated right between his legs, blowing full speed on his crotch, and

Rick rapidly sprinkling powder on the affected area. "The powder was flying everywhere," Rusty said. "It looked like a damn sand storm in 'the tent. I could write my name in the powder on Rick's . . ."

Zack's glass hit the bar, splashing liquid over my arm. A hush fell on the group like a vaporous cloud. I wiped at the bourbon on my arm, glancing at Zack's piercing eyes. He was staring at the door as if in suspended animation – and in came Colonel Norwood, Major Lynch, and Captain Hazelwood. Looking back at Zack's hand holding the glass, I saw it was shaking. I placed my hand over his. Alcohol had diminished his usual control. I could see in his eyes that all inhibitions had vanished. I moved in front of his penetrating gaze. "You remember what you told me this afternoon? Do you?" I grabbed his flight suit. "Not now, Zack, you've had too much to drink." My voice lowered. "Not now, goddammit. Cool it."

Zack slapped the glass off the bar with the back of his hand, causing the bartender to jump to one side. "I need some air," he bellowed. "The stench in here is gettin' to me." He swung off the bar stool as Norwood glared at him. I walked with him. By the time we got to the door, every member of the flight was in trail behind us. As soon as we stepped into the hot night air we let out a resounding war-whoop. Now, even if for just this moment, we adjusted to our loss.

As Zack and I entered the operations tent the next morning, Major Lynch looked up from the mission assignments and stared at our flight suits. A frown formed instantly, but he looked back at the frag sheets. He slammed the papers down and moved toward us. He cast a worried glance over his left shoulder to see if Colonel Norwood was there, then motioned me to the back of the tent as Zack lingered close by. "Your crew's assigned night alert. You're released for the day." He stopped talking as his eyes moved up and down, assessing my flight suit. "Is there some reason you're not wearing the prescribed uniform today?"

"Sure is, Major. Tactical Air Command regulations state this *is* the prescribed uniform for all flights, except VIP aircraft, where a class A uniform may be worn. I'm assigned to the Tactical Air Command—here only on temporary assignment."

"But you know Colonel Norwood wants us to set an example." He looked away, then back at me. "David, as a flight commander, every member of your flight will emulate your actions. They follow your lead in everything. Why the hell can't you just cooperate, David? I don't need to point out you're a regular officer."

I was momentarily taken back by his use of my first name. He'd never referred to me by anything other than my rank. "Colonel Norwood has no authority to supercede Tactical Air Command regulations—and being a regular has nothing to do with it. For your information, I've not mentioned this subject to anyone in my flight. They make their own decisions." I stared at the squinty green eyes that darted nervously back and forth. "But, just so we don't have this discussion again, Major, I *will* be wearing a flight suit for all future missions—as stated in the regulation."

He turned to Zack. "Lieutenant, you've got a promising career. Don't you realize this kind of action can have an adverse affect?"

Zack strode over, almost to the man's nose, looking him in the eyes. "Major, I'm a *reserve* officer—from the Latin; I don't give a rat's ass."

We both turned suddenly, leaving the Major staring straight ahead, in an obvious state of confusion as to what action he should have taken. We glanced back at his bewildered look as we ducked out of the tent. Zack was grinning ear-to-ear. Suddenly, he broke out laughing. I looked at him in awe. "You've got that arrogant look of complete satisfaction. Are you satisfied?"

"Satisfied? Satisfied? Is Norwood a Colonel? Am I handsome? Are you ugly? Hell, yes, I'm satisfied!"

"Zack, you're something else—I've got me a co-pilot with a very weird sense of humor."

Zack kept laughing, slapping the side of his leg. "That Lynch shouldn't be allowed to breed."

I thought about Zack's humor at the expense of our Operations officer. Even though amusing, it was too incredible to be funny. "Zack, we laugh at the leadership in the squadron and do our damndest to dig at 'em when we can. But this whole friggin' war's being fought this way. You know the rumors flying around about Saigon—the General and his staff having their own whorehouse. They sit around drinking at the Saigon clubs all night, next morning give their usual PR briefing, for the rest of the day they dream up stupid missions for all Air Force units. The ARVN troops, with their advisors, take a hill, fight to hold it for two days, then retreat. The Special Forces camps are small forts in the middle of Viet Cong territory. They can't even operate in daylight—much less at night."

Zack stopped right there on the gravel path. "Yeah, but the worst thing is men die for no goddamn reason." I didn't respond. "David, we need to do something about Rick, Jeff, and the others—it shouldn't just be pushed aside."

"Right now, there's not a damn thing we can do about it. Norwood can cover his ass six ways from Sunday." Zack stomped at the ground. "I've got an uncontrollable urge to go kick his Colonel ass into next week." He chuckled. "And I thought that's what you were about to do yesterday."

"No. I probably would've just told him what he already knows—and you were right, it would've been for nothing. One thing's for sure. He's got to think about these days the rest of his life."

"I can excuse Lynch," Zack stated. "Stupidity is considered somewhat of a defense, but a total lack of character or integrity is inexcusable." He looked off into the tent area as if thinking about the whole issue, then turned back to me, with a look of quiet desperation. "There's no way in hell we can win this war. There're no sound objectives, no goal. We flounder with different plans of action every day, and kill good men. What th' hell are we accomplishing here?"

"It appears we're tearing up lotsa jungle, and killing lotsa people, furthering some careers, and keeping McNamara satisfied." My smile left quickly. "Let me give you something to think about, Zack. This is the first war we've ever fought with regular officers in all the leadership roles. World War II was the generation of citizen soldiers, guys who were willing to make the extreme sacrifices, and they became instant leaders when we had to have 'em. In Korea, there were only a handful of regulars. The Air Force had to crank up fast with recalled reservists and a bunch of us neophyte Second Lieutenants. But we had able leadership and superb morale. I would've followed my squadron CO to hell—in formation, yet. Maybe we novice fighter pilots were too dumb to know better, but we did whatever it took. Even when we knew we were sold out by Washington, we all went 'balls to the wall' to get the missions done. We won a moral victory there, even if the folks back home were ambivalent."

I pointed toward the orderly room tent. "We've got a CO sittin' in there who's been getting his ticket punched, year after year, with just the right staff jobs. He's kissed every butt in TAC's chain of command, wouldn't think of ever questioning the system, and never made a tactical decision in his life. The system created Norwood. He's a product of the structure, more typical of the regular officer corps today than you realize. The few good regular officers are squelched, passed over, or ignored. Some buck the system, thinking they'll make a difference. They learn too late it aint gonna happen. When one slips through the scheme of things, like Colonel Adams, it's a damn miracle."

Zack stood there captivated by the supposition. "It's not just us, is it? It's all those who'll follow us into this damn war." His eyes took on that faraway look of resignation. "You know, it's not the truth that hurts, it's the sudden realization of it. But what's that quote? 'Weep for the quick and the dead."

"Weep for the quick—not the dead. The quick have to keep running."

"On that note, let's chow down at the 'greasy spoon'," said Zack. "No matter what the system is—Norwood's a worthless bag of shit." He stopped again on the gravel path. "Come to think of it—when has he flown a mission?"

"He flies the Saigon courier run occasionally," I said. "Hazelwood hasn't flown one either. That leaves us with the illustrious leadership of one Major Frank Lynch. Doesn't that make you feel real good?"

"It makes me wanta puke." He laughed. "But I'm still hungry. Let's go."

Two nights of scheduled flare drops told me we'd be getting our share of the nasty ones. The first night went smoothly, just long into the night. It was after midnight when control released us to head back to DaNang.

We tried to be quiet as we stumbled around the darkened tent. Tom, Zack and I were ready for sleep as we sprayed the bunks for mosquitoes and tucked in the sides of the netting. There were thuds of side arms hitting footlockers, causing a stirring of those asleep. Flight suits were tossed on top of the pistols, as we crawled into our cocoon of netting. Even in the heat, sleep came fast.

A voice invaded my sleep-induced stupor, but I was resisting it. The voice came again and I rose up on one elbow to see the First Sergeant's face against the netting. "What's the trouble, Sergeant?" I said groggily wiping at my face.

"You haven't signed the tent roster this morning."

"Say that again, Sergeant."

"A notice was published yesterday that the ranking officer in each tent would sign a daily tent roster, certifying all were present and accounted for."

"Excuse me for being pissed, Sergeant, but we flew last night and I just got wakened for some dumb-ass statement like that? Besides, it could have waited—couldn't it, Sergeant?"

"Sorry, Captain, but Colonel Norwood wants every tent accounted for by 0800. It's already 0840."

By then I was out of the mosquito netting, standing there in a pair of shorts. It wasn't my best display of a military presence, but I was going to make sure I got my message across to the First Sergeant, and eventually to Colonel Norwood. Tom rose up, watching the exchange. Zack, however, rolled over and buried his head in the pillow. I inched closer to the Sergeant. "Let me explain something, and Sergeant, listen carefully. I don't want you to make a mistake when you repeat it to the good Colonel." His chin tightened as if he wanted to bark some order back to me, but he didn't. "This piece of canvas, stretched over us right here, is a miserable excuse for quarters—but that's exactly what it is. This is a damn BOQ. It may be in the middle of Vietnam, it may leak like hell when it rains, and it stays about a hundred and ten degrees inside—but it's a damn BOQ. Now tell Colonel Norwood that there's a long-standing policy that officers don't have to check in and out of their BOQ."

He stood there glaring at me. "I'll tell the Colonel exactly what you said."

"Do that, Sergeant."

Tom rubbed at his eyes. "What the hell was that all about?"

"How would I know? That SOB must lay awake thinking up this ridiculous bullshit." I nudged Zack. "If we're awake, you are too." I nudged him again with my foot. "Let's go get some chow before they close down. They'll usually fix us some eggs and toast even after they stop serving. Get a move on."

Indistinguishable mumbling came from Zack's bunk as he moved methodically toward his towel and boots. He was still mumbling as he headed for the shower.

The second night of operations ended quickly and we were lucky enough to be released from alert status. We landed early and headed to the club. It gave Tom, Zack and me a much-needed break and a drink with the rest of the flight at the club. We ambled in and found a stool among the others. I couldn't help but notice Major Lynch's stare across the u-shaped bar, now that nine officers were dressed in flight suits. There was never a challenge mounted about the flight suits after that first day. I waited to be called on the carpet by Colonel Norwood, but it never happened. They obviously checked the regulation.

One thing that held Major Lynch at bay, other than regulations, was the way we performed in the air. We went all-out on every mission. Our motivation was the support being given to the Special Forces, not the squadron. They had our respect and a rapport was quickly established. Several times we pushed the envelope to complete missions, giving us a keen sense of satisfaction for doing more than required. It was for the Special Forces troops more than our duty. The camaraderie with them was infectious.

Relaxed aircrew gathered around the bar, where jokes flowed as freely as the alcohol. Wild tales of flying were being explained, complete with hand gestures. As more drinks were consumed, the bawdy songs began. I was in no mood for this. My images were of another life, and Leslie. I eased out of the group and slipped away as inconspicuously as possible. I had a compulsion to write her – to tell her how much I loved her. Zack looked at me, then back at his drink, but said nothing.

I sat on the edge of the bunk spraying insect repellent all over my body. That way I could sit there in my shorts on the edge of the bunk and write without being eaten alive. The pen stayed poised ready to write for a long time. The words never came easy, emotions stayed fixed in my heart, not easily placed on the paper. Tonight, pen and paper were not enough for me to express my feelings to Leslie. Staring into the night outside the tent, I clenched the pen tighter, rethinking what I wanted to say. Pen finally met paper, as I started to write.

*Dearest Leslie:*

> *I know you and all the wives were there for Betty and the others. You and Betty have been friends for some time, but I don't think you knew the other wives that well.*
>
> *There's one thing for sure—the Air Force family sticks together in hard times like these. I know there was sadness at Pope. There was much of it here. As Flight Commander, I felt responsible. It haunts me that I couldn't prevent the loss of that crew.*
>
> *With our situation here, we have to maintain a sense of humor. If you see Colonel Adams, tell him we'll have some strange stories for him when we get back. He'll know what I'm talking about. We all wish he'd taken the unit over—we*

*wouldn't be having the problems we face on a daily basis. It goes from the sublime to the ridiculous!*

*Since being here, I've spent many hours thinking about us. I have a much better appreciation for what's important in life. The basics of what's valuable revolve around love. Even though you once said that love alone is not enough—I know nothing is possible <u>without</u> it—and everything is possible <u>with</u> it. The road in life is full of bumps. It's how we handle those difficult times—the ones that wrench our insides—that matters. We haven't always done that very well—have we? The decision to do that is up to us.*

*I've got a long leave due me when we get back. Let's go somewhere isolated from the world. We need some time alone to find that special magic that used to be there. Think about it. I miss you.*

*With love,*
*David*

Morning came too quickly. Without shaving, I rushed to the mail drop, even though the mail was never picked up until afternoon. Then it could sit waiting in the orderly room for the next courier. I approached the thatched bulletin board area, and reached toward the blue box on the post. As I dropped the letter in the hole, I turned toward the sound of boots on gravel. The First Sergeant was approaching at a brisk pace, calling my name as if I were about to leave the area. "Captain Barfield, could you wait up a minute?"

Since I wasn't going anywhere, I stood there waiting. He stopped suddenly and saluted. "Captain, you still haven't signed the tent roster. Since you're the only one who hasn't done that, could you please just stop by the orderly room and sign the blasted thing?—Please."

"Seems we had this conversation yesterday, didn't we, Sergeant?" He nodded. "That tent we talked about," I pointed behind me, "is still a BOQ. I don't plan on signing anything as ridiculous as a damn tent roster." I smiled. "If, however, someone turns up missing—you'll be the first to know."

He shuffled back and forth, ill at ease in not getting the response he hoped for. I could see he was a man caught in the middle. "I told the Colonel what you said." He didn't make eye contact as he continued. "He said if you didn't sign the roster, he'd fall the entire squadron out at 0500 every morning for a head count."

The idea hit me as so absolutely hilarious that it took a while to stop laughing. "You know, Sergeant, that little maneuver is certainly within his rights as CO." I could hardly stop laughing long enough to continue. "He has the power to do just that—let's see if he has the balls. I don't think he wants to face about a 100 hostile faces at 0500 each morning."

"You won't sign the roster?"

"How many ways do I have to say it? Hell no, I won't sign it."

The salute was abrupt, as the Sergeant trudged back to the orderly room.

Two days later, a notice was placed on the bulletin board that the Commanding Officer had decided it was not necessary to have the ranking officer sign a tent roster. He had devised ways to do the same accounting and save the ranking officers in each tent the time and responsibility.

Zack ripped it off the bulletin board and handed it to me. "Save this. You rammed it home on him again. You'll look back on this for a chuckle one day."

I didn't smile or take the paper. "There's nothing to chuckle about—and no damn victory. It was the right thing to do; just that simple." I looked at Zack. "Before we get outta here, I'll end up paying for it. If you don't believe that, you really underestimate Colonel Douglas Patrick Norwood."

# 11

## Plateau G

The heat, even at 0430, was becoming uncomfortable as the sun's earliest rays illuminated the horizon. With muffled conversation and laughter, shadowy figures moved toward Operations. Up ahead, in the dim light, the formless blur came into focus as a tent. Moving through the side opening, the air inside was heavy, hard to breathe. Perspiration soaked my flight suit as it became clammy against my skin. I spotted the vacant seat beside Zack and sat. He shook his head, "God amighty, it's already hotter than a goat's butt in a pepper patch."

In the front of the tent, Major Lynch fumbled with his briefing notes, perspiration dripping down his cheek. Standing behind him like a puppet master, Lieutenant Colonel Norwood waited to add his usual words of encouragement at the end of the briefing. Glancing around I saw the remnants of—Flight, scattered around the tent. Immediately behind Zack were Phil Merc and his co-pilot, B.L. Connors. The crowding in of bodies elevated the temperature. There was uneasiness in the air you could taste. Looking around the room, at the number of aircrew wiping at sweat and waiting for the inevitable, it was obvious this was a maximum effort.

His arm raked across his forehead at the beaded sweat, as Major Lynch moved to the front of the assembled aircrew. He wiped hastily at the perspiration with his other arm. "Gentlemen, this mission's critical to cutting off the VC in the highland area above Kontum. The Joint Staff in Saigon places the utmost importance on our success today." He glanced over the squadron. "Hey, Guys, we're gonna' do the almost impossible—note I said *almost* impossible. We're going to airlift a Vietnamese Ranger Battalion and its American advisors from Quang Ngai to Plateau G—a landing zone on top of a 6,000 foot mountain and make a max performance take-off five minutes after engine reverse."

Maps popped up in front of the aircrews as they searched for this plateau. "Navigators, Lynch continued, "take a careful look at the location and landmarks. You've got to help pilots zero in on the objective without delay." He looked out at several pilots searching for the LZ and this mystical Plateau G. "It's eighty clicks straight north of Pleuku—got it?" As heads bobbed up and down, satisfied the crews knew their destination, he continued, "We're going in with five-minute separation. This runway's gravel and dirt, 2,600 hundred feet long—and room for only one aircraft at a time."

"That's pretty damn short, especially for six thousand feet elevation, in this heat, " said Phil. "Who says that's the length, Major?"

"The Army says it's 2,600 feet," Lynch said.

Colonel Norwood stepped forward. "If the Army says the damn runway's 2,600 feet, that's the length, Lieutenant."

"Like the Army's got a bridge in Brooklyn they'll sell us too," Phil said. Laughter rolled through the tent.

Norwood scowled at Phil. "Get on with the briefing, Major."

Zack turned and whispered to Phil, "You're about to land on that damn bridge."

Major Lynch droned on with the details. "Five minutes gives you time for a quick unload of the Rangers and taxi back, making an immediate take-off. If something happens to your aircraft, taxi off the edge as far as possible and abandon it. The next aircraft's right behind you." Heads moved around as mumbling rolled toward the front of the tent. Major Lynch hurried on. "With that altitude and that length of airstrip, we've loaded only enough fuel to get off the ground and land at Pleiku for refueling. In fact, you'll have 50 gallons in each wing tank at take-off from Plateau G. Take-offs are gonna' take water injection and all 2,600 feet at that altitude. It'll take a real maximum performance take-off, probably rotating at 70 knots. There's no room for error on this one."

A hand grabbed my shoulder as Phil shoved the dash-one, pilot's handbook for the C-123, at me. His finger pounded a paragraph with red dashes surrounding it. I read the danger notification quickly. As Phil stuck his hand in the air trying to get the Major's attention, I scanned the highlighted notation: "*No maximum performance take-off will be made with less than 55 gallons of fuel in each wing tank. Centrifugal force will push fuel to the rear of the tank, preventing the standpipe from picking up fuel. In cases of maximum performance take-off, the engine will quit from fuel starvation.*" I shoved the book to Zack, who read quickly, then glanced back at me. "Goddamn," he exclaimed. "He's about two bubbles off plumb."

"What the hell's the commotion back there?" The Major asked, straining over his briefing notes to see who was making the noise. "What's the problem Lieutenant Merc?"

"Major, you might want to read the warning notation on page 21," Phil said and sat down.

Major Lynch thumbed quickly to the designated page. Blood drained from his fleshy face, leaving a yellow pallor under the suntan.

"What's he talking about?" asked the CO, looking over the Major's shoulder.

Phil took over at that point. "There's a notice that got overlooked in the planning of this mission. I hope to hell there're no more."

Norwood's eyes moved up from the page and fixed on Phil. His eyes carried the message. Slowly they moved down to the book again and he continued to read. Everyone scrambled for their dash one, reading the notation. Cursing, moans, and sporadic laughter caused Major Lynch to beckon to the Maintenance Officer. There was a quick conversation and Major Lynch turned back to the 30 officers in the Ops tent. "The tanks will be topped off to give you sixty gallons at take-off from Plateau G." The Major's voice trailed off, losing its strength. Norwood hurried to the side entrance looking back for the Adjutant. Zack leaned toward me. "Looks like he's about two jumps ahead of a fit. Reckon he doesn't have his usual words of wisdom to add to this briefing." His elbow nudged my side. "Or maybe that torqued look on his face is due to some flaming hemorrhoids."

"He doesn't have hemorrhoids, Zack—he's a *perfect* asshole."

A voice came from the rear of the tent. "What about intelligence? Can we expect any ground fire?"

"The area is supposed to be secure as of now, but they say the VC's closing the gap," Major Lynch said. "You'll have more than ground fire to worry about just getting in and back out on that short strip."

The formation leveled off at 5000 feet, heading south to Quang Ngai. Flights of two were slightly offset as the formation of ten aircraft stayed well out over the water. The sun, rising slowly off to our left, showed through the formless gray cloud bases, the colors changing from light pink to a fiery red. I had no appreciation for the beauty contained in the sunrise. I was anxious about the mission. I hated having too much time to dwell on uncertainties. My hands shifted their grip around the control column, restlessly fidgeting as I fought the apprehension. *I hate this goddamn feeling.* I looked at Zack who was calmly opening another pack of Marlboros. He pushed the smokes into his left sleeve and smiled. His calmness was infectious. It was like having a companion when you're walking down a dark street at night. His presence reassured me.

After touching down, we taxied up, forming a line on the grass facing the runway. The Loadmaster lowered the ramp as engines coughed to a stop. Zack slammed open his window. He sucked in the freshened air, taking deep breaths. As the last aircraft shut engines, we could hear the shouted commands of the troops forming behind the aircraft. They were indistinguishable in the early light as their camouflaged uniforms blended with the dimly lit jungle. Four tall Americans emerged as moving vegetation from the jungle; their camouflage uniforms becoming distinctive in the budding morning light. The closest one spun around and shouted commands that were then translated into Vietnamese. The staccato commands trailed off, becoming indistinct sounds down the line of troops.

The long lines of Rangers formed quickly and broke off in orderly rows toward the aircraft. They walked hunched forward under the tremendous weight of equipment and ammunition. Two lines formed behind our aircraft and started to board the ramp. I swung out of the seat, down the ladder, and ran back to stop the tall blond American in front. "Captain, its too damn hot to wait inside this sheet metal oven. We've got five minutes between aircraft take-offs, and number one hasn't even started engines yet."

He swirled around and snapped a command to a Vietnamese with a Lieutenant's pip on his collar. Equipment hit the ground as the Rangers silently sat on the grass. He turned back to me. "Give us a five-minute warning and I'll have the platoon on board."

"Okay, I'll have the Loadmaster come back to give you the word. He'll make sure everyone gets strapped in." The Captain, his green beret pulled low to the right side of his head, had an M-16 slung over his shoulder, a .38 caliber revolver in a shoulder holster and two hand grenades hung loosely from the webbing of his harness. His face was browned by days of squinting into green landscape, searching for a phantom enemy. The sun had etched fine white crows feet lines on his face, which disappeared again as he squinted. The dirt and stubble of a beard insinuated more age than his obvious youth. "How long have you been with this Battalion in the bush?" I asked.

"We've been out—let's see—about two months."

"Now you're going on another operation. When the hell are they gonna relieve you?"

He adjusted the M-16 on his shoulder and scratched at his beard. His eyes looked into the distance, not focusing on me. "Don't know. They send in replacements and we move on to another firefight. Reckon it depends on the tactical situation." He looked hard at me. "We're about ready for a break."

What could I say? I felt sympathy for this exhausted Special Forces officer, and awed by his commitment to an ambiguous mission. It was difficult to fathom his dedication, knowing how little his country appreciated him or his mission. As I stared at this tough, battle-weary

Captain, confidence shone in those bright, clear eyes. What drives a man like him—*what drives all of us?* The question, at first, seemed irreconcilable. But as I stood there in the glare of a burning sun, in a place most people had never heard of, it became clear. It's not dedication to some mystical code of honor. We simply do what we have to. We do it because other guys out here count on us. There was no mystery after all. It was really fundamental.

I called over to Jocko's replacement. "Sergeant Milliken, we'll start engines in six minutes, start getting 'em on board—and take-off your chute."

"Take-off my chute? Why, Captain?" Sergeant Harry Milliken wiped off the smile he was working on.

"Because of the weight thing, we don't have chutes on board for them." I nodded toward the troops. "How the hell would it look if we wore 'em?"

His unbuckled chute hit the deck of the aircraft. "We don't need 'em anyway." He tossed the chute to the side.

I called for the start-engine checklist as our Navigator leaned between Zack and me. "What's the matter with you, Tom?" I asked.

"I'm gettin' sick. I never smelled anything like this. God, those guys stink in this heat."

"Tom, you'd stink too if you'd been where they've been. And you wouldn't give a shit who's sniffing the air around you."

"I'm gonna puke."

"Not here you won't." I pushed his head back with the palm of my hand. "Starting number one."

The aircraft lurched down the runway as the air gushed through the open windows. Tom's color returned and he could breath again. We turned on course for Kontum, our major checkpoint, climbing to altitude. Zack crosschecked the instruments and set cruise power on the large radial engines, and then turned to Tom. "Hey, let's find that little ole LZ."

As we turned over Kontum, the radios crackled staccato messages. We heard Blocker one call airborne as Blocker two called on approach. The co-pilot's voice was tense as Blocker one cleared the LZ. "Blocker formation, Blocker one. Be advised there's hostile fire on final. Keep a steep approach."

"It gets more interesting all the time, Coach." Zack said, shaking his head at the transmission.

"You should have the LZ at twelve o'clock, ten miles." Tom said, leaning forward to see out front.

"We got it dead ahead.'

"Roger."


The radios came alive with crackling transmissions from ground forces mixed in with those of our formation. Confusion crept into the operation with different call signs mingled with ours. "Air Force aircraft on approach, this is Roundtree. Do you have contact with any of our helicopters? We've got nine more bodies at the bottom of this mountain to get out."

"Negative contact, Roundtree," Zack said.

The radio crackled again. "Roundtree, this is Eagle one. I've been reading you the whole time. Those bodies aren't going anywhere and we're pretty damn busy up here. Got more friggin' VC around us than the door gunners can handle."

Zack's hand shot forward to the flap handle, his eyes jumped at me. "Gear down and locked, full flaps, cowl flaps trail, landing checklist complete." I nodded and encountered his eyes, looking as if they expected something more from me. *I have no more, godammit.*

"As soon as the nose wheel touches, Zack, hold forward on the yoke and help stand on the brakes. I'll hit reverse as soon as possible."

"Roger."

There, in the middle of dark green vegetation, was a mountain with its top sheared off. A raw-looking gravel landing strip appeared in front of us. The ugly brownish scar looked extremely short as we approached it. Rugged mountain ridges fell off sharply into dark green jungle. Shells exploded beneath us in the jungle. "I think we're taking small arms fire, Captain." Sergeant Picardo became silent for a second. "Everybody's okay back here."

Too busy to acknowledge his transmission, I aimed for the first few feet of this supposed runway, easing back on power. The aircraft skimmed across the cliff's edge as I slammed it hard onto the gravel. My right hand snatched off the throttles, as Zack shoved its nose into the dirt, gluing the nose wheel to the irregular surface. Instantaneously, I lifted the throttles over the detent position, into full reverse. The aircraft vibrated awkwardly through the maze of earth blown up in front of it, shaking violently, finally coming to a stop. There, no more than twenty feet in front of us, was the end of the LZ. Just beyond the runway's end was a drop-off down the mountain. "Jesus H Christ, that wasn't 2,600 feet," Said Zack. "A few more feet and –."

"You wanna die in bed like my grandfather?" I interrupted.

"Damn right. A lot better than bobsledding down a mountain side."

Milliken had the tailgate coming down as Rangers dashed into the swirling dust and the unknown. They quickly blended into the terrain, and were soon swallowed in the foliage.

"Tail gate coming up", shouted Sergeant Milliken. Clear to taxi."

"Roger."

As we turned to taxi back for take-off, the Flight Engineer was visually checking for damage from gravel and the ground fire on approach. "Engines look okay, Captain. Can't see any damage."

The familiar crunching sound of a mortar round erupted from our left rear. I glanced back, looking where the round hit. A louder crunch came from our eleven o'clock position, as rocks and shrapnel pelted the aluminum skin. My muscles tightened as I waited for the next round.

"Where's that brilliant Intelligence Officer that said no VC here yet? I'm gonna be lookin' for a piece of his ass." Zack mumbled. I taxied faster.

"Let's get the hell, outta here," yelled Tom.

"Cool it. We'll be airborne soon." I said.

The aircraft swung into the wind. I pulled the throttles into reverse, backing the large machine back to the edge of the ill-defined runway.

"We'll use every foot available," I said.

"This damn thing's not 2,400 feet long," Zack said while setting full flaps and calling out the checklist.

"You saying the Army'd lie to us?" I asked.

"No, those weenies wouldn't do that just to get us on top of this friggin' mountain, would they? Here's the TOLD card—we should break ground at 70 knots."

"Roger. Follow me through. You know there's no abort on this one?" Zack nodded as I continued, "There's 62 inches, water injection coming on." I edged the throttles to 63 inches of manifold pressure." The aircraft vibrated anxiously under all the power it could deliver. It was sliding forward on the gravel in spite of holding the brakes.

"Blocker four on final. Get movin', David."

I released the brakes as the engines clawed at the hot humid air delivering all their energy. The LZ disappeared rapidly as we lumbered to 70 knots. With no warning there was the end of the runway. I glanced down to see only 68 knots on the airspeed indicator. Zack swore unintelligibly as I hauled back on the yoke. The aircraft sank with lack of airspeed, dropping rapidly, following the outline of the mountain. The mushy controls suddenly stiffened as we increased airspeed. We were flying.

"That's a maximum performance take-off if ever I saw one." Zack shouted. "I wasn't sure there for a minute."

"Me neither." I wiped the sweat pouring down my face.

"Blocker four, be advised there's mortar fire on the LZ." Zack transmitted.

"Roger, three. Go ahead and make me feel real good." Blocker four responded.

"We're thirty miles South of Kontum." Tom said.

I looked over at a relaxed Zack, who was reaching in his sleeve for a cigarette. "Call Pleiku tower and tell' em we're inbound for landing—and a good cup of coffee."

We walked along the dust-covered aircraft, examining the four holes in the ramp and two in the horizontal stabilizer. Sergeant Picardo evaluated every part of the engine for defects. As he continued his inspection of possible damage, the four of us looked at each other, saying nothing. We knew. When you know how close it comes, it makes you humble and grateful. Every day in this country I felt less invincible, and on this particular day I felt humble, very humble indeed.

We relaxed, laughed at the mortar rounds as if they were mere fireworks. It was over and we were on the ground again. Moving steadily to the Operations building, the banter continued. It was the escape valve for tension. We headed for the coffee pot on the counter. I enjoyed watching the emotional letdown set in after a mission like this. I could see it in their faces. We sipped our coffee, waiting for our turn for refueling. Milliken left with Sergeant Picardo to make sure of the refueling. Zack, Tom and I leaned against the Operations office wall, talking about the chow waiting at DaNang. Major Lynch moved in our direction from across the room. His presence unconsciously stopped our conversation. Zack looked up at him. "He'd be outta his depth in a parking lot puddle. Besides, just looking at the booger, I figure he fell out of the ugly tree and hit every branch on the way down." We stifled our laughter as Lynch stopped directly in front of me.

"OPs just got a message from the Rangers we dropped off. The last aircraft made it out okay." He glanced out the window and back self-consciously. "They're under heavy attack and almost out of mortar rounds. You're gonna have to take in a resupply load immediately."

"And just what the hell's wrong with the other nine crews on the friggin' gaggle, Major?"

"My aircraft is already refueled and too heavy to go back," said Lynch. "And—Colonel Norwood told me to give the mission assignment to you."

My coffee cup came down hard on the counter; the contents spilled out and ran over the wood, dripping onto the floor. "You know, Major, every mission has to have a 'frag order' from Air Division. Tell Colonel Norwood to come up with a 'frag order' real quick—or forget it."

He glanced around as if there was someone to give him advice. "There's no 'frag order'."

Zack grabbed my sleeve, spinning me toward him. "David, remember what you've always said: 'Get the job done and to hell with the paperwork bullshit.' Did you really mean it, or were they just words?" He waited, as I stood speechless. Zack glanced over at Major Lynch, and then whispered, "To hell with that toad who just told us to go. Those Rangers need mortar rounds—let's get 'em there."

"No way, Captain," Tom shouted. "You said there's no 'frag order'. We don't have to do this."

I looked hard at Zack, never looking back at Tom. "Yeah, we do." I slowly turned toward Tom. "As much as I hate it, we damn well have to do this." His face turned sallow as I talked. I could see his hand clutch tightly to the map he was holding, his hand shaking. "Tom, you stay here and arrange our fuel and figure us a flight plan straight out over the water and up to DaNang—we don't need a Navigator on this one. Besides it'll be less weight."

My gut churned with an uncomfortable feeling that this might be the one that gets you. Fear is a bad companion. It was not a new feeling. I'd dealt with it before. Today, it was a skilled adversary. The feeling starts in your gut and works slowly up to your brain. There it has to be subdued. *Damn, I don't want to do this. Duty can damn well be an ugly word.*

Sergeant Milliken dashed through the door, breathing heavily. "Captain, some moron just pulled up in a truck loaded with 60 millimeter mortar rounds. What kinda crap is this?"

"Load us up to max take-off weight. We're going back to Plateau G."

He looked at me as if I'd gone nuts. I looked him in the eye, waiting for his rebuttal. He looked hard at me, as I wondered how I'd answer his objections. His solemn look of despair showed itself even more than this morning. "Roger, Captain, we'll be ready in 20 minutes." He ran through the door, and I watched him dash for the aircraft. We missed Jocko, but Milliken was proving to be a damn good Loadmaster. I didn't always understand him, and he hadn't been put to the test until now. Given the right circumstances, you get to know a man in a hurry. I'd know Millken pretty well before this day ended.

I turned to Zack. "Figure us a TOLD card and one for the LZ. Since this was your brilliant idea, you'd best get your butt hoppin'."

He laughed. "I'll figure one for here—as for that LZ, just haul back on the yoke at the end of the runway and pray." He put his face in front of mine and squinted. "You *are* in good with the man upstairs—right?" I hit his shoulder. He looked at me, a smile running across his face. "I didn't know teaming up with you would put both of us on Norwood's hit list. Reckon he's trying to get us killed, Coach?" Zack took on that look I could never decipher. It could denote a serious question or serve as a facade for his usual facetious analysis. "Did you ever figure it's me he's really after, and you're just along for the ride, Coach?"

"What th' hell are you talking about?"

"Forget it. Let's get on with this thing."


Our objective was ahead of us. My gut tightened, knowing things I didn't know the first time. I caught myself grinding my teeth, as Zack called off the checklist. The gear went down with a solid thump, the nose lowered with full flaps extended. My gut tightened more as we headed toward the runway. I leveled off as we skimmed the ridgeline, with slightly too much airspeed. The aircraft bounced as I forced it to the ground. The nose gear finally touched as I slammed the throttles into full reverse. The aircraft vibrated and oscillated down the strip.

"Stop, you bastard." Zack yelled.

The aircraft shuddered to a stop and we exhaled for the first time. The engines, coming out of reverse, pulled the cloud of dust behind us, and we stared out at nothing but sky. Sergeant Picardo looked out between us. "Where's the friggin' runway?"

"You'd best look out the back, Sergeant," Zack laughed, "there's none up front."

The nose was actually over the edge of the plateau. We had to use reverse and back up enough to turn around. We taxied back, looking for someone to unload the cargo. I turned the aircraft into the wind and cut engines, waiting.

Finally, a truck moved our way; mortar and artillery could be heard in the distance. The Vietnamese began unloading the heavy boxes of mortar rounds. They moved slowly and methodically, placing each box carefully onto the truck bed. They were not Rangers from the Battalion we dropped off and acted as if time was of no importance. A mortar round found the range, exploding 50 yards from us. I leaped to the back of the load and screamed at the closest soldier. "Get this crap off here—now." He looked back at me with a blank stare. He obviously understood no English. The next round smashed into a bunker, less than 30 yards away. Shrapnel fell around us like hail. "We gotta get outta here." I yelled at the figures moving like zombies.

Suddenly a jeep skidded to a stop in back of the ramp. A muscular Vietnamese Officer jumped from the jeep and walked through the dust. I could see the Lieutenant Colonel pips on his "Tiger suit" fatigues. He had a black mustache and sunken dark eyes that showed no emotion. His voice was hard. "There's a counter attack. Get off as soon as you can." He spoke perfect English.

"Damn right, Colonel, we'd like to do just that. Get these mortar rounds off the aircraft, and I don't care if they throw 'em on the grass." Another round walked its way closer to the C-123. "Can you get 'em movin', Colonel?" My voice involuntarily changed pitch.

He turned toward the soldiers, swatting his leg with the leather swagger stick he carried in his left hand. He barked a few words and all snapped to attention. He growled a few commands in Vietnamese, and the men erupted into action as boxes flew off the aircraft and bounced onto the grass. It took less than four minutes to clear the belly of the C-123. I glanced at the Colonel, smiled, and saluted. He returned it, never changing his grim look.

Zack and I hurtled forward, strapping quickly into the seats, at the same time hitting switches. "He sure 'nuff put the fear of Budda in 'em," Zack said, as he buckled his shoulder harness. "He's either one real bad ass or he's got a good case of testosterone poisoning."

The engines groaned under maximum power as they pulled us toward the end of the strip. I kept glancing at the airspeed as runway disappeared rapidly—60 knots—65. The end was almost under us. 67 knots. I hauled back on the controls and the nose raised slightly, the wheels still fixed to earth. We shot off the end and sank sluggishly off the precipice. We were barely flying, on the verge of a stall, the warning horn blaring its admonition. The controls shook in my hands as we plunged down the slope of the mountain. The airspeed began to build as I felt some positive control pressure. The aircraft was flying. We climbed to 6,000 feet and turned south toward Pleiku. Zack lit a cigarette, blew the smoke out slowly, and smiled. "If Norwood's trying to do us in, he just missed a damn good opportunity."

Ignoring the comment, I looked out the side window. The pristine jungle below was darker where clouds cast shadows. Its vastness was assertive. It hid the misery that took place beneath its dark green canopy. We had a quick glimpse of the valley of death, but for right now, the jungle was pastoral. For now, for this minute, I needed my mind to transcend the grim reality of this ill-defined war.

As I stared into the cobalt sky, Vietnam was tranquil for this moment.

# 12

## Confrontation

The Pleiku runway disappeared underneath us as I pulled the nose into the sun, peeking from behind a group of cumulus clouds. Rambling conversations began over the intercom as soon as the landing gear bumped into the wheel wells. Humor, coursing through the crew, abruptly provided a relief valve for suspended anxiety, discharging tension spontaneously. Laughter erupted from Tom at the silliest of comments. A successful mission usually provides a feeling of satisfaction but as the stakes are raised, as this one was, it becomes more gratifying. We beat the odds this day, and it felt damn good.

Major Lynch met us as we walked toward Operations. He began talking to me before he reached us. "Colonel Norwood wants to see you ASAP."

Zack leaned into my ear from behind. "He wants to tell you how very sorry he is for having to send us back into Plateau G."

I glanced over my shoulder, frowning at Zack. Looking back at Major Lynch, I said, "What demands my attention so quickly?"

"He just said to ask you to come up as soon as you landed."

I waited for the First Sergeant to announce me, then moved to the front of the Colonel's desk. I saluted, keeping the proper military protocol that was so firmly ingrained in me. He pointed to a gray steel chair. "Have a seat and let's talk."

"Yessir."

"You and your crew did a damn good job taking that second mission back to Plateau G. I hated like hell to send *anyone* back, but the Rangers had to have those mortar rounds." He leaned forward. "Your aircraft was the only one not refueled and too heavy, and the other birds behind you weren't even on the ground yet." He smiled and looked intently at me. "I'm recommending you for a Distinguished Flying Cross and your entire crew for a decoration."

"That would be nice for the crew, Colonel. They performed well under the circumstances – they deserve some recognition."

He took a piece of paper, which had been strategically placed, in the center of his desk. He lifted the page in his left hand, playfully glancing at it and back at me. "This list was just pulled down from the Saigon message traffic." He smiled ear to ear. "This is the promotion list to Major—and your name's on it, Captain Barfield. Congratulations." He stood, extending his hand.

"Thank you, Sir. What a surprise."

"You've had a good day, Captain. I realize you won't be pinning those gold leaves on until after you leave here, but the fact is you'll soon be a field grade officer." His eyes focused directly at mine. "Start thinking like one." His vague smile disappeared.

"Colonel, don't expect my thinking to change because I'm on a promotion list." I could see hostility building in his eyes. I could almost feel an electrical charge. "There shouldn't be some sudden change in your thinking or your value system because of rank. The Air Force shouldn't require, or expect, that from any officer."

"In other words, you have no intention of cooperating. "

"That's not what I said, Colonel. I was just trying to be honest about my thinking. It won't change my integrity. Some things one should never compromise."

"You're just a damn maverick, Barfield." He shoved the list toward me. "Don't think this promotion can't be changed—all I have to do is report your attitude and lack of cooperation in my reports back to Wing Headquarters at Pope." When I refused to be drawn into his supposition, he slammed the paper onto his desk. His face turned crimson. "Forget that DFC. You've bucked me since the day we formed this group. You fail to wear the correct uniform, you don't file flight plans at mission sites, you refuse to sign the tent roster, and your whole flight insists on making a fool of the Operations Officer." His neck veins pulsated. "Your conduct borders on insubordination. I'd say you're a damn site closer to a court-martial than a promotion."

I stood and leaned across the desk. The blood coursed toward my face, but I tried to maintain composure in my voice. "If you want to prefer charges against me, Colonel, make damn sure of your accusations. My flight executes every mission assigned, pushing past the envelope on some. Plateau G today was a pretty damn good example." My face came closer to his. "My flight has the lowest abort rate in the squadron. We bust ass doing our job, Colonel." His face was splotched with the rush of blood. "I wear the uniform prescribed by Tactical Air Command regulation, not one devised for personal ego. There's absolutely no requirement to file a flight plan at a combat mission site with no operations, or anyone to give it to." I pointed to the phone. "I think Wing Operations would love to hear about the Major's suggestion: 'Just place it under a rock'. What a sterling piece of advice." I saw the anger in his eyes, but I kept on. "I explained to the First Sergeant about the tent quarters being a BOQ. Since when do officers have to have a bed check, Colonel? And—as for your Operations Officer, there's no need for my men to make a fool of him—he's a self-made man. The fuel requirement mistake for the planning of our mission today would tell Wing Operations enough."

He leaped from his chair, grabbing hold of the desk as if using it for leverage. "Goddamn it, Barfield, you can't talk to your Commanding Officer like this." He looked toward the door. "Let me get Sergeant Stone in here to witness this conversation."

"Good idea, Colonel. Because I want him to hear about the numerous witnesses in this squadron who'll declare you deliberately ordered five men to their death. They'll testify in a heartbeat to the circumstances surrounding that mission." I clinched my hands into a fist as they supported my weight on the desk. "I'll never know your motive for that travesty. It could have been pompous arrogance in not wanting to cancel a mission, it could have been reprisal toward me, or it could have been because you just don't give damn about anyone or anything but your career." I waved my arm toward the entrance. "Call him in, Colonel."

His face came within inches of mine. "Get the hell out of my office, Captain." He pointed to the door. "You may have crossed the line this time, Captain." His voice quivered slightly. "We'll see, Barfield. We'll see."

I looked back at I reached the doorway and saw him visibly shaking as he tried to control his anger. I'd never seen hate in a man's eyes before. I smiled softly, looking at a wretched individual who happened to wear the same uniform I did. I was sorry for that fact.


As I entered the tent, "Well, what did he want?" Zack asked. "Did he tell you he was writing all of us up for a DFC for going back into Plateau G?" "No Distinguished Flying Cross, but I'm on the list for Major," I said, not wanting to go into Norwood's veiled threats in front of the crew. They'd had enough crap thrown at them this day.

"Hotdamn," said Tom, as he ran over to me. Rusty and Mac joined him, slapping me on the back and shouting congratulations. Zack sat on his bunk with mouth agape. When the commotion died down, he placed a hand on my shoulder and looked at the other three men. "You guys should start showing the proper respect for our leader here. " Zack tapped on my shoulder. "You don't go slapping field grade officers on the back—and I didn't hear one of you say, 'Sir'." He was grinning from ear-to-ear as I pushed him down on his bunk. Zack was dying laughing as he bounced in the air. "Easy there, Major, this is assault on a subordinate."

"I'll assault your sorry butt." I straddled his body, pretending to get a chokehold. "Get up and let's get some chow." I leaned close to his ear and whispered. "We need to talk."

We walked together in silence; the only sound was our boots crunching the gravel. Zack was a guy you could sit with on a bench for hours, saying nothing, and both feel comfortable with the quiet.

"I want you to keep your guard up, old Buddy, I figure Norwood might nail you too – you know – guilt by association. Just be alert for whatever actions he can cook up." He watched me but made no comment. "Don't overreact to my suspicions or distrust, but I damn well want you to be aware of the prospects for retribution." I tapped him on the shoulder. "Okay, let me explain this . . ."

"Lieutenant. Hey, Lieutenant." The man moved toward us. "Lieutenant Williams, you musta' paid those doctors over at the hospital on China Beach. They said I'm fit for duty, just like you said." Jocko stopped and saluted.

"I told you a band-aid and two aspirins would do it, Zack said. Now you're back with the first team. How'd you get so lucky, Jocko?"

"Milliken told me about your wild mission today. He was glad to see me back." He chuckled. "Captain, I think you and Lieutenant Williams scared the crap outta old Harry today."

"We all puckered a bit on that one today, said Zack. You can be glad you missed it."

"Glad to have you back, Jocko," I stated. "What about the knee?"

"Oh, they x-rayed that 'sombitch' enough. After talking it over, they decided it was too close to the back of the kneecap to operate. They said an operation could do more damage than just leaving it there. From looking at the x-rays, it was a small piece of a round that split off and hit me." He smiled. "It really don't matter, 'cause that little old piece of metal's gonna stay right there." He saluted. "See you tomorrow at Operations."

"Okay, Jocko—and we're damn glad to have you back," I shouted after him.

We walked for another few moments while I gathered my thoughts. "As I started to tell you—the conversation with the good

Colonel turned ugly. He was thinking that my upcoming promotion to major could be used as a hammer to beat me into line. The more we talked, the worse it got. He threatened to send in a negative report to Wing to stop my promotion, even said my behavior bordered on a court-martial."

"That sorry son-of-a-bitch reached rock bottom but continues to dig," said Zack.

"When he threatened to bring in Sergeant Stone as a witness, I told him to go ahead. That's when it really came to a head—I basically said he was responsible for Rick, Jeff, Carey, and the rest of the crew."

"I'm glad, David. It needed to be said, and dammit, who else in the squadron was gonna do it?"

"You mean who else stupid enough?" I touched his shoulder. "He won't let this one go. I don't know when or how the reprisal will come—but it will. And it could affect you too, Zack."

Zack stopped and the sun glistened off the beaded perspiration on his forehead. He wiped his sleeve across his face, then pointed to a shady spot beside the shower enclosure. "Come over here and sit a minute, David. There's something I should have told you a long time ago." He took off his hat, plopped down, leaning against the wooden sides.

We sat for a while in the humid heat. A radio playing from a nearby tent was the only sound. I knew Zack was wrestling with whatever it was he needed to tell me. He would get there at his own pace.

"You're right about guilt by association." He still looked straight ahead. "But it's me he wants, David. You just happened to be in his line of sight."

"How did you know Norwood before all of this?"

"It's a long story – one I'm not proud of." He slowly turned to look at me. "You won't like it either. It happened almost two years ago, when I first got to Pope. There was this little bar south of Fayetteville where several of us hung out. One Friday night, three of us stopped there for a drink and a bite to eat. We just wanted to relax and unwind from the weekly grind. We weren't on the prowl. There was a table near the bar with four girls laughing and talking. One kept looking in my direction – you damn well know the look I'm talking about."

I nodded, waiting for the story to unfold. "I got up and went over and introduced myself. One thing led to another and I asked her out. Hell, I knew she was young, she said she was nineteen. We dated a few times, always meeting me at the bar. I thought that was a little strange, but she explained her father didn't like for her to date service men, even officers."

"Zack, you didn't suspect something from the git-go?"

"My raging hormones had already taken charge. One night we ended up back at my apartment, and you know what happened. It was late and I offered to follow Laura home to make sure she was all right. She was very nervous and insisted on driving home alone.

The next morning, Bob Grimes stopped by for a cup of coffee. It didn't take long for him to let me know the real reason for the visit. He told me Laura's friends briefed him that night I met her. He didn't want to interfere and thought I'd find out that she was only seventeen. I damn near flipped when I heard that. Her name was not Laura Woods – it was Laura Norwood. I didn't know her father, only that he was a Lieutenant Colonel in Wing."

"Jesus H Christ, Zack. Why didn't you check her out before getting that involved? You didn't have a clue she was seventeen?"

"Good God, David, she had the body of a 25 year old. She was poised and acted older – hell, I had absolutely no idea."

"Norwood found out?"

Zack's fist hit the building with a sickening thud. "When she called that night, I told her I could never see her again."

Two months later I'm walking back from the flight line and this tall lieutenant colonel meets me. He doesn't stick out his hand with his introduction, he simply says he's Laura's father. He pointed to his car and said, "Let's take a ride." My first impulse was to run like hell, but I knew I had screwed up and might as well apologize and accept responsibility for being terminally stupid."

He said nothing for the first five minutes as we drove off base. I finally initiated the conversation with an apology for going out with Laura, explaining I had no friggin' idea she was only seventeen. Man, I was groveling to make sure he understood I was sorry."

"Suddenly he pulls the car off the side of the road. He turns to me; his face contorted with his lips pulled tight – a look I'll never forget. He grabs my jacket and snatches me around. Just as I was ready to hit the SOB, he says: 'My daughter is pregnant, you stupid bastard.' I was stunned. 'You ruined her life, Lieutenant. She has this warped idea she's in love with you and that you love her.' His eyes – damn, I'll never forget those eyes. 'I told her she could never see you again. She had an abortion yesterday. Now listen up real good, you stupid SOB. Stay completely out of her life – never contact her again. You understand me Lieutenant?'"

Zack's head dropped into his hands. I put my hand on his shoulder and squeezed hard. "I'm sorry, Zack. That's a helluva story and having Norwood as our CO is real irony. But look, we've all made mistakes in this life – probably gonna make more. It's not like you were some callous bastard who knew her age and did this – you just didn't know."

He looked up. "David, she had a nervous breakdown right after that. She called several times and I just hung up." He looked at the ground, his head shaking back and forth. "Just hung up the phone." He continued to stare at the ground. "I could've made a difference."

"Think about it. Don't you think she had some small damn responsibility in what happened? She lied to you. Learn to forgive yourself, Zack and forget it. Time to move on."

"That doesn't take away one iota of the guilt I feel about Laura. So you see, Coach, it's you who are guilty by association. Norwood hates my guts but he never lets it show. It's hidden somewhere deep inside that steely facade, waiting for the right time to . . ." He swallowed hard. "As you say – it ain't over yet. Norwood's one dangerous SOB."

"Roger that. I earned his hate on my own. Don't blame yourself. Now that it's noted, let's get a drink and forget that bastard, the heat, and Charlie for a few hours." I jumped up, extending my hand to pull him up. "And drop the guilt. I earned that bulls eye on my back." I watched his smile erupt. "C'mon, Zack, let's go."

Larry Hazelwood slunk into the bar. His mouth drooped at the corners as he scanned the crowd for a friendly face. Guy Mapp was sitting alone and we watched him pull up a chair next to Guy. We turned back to our drinks, ignoring their muted conversation. Zack sipped his beer and tilted his head in my direction. "I wrote my Dad yesterday." I watched him rotate the bottle slowly, then take another sip of beer.

"So, what am I supposed to say? That's great, Zack? I'm sure you feel better for doing that?—or what?"

Zack slammed the bottle down on the bar. "What got your shorts in a wad?" "Look, if you want to talk about your letter, fine—go ahead—I'm listening."

"Screw you." Zack jumped off the bar stool, slamming directly into Guy, who was coming up from the rear. Beer went all over Guy. "Damn, I'm sorry," said Zack, glancing back at me. "I should've looked where I was going."

Guy swiped at the beer on his shirt. "Get back on that bar stool. You both need to be sitting down."

We noticed Hazelwood standing behind him, almost hidden. His presence was always a bad omen. Guy moved between us, placing his hand on our shoulders. "Budnik just bought it."

We sat in stunned silence. I thought back to the funny-looking broken nose the night he bought us drinks after we got his crew out of Khe Sangh. I cleared my throat. "How?"

"That's the shitty part. They flew a mission over to the firebase near Kontum. Just before take-off there, Jim Keel, the navigator, asks the Special Forces grunts what they had flying on top of a bamboo pole." He shook his head. "It was a pair of panties. According to the reports, Gene told the grunt captain they were gonna knock those panties off that pole after take-off."

"Don't tell me they tried it," Zack said.

"Did it. The first pass, they came in low and rocked the pole, causing it to sway back and forth. Then, according to the grunts, on the second pass, they got the panties—and the right wing caught a large tree just as they pulled up at the end of the compound. The aircraft cart wheeled across the area, disintegrating on impact."

"Any survivors?" I asked.

Hazelwood stepped up, sticking his head beside Guy's. "None."

"All for a damn pair of panties," said Zack. "And after we almost got our ass shot off getting them out of Khe Sangh." He starred out the window, oblivious to the rest of us.

"It's a helluva war," said Guy.

No one commented. Zack slid off the stool and started for the door. I followed a few yards behind, leaving him to his thoughts. He had to deal with it in his own way.

There was no doubt about the 0700 briefing time the next morning. The word had been spread by every means available to Colonel Norwood. The Operations tent filled with aircrew before the prescribed hour. Colonel Norwood walked to the front, followed by Major Lynch. Norwood held the makeshift rostrum, holding it so hard his knuckles turned white. He stared out at his audience, glancing swiftly side-to-side to scan each individual. Suddenly, it was quiet enough to hear breathing. Every eye was on the CO, waiting for him to speak. He pointed to Major Lynch. "Hold those up so everyone here can see 'em." From the envelope under his arm, Lynch pulled out some pink panties. "Get a good look at those. Two Air Force Lieutenants thought this was worth risking their crew and aircraft for." He shook his fist in the air. "How many more goddamn idiots do we have in this outfit? It's not enough we're in a combat situation—these hotdogs go out and make a fool of the whole Squadron. They disgraced themselves, me, this unit, and the Air Force."

Mac rose to his feet, fidgeting with his hat. "Colonel, there's no doubt a mistake was made here—a huge error in judgment. But we just lost five men. Our friends. We're sad about the loss, and I don't think it's appropriate to talk about them in this manner."

"I call it like it is, Lieutenant. They were damn stupid. Hear that, Lieutenant?—damn stupid. And, oh yes, you, and the rest of this unit, can assume some of the responsibility. This kind of hotdog shenanigans must be the mind-set around this squadron." He held up a message. "I've got to report to Saigon this afternoon and explain this fiasco to the General." He looked back at Mac. "Maybe you can explain why we have no discipline in this unit." Mac sat there, knowing not to respond to that one.

"Well, Gentlemen, you can bet your butt we'll have discipline in this squadron from now on. You'll act like professionals and fly like professionals. You'll turn in a copy of all TOLD cards to be checked before each mission, there will be a debriefing after each mission, any deviation from the briefed mission will result in an Article Fifteen of the UCMJ, and we'll have a stand-by inspection every Saturday morning." Then he smirked. "For your information, the clever ice-making scheme has been uncovered, dismantled, and the parts turned in to disposal. Eventually, I'll find out who was responsible for that—never doubt it. Dismissed."

# 13

## Retribution

Two weeks of monsoon rain had dampened our spirits to a low unsurpassed by Colonel Norwood. Rain came down in sprawling sheets, blowing in under the tent top. It cascaded down the tent walls, splashing mud into a soupy mixture around each one. We moved our bunks to avoid the overhead leaks, only to find new sources of moisture falling on the bedding. The gravel paths were the only place you could step without miring ankle deep in mud. Missions were being scrubbed due to low-hanging clouds slithering down the mountains into the valleys in northern Vietnam. Time stagnated. When sunshine pierced the gray above us, which was rare, we could expect a maximum effort. In spite of the weather, we still supported the Special Forces' acute needs, and cases of beer were always stashed on board.

The weather, however, was not a factor in this operation. The ceiling was high enough to get the mission off. We were sure of the planning this time because two flight commanders assisted in the minute details. Every aspect was covered in the briefing. We knew we were ready. It was with complete confidence that we preflighted the aircraft, and sat waiting for the Vietnamese to climb on board.

The Vietnamese Airborne Brigade lined up behind the 10 parked C-123s. We were told these were the sharpest troopers in the Republic of Vietnam's Army. They stood erect, with their helmets tight, laden with equipment, rifles, grenade launchers and parachutes. Given the command, they jogged up the ramps and took their places quietly. When Jocko gave the word, the ramp door closed.

We fought the mountain thermals to stay in loose formation, four aircraft abreast in two flights. The first flight was to drop the troopers and the second wave was rigged for equipment drops along with troopers. Tom was the lead Navigator, placing considerable pressure on a second lieutenant. He concentrated on his charts, glancing out occasionally for confirmation of terrain identity. He yelled for a correction to a heading of 218 degrees, then: "DZ dead ahead. Drop in four minutes." Zack keyed his mike, "Backfire flight, drop in four minutes. Drop on lead aircraft."

The Vietnamese Captain stood in the back facing the troopers. He barked the commands I had heard so many times at Pope with the 82$^{nd}$ Airborne Division. Even though spoken in Vietnamese, I could understand his directions. "Stand up—Hook up—Face the door—Standby for green light." Tom shouted in his mike, "Ten seconds." Jocko held up ten fingers. The Captain nodded and translated the time in Vietnamese.

The troopers were lined up, facing the rear, touching each other back to front in a tight line, as they waited for the jump signal. Tom flipped the green light on. The Vietnamese Captain yelled: "Go," and troopers filed out so rapidly that the aircraft was emptied in eight seconds. Zack quickly checked for malfunctioning static lines, which would leave a trooper twirling helplessly behind the aircraft on a static line that failed to release the chute. Seeing the 26 empty lines trailing like streamers in the slip stream, he shouted: "All clear."

As we turned left, in a wide arc to accommodate the formation, we saw the chutes collapsing, as the last soldiers were hitting the ground. The equipment chutes, from the second wave, blossomed in the air like giant multi-colored flowers, floating lazily in the air. The mission went like clock work with all troopers and equipment hitting on the DZ.

A message was posted in operations that the Airborne unit had secured the area around Khe Sanh and casualties were extremely light. The next message was from Saigon, stating a "well done" for the 309th Air Commando Squadron. The message from Saigon was the only excuse quoted that night, but there were many others, tucked away in our individual minds. We all were sky high with elation over the perfect Airborne drop to relieve Khe Sanh, the first airborne operation to take place in Vietnam.

As the crews exchanged stories of the mission, laughter filled the bar. The boisterous exchange died down quickly, and the moment of quiet resolve settled over the bar like a specter. Reality of what we just did, what we do every day, reached out for the recesses of our subconscious. It took little time for the drinks to stop flowing and individual conversations to take over. It became just another day at the office for us. I glanced around the bar and watched the guys break into small clusters, talking about every topic under the sun. It never ceased to amaze me how aircrews could one minute be engaged in a life or death contest, and a few minutes later, talking about the best way to fight crab grass in your yard. I snickered to myself as I caught bits and pieces of nearby conversations.

Zack looked at me dubiously. "What's got you so tickled, Coach?"

"Life, Zack old boy. Life. Freud would have a blast with these guys." I tugged his sleeve. "Let's go grab a table back there and relax with another drink."

"Let's go," said Zack, holding up his beer, "I got a fresh one."

We took a small table in a darkened corner of the club, pulled a second chair around and put our feet up. We sat there as a subtle calming came over me. I sipped the bourbon and let my mind be still. Zack was content with no conversation, looking fixedly at his beer, his eyes focused on some distant place and time. We sat there several seconds, then looked at each other and both started to speak. I stuck up my hand for him to wait. "Tell me how Jane's doing these days. Has she found some local guy who doesn't fly off to the outer reaches of the globe?"

"She knows a good thing when she sees it." His eyes got serious. "I'll never understand how I got lucky enough to have her in my life. We have something going I never expected. There must be some truth to that old story about love being for real." He sipped his beer. "I sure don't want to screw this one up."

"Not everybody does, you know."

"Christ, I'm sorry. I didn't mean you and Leslie, I . . ."

"I didn't think you did. Besides, this will work out—one way or the other." I swallowed hard. "We both know what's important in this old world. It's just a matter of grasping it. I know I've learned some things about life since we left Pope—and about me."

Zack looked hard at me. "I can't wait to get back. There were several times I wondered about staying in, but I've found the real reason I won't make the Air Force a career. It sure as hell won't be a factor in my life with Jane. I'm going with the airlines."

"Military life can play hell with relationships that aren't very strong," I said. "But so can some of those 'stewardi'." I laughed.

He nodded and began to laugh. "I was dating a stew just before I started flying with you. Did you meet Kim?"

"Zack, I lost count of your other women way back there."

He slapped my shoulder. "Hey, I was just gonna tell you about this stew. That was the coldest woman I ever met. Hell, I could get an ice cream headache from kissing her too fast."

"That did it," I said. "Let's go hit the sack. It's been a long day."


It was one of those ill-defined weather patterns that made predictions of longer than one hour a mere guess. We watched the rolling clouds and torrential rain, seldom interrupted by the sun splintering the gray with bright shafts of light. The forecast today never varied from low-lying clouds obscuring the mountains in I Corps area. Missions were scrubbed again. Meteorology would not risk a forecast that would permit a "go".

"Well, it looks like we won't be able to get off any missions except down the coast. To the north we're socked in," said Major Lynch.

"Just a minute, Major," Colonel Norwood stated, as he walked briskly to the front of operations. "Are there any High Priority or Critical missions?"

"No Critical, only one High Pri.—to reinforce ammo to Khe Sanh." He looked back down to a frag order in his hand. "It's doesn't become High Pri until tomorrow—this stuff may break by tomorrow."

"What's Weather calling for in that area?" Norwood asked.

Major Lynch fumbled through sheets of paper, pulling one from the stack. He touched a finger on the map in the location of Khe Sanh, and then glanced back at the weather sequence. "It calls for broken deck at 1,500 feet, overcast layer at 6,000 feet, and visibility less than two miles, in rain, under the cloud bases."

"If the broken deck has a few holes, an aircraft could let down through the stuff and fly down that valley." He looked harder at Lynch. "Maybe someone would like to give it a try—they can always abort the mission if there's no hole when they get there." Before the Major answered, he turned to me. "Captain Barfield—soon to be Major Barfield – do you think someone in your flight could give it a try?"

"I wouldn't ask anyone to try it, Colonel. That weather leaves little room for error in these mountains."

"If you wouldn't ask someone to do it, does that mean your crew would take the mission—of course, you realize it's voluntary."

"No, Sir."

"I'm sorry to hear that, Captain. I figured on more from one of our squadron leaders. You once told me that your flight busts ass to always get the mission accomplished. Isn't that right?"

I could see the trap he was building, setting me up for my ego to rebound. I knew I couldn't let him goad me into a mission that had almost no chance of success. "Colonel, there are times when circumstances dictate the use of discretion—this is one of those times."

"Lord, when did discretion become another word for—let's see—no, I won't use that word?"

Zack grabbed my arm and whispered, "Don't let him do this."

"Colonel, maybe Major Lynch would like to give it a 'try', as you call it." I worked at showing no emotion. "He's got the inside on the weather—as well as your burning desire to get this mission off."

"I'm sure Major Lynch would jump at the challenge—if he weren't essential here." The thin smile stretched across face, making his lips tight. "So, I'll ask again, Captain Barfield, are you leader enough to make a try at this mission, or are you going to use some flimsy excuse to dodge that challenge." He looked side to side at the crews gathered there. All sat motionless, watching the building repartee. "The others are waiting for your decision. I'm sure, Captain, you're not the kind of officer who would use questionable weather to expunge your duty. I'm confident you're pilot enough to take this one on."

I knew I was had. I had fallen to my bruised ego, goaded into showing my machismo for no reason, except pride. I fought the feeling. Yet, there was no way I was going to let the squadron and my flight watch any further humiliation. Colonel Norwood had outmatched me. "We'll take the mission, Colonel." He smirked, knowing I'd fallen for his cunning. I immediately wished I could suck back those five words. I wanted so badly to undo this thing. It was too late.

"Good." The smile stretched broader. Our eyes met, a window to his soul, they flashed with gratification. "Major Lynch will brief you on the details," then strode out the door.

As Lynch stated the particulars for the load, expected departure time, and fuel loading, I only half-listened to his mono-tonal voice. My mind focused on the weather. If we could stay under the overcast layer, we might find a hole over the valley. I turned to a worried Tom Johnson, the concern in his eyes was apparent. "We won't need a navigator on this one. You can't take a fix in this weather. We'll leave you here on this trip."

"I'll go, Captain," Tom stated quickly. "I can help with radio bearings."

"No, Tom. You'll have to miss this one."

Zack and I ambled to the aircraft being loaded with various ammo requirements. Jocko was critically examining the load to make sure of weight and balance. Sergeant Picardo was double-checking fuel and the engines. No one was making conversation, just methodically preparing for a mission. I joined Zack on the flight deck. He turned toward me. "Ready to start engines—you want to brief me on this gaggle?"

"We'll establish a radial off the VOR on Monkey Mountain. I've calculated we should be over the Khe Sanh valley at take-off plus forty-three minutes. We'll try to stay at minimum en route altitudes and between layers. Any questions?"

"Yes. How th' bloody hell did you let Norwood get to you like that?"

"We all have feet of clay, Zack. We keep finding that out at the oddest times."

"You couldn't just say: 'Hell no, Colonel.' Why?"

"It's done."

"That's for damn sure."

"I'm sorry, Zack."

"Hell, we'll get it done." He smiled. "That doesn't mean I'm not pissed at you."

"You were overdue anyway – it's been about four days since your last 'pissed' mood."

"Bite me. Now, let's get this thing in the air." Zack fumbled with the chart, moving his finger over the area. "Minimum altitude is five thousand. No use meetin' a mountain out there."

"We sure as hell can't find a hole if we're in the soup," I said. "We'll do our damndest to stay between layers. Ready to start number one."

"Roger," Zack said.


The runway disappeared as we turned to the heading. The base of the solid overcast was right above us, as we skimmed between the layers of wispy gray clouds. We settled back for the remaining 36 minutes to the target area. Zack placed his hands on the control column. "I'll take it for awhile."

"Okay, I'll monitor the time. Keep looking for some breaks below us."

"It'll be O.B.E. pretty soon," said Zack.

"And exactly what is an O.B.E."

"O.B.E. is 'overcome by events'. Thought you'd heard that expression." I gave him a withering look. "Look out there. We're skimming the base of this crap now. Any lower and we'll be doin' some mountain climbing."

"Keep on course and we'll see if it gets better up ahead." I shot a glance at the clock. "Twenty one minutes to go."

Zack took out a Marlboro and lit it; lifted his chin as he blew the smoke out. "I never finished telling you about writing my dad. It was easier than I thought. Once I got started, I told him I looked forward to a visit and a long talk. In my feeble way, I told him I understood his grief, anger, and hostility after my brother's death." He pointed at me with the Marlboro. "Even though I don't—he needs to hear that."

"Is that being honest?"

"There's no place for honesty at this stage of the game. He's dying, David. Why should I try to justify my feelings and explain the hurt? There's a time in life when you let the past stay just that—the past. I just want to spend some time with him, to make him feel like he never let me down or made me feel like a poor excuse for my brother." He drew in a long breath, exhaled, and looked out the window. "Maybe I can find some satisfaction in our relationship if we can have it end well."

Zack wanted to talk and I let him. I knew he could only go so far with this subject before it cut down to the quick, hurting enough to stop. I listened.

"I figure we've got about six more weeks before we get relieved here in Nam. The first thing I'm gonna do is get Jane and take her with me to Mom's. I'll let them get acquainted while I spend a couple of days with Dad. If there's time—and he's up to it—I want her to meet him. I want her to know that part of my life—a part I've never been able to explain to her. I've got to use all the time left for Dad and me. I . . ."

When I saw the moisture building in his eyes, I said, "Sounds like you've put some thought into this." I smiled at him. "You'll have your time with your dad, and it'll be great for you both." I looked ahead at a speck of terrain showing. "Hey, let's see if we can squeeze through that opening."

"We're five minutes before reaching the valley according to my calculations," Zack said. "I'll get a better look in a minute."

"Well, hell, maybe we can get visual further up ahead and get this ammo in after all." Zack laughed. "That'd frost old Norwood's nuts if we made this a cake walk."

"Hold it. I think there's a break right up there."

"Bullshit. That's a sucker hole," said Zack. "We're still three and a half minutes early on the time and distance estimate. Except for that small hole, it's turned to solid overcast under us and we don't know for sure where we are. Let's abort this thing now."

"But we've gotta be right over the area," I said. That's enough of a break in the layer. I'm gonna try it. If there's any doubt, we'll climb back out and head for DaNang."

"Norwood really did a number you." Zack's eyes found mine. "You don't have to prove a damn thing—not to him—me – or yourself, for that matter. We gave it a good try." He leaned close. "Come on, David, use your head. That hole's not large enough to see which valley's down there."

Ignoring his plea, I pulled back the throttles and started down through the break in the broken layer of clouds.

The clouds engulfed us as they shifted in the sky. "Where's that hole we had?" Zack said. "It sucked us right in."

"We'll break out—if no visual at 2,500, we're going back up—quick like."

We broke into a hazy visual with the jungle below. We quickly dropped down to 2,000 feet into a large valley with mountains rising up on both sides. The valley was wide, gently rising into the mist. I searched for some familiar landmark but it all looked like jungle at this altitude, with absolutely nothing to distinguish the approach to Khe Sanh. "Keep looking," I said. "Khe Sanh should be right up this valley. See anything familiar?"

Zack stared straight ahead, looking into the murky horizon. He was looking for something familiar, something about the terrain that would confirm we were in the right area. He was not happy.

The rain reduced visibility as fog rose from the valley floor then crumpled gently into the rolling mountains. Heavy rains had left pools in the crags of the valley floor. I fought to keep a visual reference and follow this cut between the two mountains that were disappearing into the gray clouds on either side.

The clouds slouched into the valley and visibility dropped to less than two miles. We peered in the direction the valley was taking us. Doubt crept into my thoughts. *God, it must be right up ahead—if we just had more visibility.* The valley came up to meet us. It rose toward our altitude surreptitiously, reaching up slightly, gradually, like it stalked us. We were running out of valley, as it rose into the foothills of a mountain.

Zack scanned the area ahead, leaning forward to attempt a better view through the moisture. He sat back instantly. "This isn't the valley—this is the wrong damn valley."

I looked at him, then out the windscreen. "Damn!" I shot the prop controls to 2,000 RPM and jammed the throttles to climb power. I glanced left, ascertaining if we could get closer to make a 180-degree turn to go back. The mountain was too close. We had to climb straight ahead and top this ridge. I slapped the prop controls to full increase RPM's and pushed harder on the throttles, even though they were against the stop. I hauled back on the controls and we started an immediate climb. Zack looked my way, eyes wide and mouth drawn tight. I had no reassuring statement as my hand continued to push on throttles already fixed hard against the stops. "Damn," said Zack, placing his hands on the control column as if the added assistance would lift us faster.

Thick clouds and rain cloaked us in a gray cocoon, blocking out everything past the nose of the aircraft. I concentrated on the panel of gauges, flying instruments, and keeping a maximum rate of climb. The engines wailed in their effort to pull us to a higher altitude. My gut tightened. In my quick crosscheck of the instruments, I saw the altimeter needle passing through 3,400 feet. I knew 4,000 would give us the clearance we needed.

Without warning, green limbs suddenly crashed against the fuselage, splintering into deafening fragments. Chaotic, penetrating sounds surrounded us as we crashed through the jungle. Ruptured metal flew around us as the aircraft sliced its way to the mountain. The noise was thunderous as metal splintered trees. The slashing sound seemed to go on forever, yet it was only a second or two. Then there was nothing.

# 14

## Morass

My eyes blinked rapidly trying to focus on my surroundings. Water trickled down my left arm from a jagged piece of metal overhead. I fought the excruciating agony in my left leg. My head throbbed and swirled in and out of consciousness. The jungle in front of me came in and out of focus, as I tried to gather my thoughts into some pattern of recognition. I turned and saw Zack slumped over, covered by the destroyed instrument panel. I reached over, grabbing his sleeve. "Zack. Zack, can you hear me?" There was a low groan, almost indistinguishable in the falling rain. I had no idea of the time lapse since the crash. I shook my head, trying to focus. Again I stared at the jungle, occupying the space in front of me where the cockpit had been. Reality grabbed my thinking.

"Jocko! Sergeant Picardo!" I yelled. No answer. I swiveled my body attempting to dislodge my leg. Pain seared through my body with every movement. One large jerk and I pulled free. At last I could get closer to Zack. I pulled his limp body to an upright position. That's when I saw his gaping head wound. Blood covered his right side. Leaning into his left ear, I called his name over and over. No response. I pulled at his flight suit, moving him a few inches out of the seat and turned back toward the ruptured fuselage, seeing an opening through the rear. The tail had broken off, leaving only half the rear section attached. "Jocko," I screamed again. I hoped for an answer, but it was no use. I pulled Zack further into the belly of the aircraft. Four more agonizing tries and I reached the soft wet ground. It took almost an hour to reach the base of a large tree with vines meandering up the sides. I touched my head on the left side and felt the swelling. I rolled Zack toward me, holding him close; I tried again to make him hear me. Occasionally, he would moan softly.

My pounding head leaned against the gnarled tree, as the realization of what I had done overtook me. I hit my head hard against the tree, holding tight to Zack as tears flowed down my cheeks. I looked back at Zack again. *God, if he'd only wake up—just wake up.*

Even in my confused mental state, I began to take stock of our situation. We were in VC territory, near a mountain top, partially hidden by jungle that consumed the wreckage. It would be getting dark soon. Even in daylight, there would be no hope of being spotted with the overcast cloud layer. There was water and a first aid kit somewhere in the fuselage wreckage—if I could crawl back for it. Zack needed medical attention immediately and with no working radios there wasn't a damn thing I could do.

I lay back against the tree and looked around at the primitive tangled green jungle. The fading sun cast blue shadows on the ferns. A lizard moved quietly up a gnarled root. It had a wide head with a projection on top. Its eyes protruded on either side of its head. I reached for a stick beside me and hurled it toward him. He spun backwards and disappeared into the undergrowth. Raindrops fell into the damp gloom surrounding us. I reached deep into my resolve for encouragement and hope for our prospects. There was nothing there to dispel the apprehension.

I crawled painfully back into the fuselage and pulled myself up onto my right leg. In the corner I spotted one water container. If I could get to it, I would have to hoist it over the crushed crates and torn metal. Using my arms and right leg to pull me over the debris, I managed to get within reach of the two gallon container. I rocked it back and forth and snatched with all I had. The crushed container broke loose, requiring all I had to hoist it up to the top of the shattered boxes. Now I had to traverse the same route back to the tree. Each agonizing step made me want to stop, to give in to the pain. Zack was the only reason I kept going.

I dropped beside him and poured water into the top and held it to his mouth. His lips made no move to take the liquid. I tried to pour a small amount into his mouth but it dribbled out the side, running off his chin. I would have to wait and try again. I drank long and hard from the cup, quenching my thirst.

The meager amount of light defining the vegetation around us was slowly being drained from the jungle as night came closer. The rain stopped and the jungle sounds took over, with strange sounds of creatures I couldn't identify. I pushed some moss under Zack's head, as he lay there, silent. He was injured badly and I knew it. I worried about Sergeant Picardo and Jocko. *Are they lying dead in the jungle? Are they hurt and need help? What a sorry-ass excuse I am for an aircraft commander. I've killed my crew.* The tortured thoughts and intense pain kept me awake until exhaustion blotted out my consciousness.

It must have been only a few minutes of unconsciousness, as the pain brought my senses together again. Staring hard into the darkening vegetation, I saw the outline of four men. Instinctively I drew my forty-five automatic and chambered a round. My hand shook as I pointed it at the four shapes moving toward me. As they came closer, my finger tightened on the trigger. *This is as good a way to go as any.* About ten feet away they stopped. I could finally see that they were Montagards, short, brown men, each with a crossbow. Their eyes moved about us, surveying every aspect of Zack and me, but they said nothing. I kept the pistol pointed at them. The one on the left walked to Zack, leaned over, and touched his head. I thought this may be the help we needed, but he moved over to me, reaching forward, he took the forty-five. I didn't resist. He walked back to the other three and they dropped to the ground in a sitting position. They built a small fire, sat there staring at us, but offering no assistance or harm. I pointed to Zack. "Can you help him?" There was no acknowledgment of the question. They stayed for approximately two hours, watching the alien visitors who had fallen into their domain. They seemed mesmerized by our presence, but wanted no interaction with us. We were only to be observed in the dim light. They rose to their feet and were gone.

Pangs of hunger hit as I tried to sleep. To thrust my mind to any place but this rain forest, I tried to think about other things. I thought about Fayetteville and familiar places, forcing my mind from this damn jungle. I could almost see Leslie. Her face was beautiful, smiling at me. I reached out to touch the illusion and everything went black.

The sunlight stabbed at my eyes through the green canopy and I felt a sense of relief that the night was over. The night had been long and disquieting and I welcomed the daylight, even though it posed more danger. Zack moaned slightly, but had not regained consciousness. My head spun toward the jungle to the left. The brush moved about 20 yards from us. A cracking sound was heard as some dead branch gave way to a foot or boot. I no longer had a weapon and it would do no good anyway if these were VC. It would only serve to get us killed. I heard muffled voices and pieces of metal being moved. It could be the Montagards, back to look search the aircraft for something useful. A large fern parted and Jocko peered through. "Picardo," he shouted, "they're alive. Come over here—quick."

Jocko ran to us, dropping down beside me. "Damnation, Captain, we looked up front after the crash and thought you both were dead. The cockpit was gone and neither of you would move or answer us."

I looked up at him. " I thought you two were thrown from the wreckage and dead. Godamighty, I'm glad to see you."

Sergeant Picardo limped slowly to the tree. His right arm was in a makeshift sling and he was dragging his right leg. Jocko, glanced back at him, then spoke softly to me. "He's got a broken shoulder, and maybe his hip. He slammed up against the bulkhead when we hit and a few ammo crates broke loose on him."

Picardo stood there looking at Zack. "He looks like he's hurt pretty bad, Captain."

"He is." I touched Zack's shoulder. "He hasn't come to since the accident and I'm concerned about him."

Jocko leaned close to Zack's head, examining the bloody indentation. "Captain, he needs some help right now—if it's not already too late."

"It's not too late, goddamnit. He's gonna be okay."

"Yessir—I'm sure he is." He stared at me. "Your eye's almost closed. How's the head?"

"It's just a lump. By the way, what happened to you two after we hit?"

He laughed and looked up at Picardo. "Once we thought you two were goners, I hauled Picardo out and fixed him that sling. We were worried about nearby VC and took off into the jungle. After a while, we realized they weren't coming for us and started back to the wreckage." He laughed again. "We couldn't find the damn thing in that thick bush out there."

Picardo said, "We flat gave up on finding the aircraft again and started down the mountain to find a clearing so Rescue'd have a better chance of spotting us. We stumbled on the wreckage again—strictly by accident." He smiled. "Sure glad we did."


Picardo joined me, leaning against the tree, as Jocko fetched wood for a signal fire and tended to us. Every few minutes, he'd check on Zack. Each time I saw his frown and his head move shake back and forth, yet he made no comment about his condition. He splinted my left leg, which did nothing to ease the pain but did manage to kill time as we waited and listened for sounds of aircraft or helicopters.

We heard the droning of aircraft engines overhead. We tried to see through the dense gray clouds, as it flew almost over our position. We searched the sky for some break, struggling to see the aircraft. *How could they ever see us through the solid overcast?*

I stroked Zack's forehead with a wet handkerchief and talked to him. "Hey, Zack," I whispered, "Come on and wake up. We'll get out of here soon as this weather breaks—c'mon, fella', talk to me." His breathing became labored and the low-pitched groans were less frequent. I prayed for a response, a movement, any kind of feedback. I adjusted the moss under his head, lifting it slightly to help his breathing. I felt Jocko tug at my sleeve. "It's not gonna help, Captain—it's no use."

I grabbed his collar, pulling him closer, turning my head so my good eye had him in focus. "I don't want to hear anything like that again—you understand that?"

Jocko pulled back, snapping my grasp, without answering. He looked over at Picardo and walked back to the aircraft. He was gone for over an hour before he returned with the first aid kit. "I managed to free this from the debris." He knelt beside Zack and gingerly placed a bandage over the gash in his head. He wet the handkerchief again and handed it to me. I laid it across his forehead. Jocko unzipped Zack's flight suit and pulled it back. "That big blue area shows he's got internal injuries too."

"He needs medical attention—and damn fast."

I shook some water on the cloth for Zack. "We'll have to go easy on the water, Captain. This is it—and there's no way to know when we'll be spotted."

"I'll just use a little to wet Zack's cloth—it won't take much." *Why was I apologizing to Jocko?*

The humidity engulfed us, sapping our energy. Every movement increased the sweat that seeped through our flight suits. We each took a drink from the cup in two-hour intervals, so we wouldn't dehydrate. Water could soon become a problem. Zack let out a muffled sigh. I wet the cloth and placed it across his face. Glancing up, I could see Jocko looking at me. His face was frozen in a stare of pointlessness. There was no way I wanted to discuss Zack's condition with him.

There was the sound of a low-flying aircraft again. Jocko jumped to his feet, peering into the jungle. "Dammit, they can't see us here even if this crappy weather breaks. Look up there." He pointed up with his arm, jabbing at the treetops. "That jungle's 30 feet thick."

Jocko moved off by himself to think. Sergeant Picardo touched my arm. "Let him be. He'll be all right after a while." Picardo groaned as he tried to roll over. He shifted his weight, his face contorted in agony. "This right side is damn near paralyzed."

"Hang on. We'll get outta here soon." *Why the hell am I lying to him and myself?*

"It'll soon be dark again," he said. "Maybe tomorrow."

The night crept through the jungle, menacingly pulling a dark shade over us. I hated the darkness, listening to unidentifiable sounds in the dark. The nights passed with agonizing slowness. There was nothing to do at night except survive and be alone with the pain and my thoughts. Both were poor company. I put my ear close to Zack's mouth, listening to his labored breathing. I looked at his face with the light coming from his side. He was now a silhouette against the failing light, still, just lying there. I watched him until the light provided no more shape to his face. Darkness broke me loose from staring at my friend. I wanted to help him and I was powerless to do any more than try to make him comfortable.

Every time Sergeant Picardo moved, he groaned deeply. Jocko fumbled through the first aid kit and handed Picardo three tablets. "These will help you through the night." He tapped my shoulder. "How 'bout you take three of these too?"

"Thanks."

I swallowed the pills and began to filter out the jumbled sounds around me. In a diaphanous dream state, my mind drifted back to my last visit to Deerfield. It was a comfortable feeling, leaving the jungle behind and letting my trance take me to another time and place. The sweet smell of spring in middle Texas drifted over me. Leslie's face was there – always there in my thoughts until sleep mercifully took over.

Jocko's voice startled me out of my dream. "It's breaking up. Look up there—sky." Groggily, I looked at the breaking light shining through the trees. Faint sunlight glanced off the vegetation and cast the first shadows I had seen since the crash.

Picardo sat up, laughing loudly, and hitting the ground with his good hand. "If they can spot us through this stuff we've got a chance."

I tugged at Zack's flight suit, pulling myself closer. "Zack, we're gonna get you out of here. Hold on." Zack was cold to my touch. I placed my ear to his mouth. There was no breath. I shook him vigorously. "Zack, for God's sake don't die here—don't die, Zack."

Jocko examined Zack closely. He took the cloth and covered his face. "He's gone, Captain. I'm sorry—damn sorry."

"He's still unconscious."

"No, Captain, he must have died during the night."

Picardo dropped his head into his free hand, mumbling incoherently. Jocko looked at him, then back at me. "Captain. Captain, are you okay?" I was in a suspended state, not in touch with anything around me. This couldn't happen. Zack wasn't going to die—not this day.

The engines roared overhead and Jocko waved enthusiastically. He jumped up and ran to the few sticks he'd piled together. He lit the moss, fanning it into a flame, as the aircraft moved away. "Dammit, he didn't see us." Jocko didn't move. He sat there, rigid, as if fixed to the spot, looking straight ahead. Then he lifted his head, listening intently.

Picardo, edged himself close to Jocko. "I hear it too." There was a low sound, a far off sound that grew in intensity. Jocko once again fanned the fire as flames leaped up from the sticks. He grabbed some green fern and laid it gently atop the flames. Smoke billowed upward in a twisting movement. Picardo lay down beside the fire, blowing to intensify the burning.

The engines made a deafening roar as the C-123 passed right over us. It circled tightly three times, and then leveled out, wagging its wings. The sound disappeared again, but we knew we'd been spotted in this greenish hell.

The loud, almost deafening "wump, wump, wump" of a "Jolly Green" helicopter hovered over the wreckage, music to my ears. The jungle vegetation bent low to the ground, vibrating violently to the rotors beating wind. Two men jumped the last few feet and ran toward us. They knelt beside Zack, but shook their heads. They moved to Sergeant Picardo. It was impossible to hear what he was asking but Picardo rose to his feet with assistance. He stumbled and fell back to the ground. The medic waved to the other one who brought up a stretcher. Picardo lay down on the canvas and they moved down the mountain under the chopper blades. They lowered the mesh basket and lifted the Sergeant up close enough to be pulled inside.

They were both beside me. I remained silent as they placed me in a stretcher and carried me to the hovering chopper. Placed in the basket I looked over the side as it rose slowly to waiting hands above. There, almost obliterated by jungle and mountain, was the twisted wreckage of the C-123. Snarled jungle already seemed eager to consume the remnants. My eyes locked onto the repulsive body bag, Jocko standing beside it, waiting for it to be hoisted up. I thought about the two medics when they placed Zack into the body bag. One smooth movement of the zipper and he was removed from us, shut off forever from our world.

They placed Sergeant Picardo and me side by side in the helicopter, Jocko sat in the door gunner's seat, and Zack's body bag was placed in the rear. The helicopter dipped and moved toward DaNang. I stared at the olive drab bag with my friend lying lifeless inside. Icy fingers were tearing at my insides. One minute a vibrant, fun-loving individual, then just a lifeless body as those magic ingredients left. Only once before was I as close to another man as I was to Zack. The hurt far surpassed any physical pain that could be inflicted. The medic touched my shoulder. "I think your leg's definitely broken. But you'll be good as new after a few months." I knew I'd never be as good as new again.

As the layered green canopy of vegetation shot past underneath the helicopter, I watched the jungles of Vietnam, looking at it as an abstract of what this war was all about. I knew this war and this jungle were ending for me but my world would be meaningless because of them. Even though alive, this country had taken from me more than my life.


The first medic met the helicopter as it touched down on the hospital landing pad. Two more ran up beside the chopper as the blades slowed down. They were waiting to take us the 50 yards to the crude hospital. The bump, as my stretcher hit the ground, awakened the pain in my leg. I rose up, looking at the two who were taking Zack toward another door. I saw the body bag disappear inside. I knew I had seen Zack for the last time. He was gone. My head fell against the canvas and I closed my eyes.


Two doctors stood beside the bed, holding x-rays. "We've been discussing your leg, and a pin would make it heal faster." He held up the x-ray picture pointing to a blank space where bone was supposed to be. "Instead of doing this here, we're shipping you over to Clark. They're better staffed in orthopedics." He touched my swollen face. "They'll do an EEG soon as you get there. How long were you unconscious?"

"What about the rest of my crew? Sergeant Picardo?"

"Picardo?" He looked at the other doctor. "The Sergeant who came in with the fractures and dislocation?"

He nodded. "He's had his shoulder snapped back into place, and his arm taped to let the shoulder blade set up—broke it pretty good. He's got a severely bruised hip."

The other one spoke again. "He'll be over to Clark later. He's not going to require any surgery and this flight's full." He leaned over the bed and lifted the sheet. He moved the foot enough for me to wince. "Sorry, just wanted to see the color of the foot—circulation's okay. Now, how long do you estimate you were unconscious?"

"Maybe a couple of minutes."

"You have any questions?"

I shook my head and they moved to the next patient.

The thumping sound of helicopters became louder as they came in steadily to the landing pad. China Beach suddenly became a busy medical facility. Medical personnel in the ward rushed out to meet the incoming patients from a major engagement near Ashau.

Those who could be stabilized for later were sedated and brought to our ward. Some with near fatal wounds went straight to surgery. Our ward filled quickly with the wounded waiting for treatment. I looked down the row of cots, a slight movement of a torso along the way, a head that tried to rise up, a face that grimaced in obvious pain, and a hand that reached up, grabbing at nothing. Quickly a gurney was wheeled in and a semi-conscious soldier about eighteen was lifted onto the surface. The dark brown hair falling across his face almost hid the pain in his blinking eyes. His hand still clutched a bloody green beret. Quickly they wheeled him through the swinging doors. Anyone standing in this room would find abstract words such as glory, honor or courage obscene. This is the disgusting result of war – maybe courage, no honor, and never glory. I closed my eyes and tried to block out the suffering that surrounded me. But no matter how valiant the effort, I would never be able to detach myself from this room of misery.

There was a noticeable difference in the ward at Clark Air base. The sterile atmosphere was all business, with people moving through the ward in martinet precision. The doctor stopped abruptly at the side of my bed. He was a muscular, short man with eyes that gleamed as he blinked. There was an extraordinary air of neatness and briskness in his manner. He raised the cover and looked at my leg. "Well, looks like we need to put a pin in that break. After several days, we find it's better for the patient and aids the healing process to use a pin in a break like this."

"Okay," I said.

"There's a notation here that they want an EEG. Probably get that this afternoon." He looked closely at the still bruised face. "Reckon they want to make sure you only had a concussion back there—nothing permanent."

Later that evening, the nurse stopped abruptly at my side. "Your EEG was not abnormal." She flipped the page on the chart. "You're scheduled for surgery at 0700 tomorrow. Here, this'll make you sleep." She pushed a small paper cup toward me and held a glass of water in the other. "You can have nothing to eat or drink after ten o'clock."

I swallowed the tiny pink pill and washed it down with water. I handed the glass back to her and asked, "Has Sergeant Picardo arrived from Nam yet—is he in the hospital?"

"I'm sorry, I don't have information on other wards," she said. She turned and was gone.

I let my head fall back onto the pillow; hoping the pill would do its work quickly.

"Hey, where'd you get it?" I turned to the side looking at a gaunt figure lying in the next bed, his left arm extended in a cast, bent at a 90-degree angle. There was a metal contraption under his hand, extending out of the cast and along the bottom of each finger. "Were you hit in the leg?" He asked again.

"It's broken."

"Sorry. The skiing over there is treacherous this time of year."

I couldn't help but smile at his humor. "What got *you*?"

"I was flying a Huey with a Vietnamese co-pilot. We turned hard right for the door gunner to get a better return fire angle." He chuckled as if it was funny. "I rolled out and looked around just in time to see part of my left arm go out the top of the canopy."

"A thirty caliber?"

"A fifty. Took quite a hunk with it."

I pictured in my mind what must be left of his forearm underneath that cast. A few ligaments and bone fragments must have held it together. Nausea kicked me in the stomach. I lay back and stared at the ceiling tiles. I didn't look back at him as I spoke. "They can do wonders in orthopedics these days."

"I figure I'll be flying again in about six months."

"Probably." I knew he'd never fly again. He knew it too, but he had to hold onto something. It gave him the spirit he'd need in the months to come.

The first recognition of this world was the recovery room nurse asking me to breathe deeply. As the room came into focus, I saw the large bandage extending from my ankle to my knee. Soon I'd be back in the ward.

A few hours later, when the pain began, I almost welcomed it. Anything to keep my mind off the last three days. I wanted some long reacting anesthesia for memory. I didn't want to think.

Two days later, a tall, skinny doctor stopped by the bed. He checked the foot and large cast showing no emotion as he looked closer. He straightened, looking at me. "You had a nasty bruise on the left side there around your eye." He touched my left temple. "In fact you still had quite a black eye when you came here. Right before surgery, I had them x-ray that area and do an EEG." He shined the pencil-sized light in each eye. "Even though the tests came out negative, get it rechecked in the States before going on flight status again." I nodded my understanding. "To free up bed space, we need to rotate patients out to the States as soon as possible." He flipped through his file, stopping at one page. "You're scheduled to go out tomorrow—FT. Bragg Army Medical Center." I nodded again. "Don't have much to say, do you, Captain?"

"Not really."

He smiled, shook his head, tucked the folder under his arm, and moved to the next patient. I lay back on the pillow, thinking of facing Leslie when I got back to Pope. There was no way to sort my feelings – I felt nothing.

A hand touched my arm and I looked over at Mac standing beside the bed. "How's it going?" he asked.

"Okay. Have you seen Sergeant Picardo?"

"Nope, I just got here. Tom wanted to take the next courier over but Colonel Norwood nixed that. I swapped with Guy's co-pilot to bring a bird over for maintenance so Norwood couldn't say a thing."

"Glad you could make it. How's Tom doing?"

"A goddamn basket case. I don't know if it's guilt that he wasn't with you, or he's just gone round the corner mentally."

"Sorry to hear that. What about Jocko?"

"Jocko was released from the hospital. He's grounded for a few days—but he's okay. Jocko's indestructible." Mac fumbled with his hat as he searched for words. "David, we're all sorry about Zack. I don't have the words to tell you how I feel. We all miss him. Morale is at rock bottom."

There was nothing I could say. I touched his hand and looked at the ceiling. Mac leaned over close so others in the ward couldn't hear. "For god's sake, don't blame yourself for this. It was an accident, David—an accident."

"Yeah."

"Anything I can get you?"

"No—thanks for coming." I rose up slightly. "Take care of Tom—please."

"Consider it done." His eyes went to the floor. "Hate to tell you this, but Norwood was on the flight over here. Don't be surprised if he drops in today."

I stared back at him as I thought of the man. I felt the anger in my gut but let go of it instantly. I took Mac's hand and squeezed it. "Take care over *there*."

"You know it." He waved as he left the ward.


I was dozing when I opened my eyes to the feeling of being watched. There, looking down on me, was Lieutenant Colonel Norwood. He didn't speak immediately. He looked at my face then at the leg cast protruding from the covers. He moved around to the foot of the bed, still looking at me. I looked into his eyes, eyes that

I would never forget, waiting for him to say something. The smile widened across his baleful face. "Sorry about Lieutenant Williams. You, and the rest of the crew were pretty lucky." I fixed on his eyes, saying nothing. He moved back around the bed toward me, his smile forced. "After the second day, we were afraid search and rescue wouldn't find you guys."

"I doubt you feel any remorse, Colonel. You're a self-centered, malicious, sorry excuse for a man, much less an officer. You got what you wanted – Zack's dead."

He stiffened. "You're probably heavily sedated, Captain. I'd better come back some other time." He glanced around the ward to see who might be listening to our conversation.

"I don't think you'll be coming back, Colonel. I hope never to lay eyes on your sorry ass again. You have no character or integrity. Frankly, you're a worthless piece of humanity."

He nervously glanced again around the room, and then looked as if he were about to speak.

"Don't say one damn word to me, Colonel." I pointed my finger at his nose. "Not one goddamn word. I'll always feel responsible for Zack's death; I'll take that off you. But remember the other men who'll never go home because of you. I want that image seared into your brain. Maybe an unfeeling bastard like you can live with that—I doubt I can."

"You're sicker than I thought, Captain."

"I might be. But as for you and me . . ." I raised myself on elbows, staring straight into those eyes. "If I ever see your sorry ass again—no matter when or where—I'm gonna put your damn lights out. That, Sir, is a promise."

His face flushed and he looked ready to explode. His jaw quivering, he leaned over to say something just as the nurse walked up. "Sorry to interrupt. Time for your pain pill."

Lieutenant Colonel Norwood spun around and walked through the door, my eyes on him as I swallowed the pill. Maybe I could sleep now.

# 15

## Turning Point

Cruising at 33,000 feet, the C-141, rigged for medical evacuation, was whisper quiet. The only movement inside the aircraft was the flight attendants and nurses going about their duties. The window screens were pulled down low by the attendants, as if obscuring the brilliant sunlight translated into some mild anesthetic; as if inviting the darkness would abate the wounds of mind and body. Light still filtered in under the shades, illuminating nearby occupants. Looking at the other patients, it was obvious I was a helluva lot luckier than most on this flight. Across from me was a lean, muscular black kid, probably nineteen. His mahogany face was contorted into a constant smile. The light from the window flickered off a bottle, suspended above him, feeding fluid into his right arm. The left one was gone. A petite nurse stopped to check the flow of the bottle. She examined it closely. "It's fine," she said. He reached over and took her hand gently, reluctant to let her go, and continued his non-stop chatter about his first meal at home. She nodded approval, pulled slowly from his grasp, and patted him on the shoulder. I was intrigued by his infectious laugh when the nurses and attendants stopped there. Even though part of him was left in the jungle, the rest of him was going home – that was all that mattered to him. I caught myself smiling back at him and his happiness, when I thought that Zack would never be going home. That realization slammed into my gut like a fist.

Lifting the shade, I stared out the window at the soft white cloud cover below, resplendent from the sun's reflection. My thoughts swirled around things I couldn't quite comprehend. Life, as I tried to contemplate it, seemed to be like walking a tight rope. One wrong step and you become a statistic in some mystic tabulation of life's events. It could be that next step, which keeps you traveling along a path of monotony, can change your life in an instant, or cut off life in mid-step. *How much control do we have. Do we stumble along, in incalculable, plodding steps, on some predetermined course? Or do we alter the course by our actions? Maybe we're mere puppets playing out some pre-designed script.*

I watched the familiar landscape slide past the window as the C-141 as it made its approach. I looked at my watch as we skimmed over the approach lights and touched down eight minutes ahead of schedule. Being back at Pope Air Force Base suddenly sent waves of uneasiness over me. Soon, I would have to explain my feelings to Leslie. Numbness of spirit sapped my ability to relate to anyone right now. No words could convey my emotions. Things that happened under a large, gnarled tree in Vietnam were embedded too deeply in my mind. How could she ever understand? Explaining incoherent and ambivalent sensibilities was impossible. Not today. Maybe not even tomorrow.

The aircraft lurched to a halt and we were lowered to waiting ambulances for the short ride to the medical center at Fort Bragg. The ten-minute ride ended at the main entrance to the huge building. As the double doors of the ambulance swung open, I saw the wheel chairs waiting at the curb. Clusters of people, some in the throes of laughter, were greeting patients. There stood Leslie and Colonel Adams. She had her hand up, shielding her eyes from the sun, looking for me. I lowered myself into the wheel chair and the medic pushed me toward the door. Leslie spotted me and broke into a run, her arms extended. She knelt beside the chair and threw her arms around me. I turned my head toward her as she kissed me.

She stared at me. I brushed her windblown hair aside. "Thank God you're home," she said. "You look great."

"I've just got a bummed-up leg. I'll be out of here in couple of days." I looked at her as if it was for the first time. Her hair was flowing in harmony with the gentle gust of wind. The sun glistened off the dark chestnut strands. Her smile was as exuberant as her personality. Leslie was always effervescent to everything in life, even the awkward. I had not seen that in the days just before I left and it was refreshing to detect her characteristic spirit again.

She walked beside the chair as Colonel Adams approached. "David, I wanted to be here with Leslie when you got back. Sorta' moral support for both of you." He cleared his throat. "We had a memorial service yesterday for Lieutenant Williams."

"It was a beautiful service for Zack," Leslie added. "You would have thought so too."

"I'm sure."

"I have a rough idea about these last few days," Colonel Adams said, "so, right now, I'll leave you two alone." He stuck out his hand. "I'll check on you later, David. We need to talk some more."

"Thanks, Colonel."

Leslie stayed right beside me as the paperwork was completed and I was placed in a room. Fortunately, there was no one assigned to the other bed and I could enjoy the privacy for as long as it would last. Leslie listened as the nurse outlined the tests and procedures for the next few days. When details of the follow-up EEG were mentioned, she frowned and looked at me for some explanation. "Just a slight concussion," I said, touching the reddish-purple tract running along my head. "Nothing to worry about—it'll be negative—my head's too hard."

"I know you'll be glad to get home where you can relax. We never did finish talking about that trip after we first mentioned it in our letters. But I'm sure, that for the next few weeks, you're not going anywhere," she said, "but we'll talk about it later."

"I need to go someplace as soon as I get out of here."

"Where do you *have* to go?"

"I need to go see Zack's folks."

"We can talk about that when you get out of the hospital."

"I don't think you understand, Leslie, I'll need to go alone."

"Hey, you just got here. We can discuss this later, can't we?"

"We'll see." I looked around the room. "Could you do me a real favor and find out if I can make a long distance call?"

"I'll try. Let me go find out."


Twenty minutes later Leslie eased into the room, walking softly as if she might disturb the patient. "Got a bit of static at first, but they explained how to get off base and make a call charged to our phone at home," she almost whispered. "Here, I'll write the directions down for you."

"I can remember it."

"Nonsense, you just wait a minute." She fumbled through her purse, drawing out a small note pad with a pen stuck through the spirals at the top. She made a few notes and ripped out the page. "Here, now you can call anyone you want."

"Thanks."

"Now, how about something that'd really taste good to you—a large chocolate shake? I know you must've missed those."

"Thanks, maybe tomorrow. I'm not really hungry."

"Are you trying to be a difficult patient, Captain Barfield?" She laughed. "That's okay, I'll work on it."

I smiled and let my head fall back onto the pillow. She touched my hand, rubbing it gently. "I know you're tired," she whispered. "Get some sleep and I'll be back this evening." She squeezed my hand hard. "I'm really glad you're back."

"Me too," I said.

She gave that little wave of hers, wheeled around and was gone.


I listened to the dial tone, clutching the receiver firmly, glanced at Leslie's detailed instructions, then started to dial Information. The receiver banged down in its cradle as I stared at the ceiling, searching for the words for this call. My mind was too muddled to express what I felt. I pushed the phone aside.

After staring at it for several minutes, my hand reached over, almost involuntarily, and pulled the phone toward me. "Operator, I'd like the number for Randall K. Williams, Scottsbluff, Nebraska. No, I don't have a street address." The pause was less than a minute and the operator was reeling off numbers. I scribbled the phone number for Zack's father.

The phone rang four times and as I was ready to hang up, a female voice said, "Hello."

"Could I please speak with Mr. Williams?"

"I'm sorry – excuse me – who's calling?"

"This is David Barfield. I was with Zack. Could I speak with his father?"

"Oh—I understand," she said softly, "I'm sorry, but Zack's father passed away two days ago. The funeral was this morning." My silence brought forth her next statement. "I'm Zack's aunt. Randy was my brother."

"Did Zack's death have anything to do with . . . ?"

"Oh no," she interrupted, "he was much too sick for us to tell him." She choked back a sob, and as she continued, "We were prepared for my brother's death. It was obvious for the last two weeks it was going to be soon." She gasped as she sucked in a breath. "But it was such a shock when we heard Zack had been killed." There was a momentary silence. "Zack's mother called to tell me he was cremated and that the memorial service had been very simple—only for close family there in Chadron."

"I'm sorry about Mr. Williams." Clearing my throat, I continued, "I wanted to tell him how much Zack was looking forward to their visit." I cleared my throat, as I felt it tighten. "There were so many things Zack talked about—things he and his father needed to resolve. He was sure they would." The tightness wouldn't go away. "I wanted Mr. Williams to know how much Zack loved him."

"I'm sure he knew that from the letters Zack wrote. He felt that they had reconciled and both had reached some closure." There was silence on the other end. "Were you with Zack when the plane crashed?"

My hand closed tightly around the receiver. I wanted to hurl it out the window and stop this conversation, but I cleared my throat again, "Yes, I was with Zack when it happened."

"Please tell me about the accident. The Air Force was very cryptic in the notification and we've all wondered about the circumstances."

The word 'accident' pierced my brain like an ice pick. My first impulse was to shout into the phone: *It was no damn accident.* But would that make her feel any better about losing her nephew? I explained the mission, and how Zack never regained consciousness. She didn't press for more details. She thanked me profusely for calling, and then hung up.

My hand found the cradle as I let the receiver fit into its resting place. I tried to analyze my feelings about Zack, his father, and the visit that would never be. *Well, maybe they're having their visit now.*

"Hey there," Leslie said as she slipped through the door. "Just talked to Mama and told her you were already back. She said to say 'hello' and she'll write soon." She stopped at the foot of the bed. "What's wrong? You don't look like you feel too good?"

"No—no, I feel okay." I forced a smile.

"You might be feeling the effects of the flight all the way from the Philippines. I'll only stay a minute, then let you get a good night's sleep. Here." She held out a paper sack, bulging at the seam.

I turned it upside down on the bed and out Hershey bars, Mounds, chewing gum, hard candy, and a yellow legal pad with a ball point pen attached. "Thanks—especially for the pad and pen."

"I figured these would perk you up. You've been very solemn all day."

"Sorry."

"Well, I'd expect you to be a little happier about being home."

I stared at her wondering why she had no clue to my feelings. *Why the hell should I play a role that gives people the appearance they expect?* I searched for an acceptable answer. "Okay, I'll smile." I stretched a forced smile, showing my teeth.

"No reason to get that look," she said and her brow furrowed like it always did when she turned serious. It was a clue I had seen too many times before. My exaggerated smile relaxed into one more natural. I understood there was no way for her to feel what was gnawing at my insides. My torment was my own. I realized that expecting anything else would be unrealistic.

"Hey, you're right. I am glad to be back." I moved the cast to get more comfortable. "Tomorrow they might take this thing off, remove the stitches, and put on a new one. Hopefully it'll be lighter'n this big thing." I grimaced and moved it back to the original position, then looked over at Leslie. "I should be out of here day after tomorrow."

"Great," she said. "I bet you could go for a home-cooked meal—even one of mine."

"Hey, you're a great cook. Don't ever sell yourself short on that one." I scrooched up my face, as if thinking hard. "But, as I think back, it did break our dog from begging at the table."

She drew back the magazine she held and flipped it toward me. "You'll get a TV dinner when you get out."

The banter broke the ice. Even though we maintained an upbeat attitude all day, it was obvious there was still a mysterious impediment that we couldn't reach through. The spontaneous humor instantly relaxed the mood, and maybe chipped away some of that barrier. As I watched Leslie, I wondered if we would ever be able to rip down that wall. Could we crash through to the passion that used to be there? Unfortunately, the slight confidence I built up that we could crash through, drained slowly. It was mingled with too many other emotions this night.

Leslie, oblivious to my thoughts, chatted on. I propped on my elbow and watched her animated stories. The soft light reflected her beauty, and for a fleeting second, I saw that girl who offered me the umbrella at the River Walk in San Antonio. That mystical, animated girl I found so fascinating.

"Hey, that's enough stories of the Base," she said. "I'm boring you." She reached for my hand, looking deep into my eyes. "I meant it when I said I'm so glad you're home." She kissed me, then turned and left. My eyes followed her through the door.

"Good morning, Captain." The nurse flipped on the lights, then pulled the blinds open. "And how are you feeling today?"

I pushed at my eyes with both fists, rubbing away the sleep. "What damn time is it?"

"Zero five-thirty and you're scheduled for x-ray, orthopedics, then an EEG later today. Breakfast will be here soon—don't tarry. The orderly will be here to wheel you down before zero six-thirty."

"Can I get some coffee now?"

"They'll bring you some with breakfast." She stuck the thermometer in my mouth, grabbed my arm feeling methodically for a pulse. She made some brief notes on the chart, then hooked up the blood pressure cuff.

"I sure could use some coffee."

"Shush." She rapidly unhooked the cuff, rearranged the tray beside the bed, and then moved to the door. "Okay, I'll see you when you get back in the room."

"Wait, I need to ask you a few things about . . ."

"I probably couldn't answer them anyway." And out she went.

I was tired when the orderly helped me back into the bed. There on the bedside tray was a note from Leslie.

*Hi there:*

*I brought you someone for company. He'll keep a keen eye on you till you get out. Now, look above your head on the top of the bed.*

*They said you'd be downstairs most of the morning . . . so
I'll see you early in the afternoon. If you think of anything
you need, give me call.*

*Love Ya*

I quickly glanced above my head to look right into the bright
orange beak of a stuffed cloth vulture. Its yellow feet had been taped
to the headboard so it was looking down on me with a revolting
expression. Leslie had a quirky sense of humor. I pushed at the ugly
black bird with my finger, admiring his brightly colored feet and beak.
"Okay, Hector, it's just you and me." I was still laughing at the bird
when I heard the gentle knock on the door.

I waited to make sure that's what I heard. Quietly, barely
perceptible, it came again.

"Come in," I said.

An attractive face, delicately chiseled features and prominent
cheekbones peered around the door. "David?" she asked. "David
Barfield?"

"Come in."

She was tall, with the lithesome figure of an athlete, her skin
sun-tanned to a bronze glow. The deep color of her face accentuated
flashing blue eyes. She wore a navy blue dress that hugged her body.
She came right up to the side of the bed and stuck out her hand. "I'm
Jane. Jane Rollins. Zack talked about you so much I feel I already
know you." Taking her hand, I swallowed hard. "I wanted to come
see you as soon as I heard you were back." She glanced up at the cloth
vulture, then back at me. "That'd surely be an incentive to get out of
here." She laughed. "Someone's sending you a message."

"Leslie's cute idea." I poked at the orange feet.

She looked down at the cast. "How're you doing?"

"I'm okay." My voice seemed to choke up as I tried to speak. I
felt my heart pound. "Jane, I'm sorry about Zack." I took her hand.
"I never expected to meet you under these circumstances. I should've

recognized you the minute you came in. Zack never stopped talking about you."

She squeezed my hand and said, "He thought the world of you. I could tell from his letters that you were Zack's best friend. He told me of some of the wild stunts you two pulled—and the problems with your commander." She tried to smile.

"Yeah, we had some great times—but there were times he wanted to shoot me." I couldn't stop my tears. "I may as well lay it on the line. If it hadn't been for my stupid decision, Zack would still be alive. I want you to know, right from the start, I was responsible for Zack not coming back to you."

"For God's sake, don't take that on yourself. Zack was a strong person, one of the strongest I've ever known. There's no way he would just go along with something he didn't think was right. This is what happens in war. This is what happens every day in flying. Zack knew the risks."

"That's just the point. Zack told me not to make that letdown into what turned out to be the wrong damn valley. He knew it was a 'sucker hole'. I was just too damn stubborn to listen."

"David, you did what you thought was right at that moment. You were trying to do your job—under a lot of pressure—that's all. For god's sake, don't keep blaming yourself." Her face became serious, her eyes flashing. "Zack wouldn't want that." She sat on the bed and looked me in the eyes. "You're not the first person to make a mistake. No one is infallible." She sighed. "I'm glad I came to see you today. You've gotta shake that burden right now."

"Zack was right. You're one strong-willed person." I chuckled. "You two would have made one helluva' combination."

"Even though we had only a few months together, they were fantastic. I believe we both knew we were soul mates that first night. It was one of those strange unexplainable feelings, but you know there's something special going on. It was so easy sharing feelings and emotions, like I'd known him forever." She laughed. "Some of my friends didn't quite understand Zack at first. One even asked me if he always spoke in 'bumper sticker language'."

"He could seem a little caustic to those who didn't know him," I said.

"Zack grew on my friends quickly and they loved him."

I listened as she described their time together, not wanting to break the trance. She continued, lost in her thoughts. "I have those times to remember. There're no unpleasant memories to contend with. It was a fantastic time in my life. Think about it. I could have gone forever and never have known a person like Zack. People live and die and never know love like that. I'm grateful for those weeks together—those memories will carry me a life time."

"You're lucky," I said, "very few people ever find what you described." I took her hand. "Thanks for coming by—and for sharing that." I rose up. "I appreciate what you said." I released my grip on her hand. "I hope you'll come back."

"Take care and consider what I told you. Life has to go on for us."

She rose, straightened her dress, gave a wave and left. I thought of the times Zack described Jane to me – she *was* exceptional.


Leslie touched my arm. "Are you day-dreaming?"

"Reckon I was. I didn't hear you come in. By the way, orthopedics had two emergencies today so they moved the cast change to tomorrow morning. I'm gonna check out of here as soon as I can. Could you wait until I call, then come pick me up?"

"Of course." Her head cocked to the side. "You're that sure they'll let you leave tomorrow?" She chuckled. "Or have you made life so miserable for them; they're ready for you go."

"I'll jolly well make it miserable if I don't get out. Hey, I sorta' cleared it with the doctor this morning after he read the x-rays. That's when he told me he would take-off the cast tomorrow—it's loose anyway from the swelling going down. The stitches come out, I hope a smaller cast, and I get me a pair of crutches." I saw Leslie looking at me with eyes narrowed and a half smile. "Okay, he didn't come right out and say I could leave—but I'm gettin' out of here tomorrow."

She sat on the edge of the bed and patted my hand. "You'll feel better at home. Familiar surroundings will let you relax." She touched my hand. "You're so very uptight."

"No shit."

She leaped from the bed and stared at me with a frown and her jaws tightened. "David, I know you've been through an emotional experience – one that will take time to get over. But I'll be darned if you're gonna take it out on me. I'm not the enemy."

"I didn't mean it that way, for God's sake. I was just making a statement for emphasis—you took it the wrong way." I looked her directly in the eyes. "I'm probably the enemy."

"Maybe you need to talk with someone—before you leave the hospital."

"Yeah, right. I should talk to some 30 year old, just out of some Ivy League school, wearing a starched white coat, a nametag that says 'Psychologist', beaming with a pretentious, self-righteous attitude. He wouldn't understand the first damn thing about real life. You know, that down and dirty business of watching people die. That . . ."

"No, David," she interrupted, "he probably wouldn't. And it would be a mistake for you to open up to someone, even if they might help you." Her eyes narrowed. "How long are you going to hang onto these hostile feelings?"

"I don't know—maybe till tomorrow. Hell, it could even be until the next day."

"Okay." She frowned. "I'll see you tomorrow." She bent over and kissed my forehead. "Goodnight." I felt cold. Many nights I lay there in that sweltering tent, drenched in my own sweat, dreaming of holding her, touching her. And yet I lay here an arm's length away, wondering what keeps me at a distance. I couldn't stop her as she left the room.


I lay back on the stainless steel table, looking up into the glare of the spherical light. The whirring circular saw bit into the cast, ripping it from knee to foot. The doctor grunted as he pried the form apart. He looked at me, then glanced over his shoulder at the nurse. "Would you go ahead and remove those stitches? I'll get the cast material ready—I don't like it too wet."

The nurse moved into position. Her hands held a pair of scissors and what looked like a set of miniature tongs. She leaned close to the target and proceeded to clip the threads, pulling them from the pink skin along the five-inch incision. There was only a light tugging on my leg, no pain. She swung around and shook some alcohol onto a bandage. "Let's clean this up before the new cast goes on." She smiled at me. "It looks good. Healing nicely."

"Okay, Captain," said the doctor stated, "let's ease the leg up so I can start this from underneath."

"Ouch!"

"Sorry bout that, just got to get this in the right position. There, that'll do it." I think I'll stop it right there. Leaving your knee to bend will give you a lot more mobility."

"Good. It was hard to keep it straight for so long."

As he dried his hands, the doctor stood beside me. "Listen, don't do anything stupid with that leg. The x-rays show a good start to healing. You don't want a setback." He tossed the towel in the hamper and took out his pen. "Continue the antibiotic. I need to see you in about four weeks." He slammed the metal pad shut.

"What about our conversation yesterday—you know—about my discharge today?" I asked.

He looked puzzled, then his eyes widened. "Hell, I'll give it a shot." He flipped open the slick metal folder and began scribbling again. "I'll see if patient discharge pays any attention to my notes." He grinned and said, "I placed a request for discharge today and I'll see you in about a month."


The phone rang only once. "Hello," said Leslie.

"I made it—I'm free if I can find a getaway car. Are you interested in helping an inmate?"

"I'll be there in fifteen minutes. Can you get in the car with that cast?"

"He put on one that stops short of the knee so I can bend it. That alone helped my morale."

"See you in a few minutes."

I cut around the pant leg carefully and dropped the left leg portion in the trashcan, then handed the scissors back to the sergeant. He grabbed the right leg and held the pants out so I could pull them on. Buttoning the shirt was easy. Standing quickly, and balancing gracelessly on the crutches, I took the first steps. I turned and eased myself back onto the bed. "It takes some gettin' used to these things." Bouncing on my right leg, I put the crutches under my arms again and took two steps and fell into the chair. "Whew. I need a little more practice."

"You're just hesitant. Don't sweat it. That cast is a helluva' lot tougher than you think," said the burly Sergeant. "You'll be movin' around good by tomorrow."

The automatic doors opened as he pushed me through. The late July sun glistened off the car's roof. The heat felt refreshing, as if it warmed my thoughts as well. Leslie opened the door and moved the seat to the full back position.

The Sergeant held onto my shoulder as I eased into the seat. He shoved the crutches behind me. "Take care, Captain."

"I'll do just that. Thanks for the help."

Leslie closed the door and moved swiftly to the driver's side. She started the engine and we drove toward the east gate of Fort Bragg. She glanced at me. "Well, you're free again."

"It feels good. Those doctors and medics did a great job, but I was sho' nuff' ready to change the scenery." I laughed. "Frankly, I hate hospitals."

"You always have."

The military policeman waved us through the gate, snapped to attention, and saluted. I returned the salute and we drove out the gate. The sunlight filtered down through the vegetation on both sides of the road and shimmered off the pine straw ground cover and delicate ferns scattered about. A secure feeling flowed through my body as I looked at the panorama. I felt serene for the first time in months. I smiled at the thought: *An antithesis as simple as a forest.* The tranquility in that backdrop changed my perspective – I hoped it would last.

"What're you smiling at?"

"The trees there," I pointed out the window, "they remind me of a quiet afternoon in the woods back home."

"I'm seldom sure what you're thinking—sometimes you surprise me."

I smiled and let the topic drop.

Leslie turned up Willow Street. I could see the house up ahead, nestled in the pines, grass as green as a meadow, the shrubs all planted and perfectly trimmed. It was totally different from the way I left it. The unfinished house in March had been transformed into a homey cottage. "You've sure been busy. The house looks great."

"I did most of the shrubbery right after you left. The grass germinated faster than I thought possible. That stuff took off. It was probably due to all that water I put on it. I remembered you said keep it wet for a while. Well, I did. I mowed it yesterday for your homecoming." She chuckled and shook her head. "I'll have to admit, it was the first time in weeks—it sure needed it."

"You done sho' nuff' good, for a pampered gal growing up," I said in an exaggerated southern drawl.

"Pampered? You know better'n that. My gosh, Daddy had me working like a cowhand before I turned twelve. Mama had me pruning roses, planting azaleas, and pulling weeds when I was eight years old. Don't hand me any of that pampered gal stuff. It's just that a green thumb doesn't rank right up there in my priorities."

"It's a fantastic job—period."


I felt restless lying on the couch, reading, watching television, or just thinking. There were ample subjects for my mind to grapple with, but was more comfortable not dealing with some of them. Leslie brought a fresh cold glass of sweet tea and asked if there was anything else I wanted. I shook my head, knowing there was something else I desperately wanted. I wanted to pull her down and make love like we'd never done before. I didn't. "Here." She held the glass out to me. "Now tell me about that trip you have to make."

"I was going to see Zack's dad, but he died two days before I got here."

She leaped to her feet. "Why didn't you tell me?"

"Didn't seem like the time."

"When, David? When would be the time to tell me?" Her hands were on her hips as she glared at me. "I've never understood why you block me out of your life so effectively."

"I was going to explain that phone call, and Jane's visit—Zack's fiancé. It's not like, 'Oh by the way Zack's father died Thursday, and oh yeah, Jane stopped by the hospital.' Goddamnit, there is a right time to discuss these things—I'm sorry you can't grasp that."

Her face softened as she touched my hand. "Will we ever communicate on any level? I wish you could just tell me how you feel."

I grabbed her hand, yanking her down to the couch. I wrapped my arms around her, pulling her close, and holding so tightly she couldn't move. I could feel her heart beating against my chest. "This level of communication never fails."

# 16

## Decisions

Three and a half weeks of manipulating two crutches, with well-worn pads at the top, improved my mobility. To my surprise, they became an effective means of locomotion. Regardless of this new skill, I was looking forward to the walking cast the next week. I ignored the doorbell, continuing to run a ruler inside the cast trying to reach an insufferable itch. Leslie appeared in the door of the den, Lieutenant Colonel Adams standing beside her. "You've got a visitor," she said, smiling broadly. I sat upright, trying to come to attention instinctively.

"Easy there," Colonel Adams said, "you'll end up flat on the floor and I'm not in the mood to pick your butt off the deck." He laughed and pulled up a chair, then stuck his hand in his pocket and pulled out a small box. "I wanted you to have these." He placed the small blue box in my hand. I fidgeted with the end until it gave way and permitted me to draw out the two gold leaves. I glanced at him, my eyes searching his for some understanding. "Those were handed down to me," Colonel Adams said, "I wanted them to be your first ones, Major."

"Damn!" What a surprise." I looked up. "Thanks, Colonel. These mean a great deal coming from you."

He stuck out his hand. "Congratulations. It's effective tomorrow. The squadron will be sending over the orders—hell, you know me, I couldn't wait." His face became solemn. "But there's a bit of not-so-pleasant news to go along with that."

"What could bust my bubble today?"

"On two occasions, I talked with Colonel Hempleman, Wing Vice Commander, about the reports from DaNang. I even suggested a Board of Inquiry based on my conversations with you and a phone call or two to DaNang. One very slick Lieutenant Colonel Norwood got to the General."

"Sir, are you sure?"

"Damn sure. Colonel Hempleman told me the General had heard all the rumors, including the circumstances surrounding the loss of Rick Haffenback's crew, and an account of things that led up to your accident. He said General Hampton told him Norwood did a magnificent job in completing the deployment against all odds and it was definitely a 'well done' the way the unit completed the assigned missions. It didn't help when the 315th Air Commando Group added their comments for the outstanding way the composite squadron has performed. They've recommended the squadron for a Presidential Unit Citation." He frowned as his face moved closer. "Norwood told Colonel Hempleman and the General that there were a lot of distractions from several mal-contents. I'm sure he mentioned your name." He touched my shoulder. "I did square you away with Hempleman. He understands you went beyond your duty over there, and you and Zack pushed the limits to complete that last mission. He understood it was just a personality clash between you and Norwood." He shook his head. "The General has recommended Norwood for a Legion of Merit."

"That bastard's a murdering sonofabitch, not to mention a totally incompetent leader! The guys in the unit were the reason those missions got accomplished. Those lieutenants and captains went out every day and night, cheatin' the odds, and bustin' butt to do their job. Norwood never—I mean *never*—flew a real mission. After Plateau G, Lynch never flew another one." I slammed my fist into the sofa. "The guys damn well did their duty in spite of Lynch and Norwood, not because of them." I searched Colonel Adams face. "Colonel, I'll prefer charges against him myself. That man shouldn't be permitted in this Air Force."

"David, I know how you feel, but Norwood's a pro. You'll lose for sure." He slapped me on the shoulder. "Let it go, David. Realize the Air Force isn't perfect. We'll always have the Norwoods and Lynchs to contend with."

"I'm not sure I can let it go, Colonel. One's a bumbling fool, and the other man has no morals, character or even an inkling of integrity. Men died who shouldn't have."

"You think that's the first time?" His jaw muscles tensed as he continued. "Good men die for no reason in every war. It's the cost of what we do. But dammit, it's the few regulars like you and me who have to keep the Norwoods from taking over our Air Force."

"We're outnumbered, Colonel," I said. "Our peacetime leaders have played the game so damn well that now they're in firm control." I laughed. "At least until there's another war—one we really intend to win. Think about it, Colonel, even in World War II, it was the Pappy Boynton types who went 'balls to the wall' in combat, ignoring the book and inept leadership. The only place for a military iconoclast is in combat. They jolly well need 'em then. In peacetime, they're aggravating obstacles who must be eliminated—if they can't be controlled. I reckon I'm one who can't be controlled."

"David, clear your mind of Norwood. You're the type officer and pilot we need. There'll be a new assignment coming down soon to go with those gold leaves and your experience. Once you get away from Pope, Norwood, and this damn Wing, things will look different."

"They'll never look that different for me, Colonel. I lost Rick's crew, when I should have had the fortitude to stand my ground as flight commander—and I was responsible for Zack's death—one of the best men I'll ever know. I've gotta live with that every day of my life."

"We'll talk some more about this." He slapped me on the back. "You need some time to heal – and I'm not talking about your goddamn leg, Major."

Leslie leaned against the doorframe, watching me rub my thumb across the gold leaves. "I heard part of that conversation. How nice for him to give you his first Major leaves." She smiled. "Congratulations. I'm proud of you."

"Thanks." I glanced at the box then back at her.

"David, Colonel Adams made a real point about your hurting. I hope you were listening. I've been here for you since you got back but I'll be damned if I'm gonna cater to your maudlin, sulking self-pity." She moved closer and stood there in front of me. "It's about time you shake that attitude and get on with life."

"You'll get no argument on that." I eased myself up on the crutches and walked out the patio door.


A week later, the walking cast, at last, let me discard the crutches and use a cane. The leg had healed rapidly in the weeks since the old cast had been replaced. My spirit was taking longer. I knew Leslie was right. I had to shake this guilt. Several times I wanted to reach out, to take her in my arms and hold her tightly. I can't explain my inability to do this, even to myself. I was caught in an enigmatic web that was holding me against my will. An unwilling prisoner of my psyche; that clandestine, complex thought process that causes us to be unable to outwardly act upon our inner desires. It was like a tug of war within, always on the verge of breaking free, but held fast by years of cognitive conditioning.


Even though the doctor discouraged it, I was driving with the new cast. I enjoyed the freedom of getting out and driving around the countryside, trying to recapture the feelings that overwhelmed me the first day out of the hospital. This was a perfect day; the air had cooled to the first signs of autumn. The leaves had taken on a first hint of color. Suddenly up ahead was a clearing to the right side. I pulled off the highway onto an old logging road. As it narrowed, I wondered if maybe it was only a well-traveled route by hunters. After a mile or so, it turned into a dubious path at best. I stopped the car suddenly while there was still room left to turn around.

I opened the door and limped to the front and sat on the hood, resting my cast on the bumper. Here, in the midst of a few gaunt pines, was an old white oak, and a cascade of sweet gums. The face of a forest when viewed from afar changes dramatically when studied up close. The early afternoon sun blazed down in indirect shafts of light through the gently moving leaves. Shadows fell indistinctly and dissolved along the ground. It brought a smile as I listened intently to sounds around me. This was a place to think, to just be.

I must have been there much longer than it seemed. Glancing at my watch, I realized that two hours had passed. I felt refreshed and renewed as I twisted the wheel and backed up several times to negotiate the u-turn. I accelerated down the highway toward the Base. Finding a vacant parking spot next to the squadron, I hobbled slowly to the low white frame building. The familiar sound of aircraft engines filled the background until I shut the door. I could see Colonel Adams standing beside his desk, shuffling through papers. He looked up and motioned me back to his office with a wave of his arm.

"Have a seat, David." He continued to fumble through the jumble of papers. "I just tried calling your house. Leslie said you were out and might stop by here."

"Well, it's been a week since I've chatted with any of the guys. Their jokes keep me from the boredom of T.V. and walks around the yard. God, I'm ready to get on with things."

"Glad you said that." Finally, he pulled out a yellow legal page with scribbling on it. "Here we go. Now, let's see if I can decipher my shorthand notes." He read quickly, and then continued. "I talked with my good friend in personnel up at Tactical Air Command Headquarters, because I know you're anxious to leave Pope." He looked up for my reaction, but I sat impassively. "There's a vacancy at Langley, in fighter ops. He said they'd really like to have a guy with your experience."

"Hmm," I said, blank faced.

"And damn it, if you're hell-bent to get back in fighters, just say the word, and he told me you'd have orders down here next week for Mac Dill—F-four's again." He waited a second, watching me rub my forehead, thinking about what I'd just heard. "There's another possibility, not one I'd recommend, but they're having a hard time filling a spot as Air Force Liaison Officer at Fort Benning, Georgia. You'd have to attend the air-ground operations course and become a qualified forward air controller down at Hurlburt Field." He tossed the paper on the desk. "You sure as hell don't want to get that chummy with the Infantry. You could find your butt back in 'Nam as a grunt, slogging through a rice paddy, marking targets for a bunch of F-4's scattering napalm in your lap."

"Colonel, I really appreciate all you've done for me. I mean that. Only once before in my career have I served under an officer I had this much respect for. It's the few officers like you, Colonel, that makes this difficult." I shifted in the chair. "Those are choice assignments, but I won't be able to accept any of 'em. I've decided to resign my commission."

Colonel Adams examined my expression for signs that I was joking. He realized I was determined. He leaned forward, his jaw muscles flexing. "David, why the hell would you throw away a career after you just made Major—and you have thirteen years active duty?"

"Fourteen."

"Why?"

I looked down, gathering my thoughts. "I loved the Air Force. I used to be so blasted proud of my profession and the officers and men I worked with that it showed in everything I did. A lot of this pride was a carry-over from Korea. I served in the best damn fighter squadron in the Far East, under some real men of honor. VietNam sure changed that perception. It wasn't just the lack of leadership at the squadron level; it prevails to the highest echelons. Look at our Wing Commander—hell, Colonel, his wife would make a better Wing Commander. At least she has balls."

Colonel Adams chuckled. "Yeah, I remember when she threw you guys out of the Officers Club one afternoon for making too much noise at the bar while she was conducting an Officers Wives Club meeting." He laughed harder. "Yeah, she does have moxie."

"What I'm trying to say is I've lost the burning desire to serve, to fly, in the present-day Air Force. I just can't play the game."

"Goddamn it, that's exactly why you *shouldn't* resign. Don't let Norwood and Lynch win. Stay and fight to make it the way it was; the way it can be again. You watch—this war's escalating every day—and the real warriors will take over when the chips are down. Just like always, this catastrophe will build tomorrow's leaders. They'll learn well from this fiasco and make a difference later. It goes in cycles, David." He moved closer. "The next damn war will be fought with that kind of leadership. The Norwoods will retire and you young officers will be in command. Count on it."

"I think I'm too jaded now. I'm sorry, but I can't wait till the next war to see how it turns out."

"Major, if that's how you feel, then I wish you luck. I think you're a fine officer, one who can make a difference. I hate like hell to see you go."

"Thanks, Colonel." I grabbed his hand and shook it hard. This was becoming harder than I thought it would be.

"We'll talk again soon, David. Nothing about your decision is irreversible."

I put my hat on and hobbled out the squadron orderly room door. I watched the aircraft taking off, their engines screaming with power as they rose from the runway. Looking at their sleek beauty and the way they climbed into the sky, I remembered how once this was all I ever wanted to do. I felt a knot in my stomach as I continued to stare at the sky.

"Afternoon, Sir." the young airman said as he saluted. I returned his salute.

"Good afternoon." I watched him move down the flight line. I wondered where his career would take him. *The Air Force's probably lucky to have men like him. And they deserve leaders with integrity and skill. I hope like hell Colonel Adams is right. My Air Force deserves it.*

I dropped the walking cane on the sofa, sat down and put my leg up. Leslie sat beside me. "You were gone quite a while. Did you enjoy getting out for a while?"

"Yeah. Yeah, I did. I reckon I solved some things that needed it," I said.

"And what did you solve?"

"I made a decision." I watched her closely. It was remarkable how she could feign being totally calm. She didn't blink an eye. "It was like popping a relief valve for what I had been chewing on for these past few weeks."

She leaned closer. "Well, tell me . . ."

"I'm resigning my commission." I interrupted.

She flung herself against the couch. "What a shocker. I can't believe you'd do that." She looked at me her eyes focused on mine. "I can't remember a time you weren't in the Air Force. It's been a part of you as long as I've known you." She touched my hand. "The only thing that worries me . . ." She took a deep breath. "Don't make huge decisions until you've worked through your feelings."

"I've worked through 'em pretty well. I have to do this—to stay would compromise my integrity. Listen to me carefully, Leslie. I need to do this."

"What do you plan to do?" Her head was shaking as if saying, no, this isn't what he wants. Doubt flashed in her eyes.

"I sent resumes to Delta, Eastern, and TWA. Delta looks the most promising."

"Knowing you and your friends," she said, "I wonder how happy you'd be flying with the airlines—a DC-Ten's not an F-four."

"What a statement coming from you." I laughed. "I never knew you were particularly fond of me flying fighters." I shook my head. "That's immaterial anyway. I won't put in my resignation papers until I'm sure what would be best."

"It's your life, David."

"I thought it was our lives?" I asked.

"This is your decision. Just yours." She rose and moved to the sink and stared out the window. She spun around and faced me. "Whatever you decide to do with your life, give it careful thought."

"There're no sure-fire decisions, nothing is guaranteed in this life. You just make the best decision you can at the time." I stared out the patio door. "I've sure as hell made my share of bad ones."

She swung around. "Is that what's driving your decision?" She crossed her arms, waiting. "David, you've never talked to me about the crash, about Zack's death. I've tried to be patient so you'd share those feelings." She walked over to the couch and sat close. "Why won't you talk to me?"

"Leslie—Leslie, for right now, let that one go. But that's not the main reason I'm resigning. I can't be a part of a system where officers like Norwood are in leadership positions—then rewards their lack of integrity and incompetence. The system's tainted, and I won't play that game. It demands something I can't give."

"David, you're such an idealist. Sometimes you have to bend a little."

"Why the hell couldn't you just say: 'If that's your decision, I support you?' God, I'd love to hear that just once."

"I'm not going to say something I don't mean just because that's what you want to hear. You know me better than that. We approach things differently. You smash into 'em head-on. I don't . . ."

The phone ringing stopped her in mid-sentence, as she spun around and answered it. I hobbled out to the patio, not waiting to hear who was calling.

It was that time of evening when the sun was setting behind the tall pines. The house was situated so the sun set right across the back left corner. Sunsets continued to fascinate me; never losing that mystique that changed the sky each afternoon into different pallets of color. The sun descended slowly behind, making a few cumulous clouds dark and ominous. I wanted to go back in and tell her I understand and know I have her support. The words were not readily available—they never were when called upon. *Damn wall.*

I walked up behind her in the bedroom. When she turned abruptly as if in a defensive posture, I stiffened immediately. And instead of putting my arms around her, I stood there close, almost feeling her breath, looking into her eyes. Tears streamed down her face, as she buried her head into my shoulder.

"Hell, I didn't mean it quite like it sounded in there," I said.

"That was Mama on the phone. The Vet had to put Rambler down this afternoon."

"Damn, I'm sorry—really sorry. I know how much you loved that horse."

"He had equine pneumonia and the antibiotics didn't work." I handed her my handkerchief and she wiped at her eyes. "Not many people understand how much you can love an animal." She gasped in a breath. "He was like family—oh, God, why?"

"No one can give us a helpful explanation with this kind of hurt. He was a great horse and I know you're hurting now. But try to focus on the good times together. Hold tight to those memories."

She pushed back. "Does that advice apply to you? Can you do that? Can you focus on the good times, and not Zack's death?"

"I try."


The next morning, we sat eating breakfast, neither talking. I knew how sad she was about Rambler, and there was nothing to take away the grief. I poured a second cup of coffee for her. "How do you feel today?"

There was a faint smile, but Leslie didn't jump on the question with a quick response. She took a long sip from her cup. "David, I called the airlines this morning before you woke up." She looked at me with red eyes; I sensed what I was about to hear. "I have a reservation tomorrow at three-ten. I can tell you don't understand, but right now I need to go to Deerfield. I need to walk through the fields and sit by the stream and let my mind rest. I need this, David."

"Why now? Is it Rambler or me – or both?"

"It's everything. I need some time, some space."

"Not the best time for this decision."

"Your leg's almost well, and you can do everything you need to do."

"That wasn't what I meant, and you know it."

"This is nothing final. You need time to work through some very important issues, and I'm no help at all. I'm a hindrance, in fact. We both need some time away from these things."

I reached across the table and took her hand. "Leslie, if that's what you need—do it. I want what's best for you. Your happiness is important to me. When you think of us, our past, our future, I hope that makes a difference."

"We just can't express that caring on a day-to-day basis. We can't be there for each other when we *need* the most."

"Do you really think time will make a difference?"

"I don't know. I really don't know."

She placed the last few items in the two suitcases, zipped the hang-up bag, and turned to me. "Looks like that does it," she said, glancing at her watch. "I think we should get going so there's no rush to check these big old bags. Don't want to miss the plane."

We both were quiet on the short drive to the small Fayetteville airport. Several times I started to speak but stopped myself. I looked over at her and she looked at me, a smile sliding across her face. Seeing her dimples made me smile back. I knew there was little to be said now. Nothing short of heaven would alter the course we had set in motion.

After checking her bags, we sat in the old waiting room, looking out onto the ramp area where the small commuter plane would load. My mind was numbed by a sense of providence gone astray. Here was an opportunity, maybe the last, to express my feelings, to lay my affection right out there in the open – yet I was emotionally paralyzed. *Damn.*

The twin-engine plane taxied up toward the terminal and shut down the engines. Baggage handlers rushed out to load and unload luggage onto a large handcart that looked like a child's overgrown wagon. Four people deplaned and walked into the terminal. The loudspeaker crackled, "Piedmont Airlines flight 347 for Atlanta now loading."

I took her arm. "Take care, tell Miss Ellen I'm thinking of her, and I'll miss you."

"Thanks for making this so easy. I'll miss you too—and I'll be in touch soon." She kissed me on the mouth. My arms shot out to pull her close, but she turned and almost ran to the plane. She didn't look back.

In the next two months, there were several phone calls. We kept the conversations routine and upbeat. We never discussed the separation or the possibility of reconciliation. In each conversation, I waited for those pivotal words: "David, I want to be with you. I need you." The anticipation was always there. The words were never said – by either of us.

My last visit with orthopedics cleared me for full flight status. It also was the last piece of the application puzzle for Delta Airlines. The interview had gone well, and I sensed their desperate need for pilots. They called and said I was hired, they only required a current flight physical to set flight status in motion. I would attend school in, and be based in, Atlanta. The timing was the only remaining problem. The Air Force had not yet accepted the resignation of my regular commission and my request for a reserve commission. It was being processed.

The November days became much shorter. As the sun disappeared the darkness slowly surrounded me. I walked back inside, sat, and pulled out the bundle of papers. I picked up the blue folder with a large silver Air Force seal on the front and opened it. I stared at the certificate. *United States Air Force—Honorable Discharge*. It was final. A lachrymose cloak surrounded my thinking. This had been my life for fourteen years. Over the course of those years, I had the privilege to serve with the finest pilots and crewmembers ever assembled. I remembered my first assignment as a very young fighter pilot. It was gratifying to be with men like those in the 68th Fighter Squadron, and an honor to fly on their wing in combat. We had a camaraderie that defied explanation to anyone not living it. Later, I had some new, eager Lieutenant, with fire in his eyes, flying my wing. The Air Force thrust me into, and brought me back out of, combat in two wars. I rubbed my hand across the document, thinking of that unique camaraderie, the bawdy bar songs and the toasts to those who went down. It was putting their loss in proper perspective for those who would be in the cockpit and go back up the next day.

As I stared at the letters on the discharge, I thought back on Colonel Adam's statement that we could make a difference. *Maybe the system will change with the young Turks who're being baptized right now in the skies over Vietnam. Possibly they'll learn from the mistakes they see.*

I sat there, bourbon in hand, letting my mind recall a collage of events, from Aviation Cadets to those last few months in Nam. Faces flashed by with smiles and laughter in the background, and then came the last image—Zack lying next to me under that gnarled old tree in the jungle. I dropped the certificate into the box, atop my old flight jacket. I folded the four sides of the top and taped it shut.

Shoving the box to one side, I jumped up and moved to the desk. Sitting, I grabbed the pen to write a long-overdue letter. I held the pen, staring at the wall, trying to gather words from my heart. No more procrastinating – this needed to be said, and the time was now. I began to write.

*Friday*

*My Dearest Leslie:*

*There are so many things I'd like to say to you tonight, feelings way too deep to put on paper, thoughts too profound for me to convey. It appears that when I need them most; I'm faced with a paucity of words. I'm sure there was love, but as you said: love is not enough to sustain a relationship.*

*It takes hard work; it must be based on resilience and trust. We found only a portion of that combination.*

*Try to remember the good times—there were many. To dwell on the other would be an injustice to something very special that once existed.*

*You were my fantasy—I just couldn't make you real. But everyone should have a fantasy.*

*What I'm saying . . .*

I grabbed the letter, crushing it in my hand. I held it there for several seconds before tossing it in the trash.

# 17

## Impulse

I sat in the loaded car, staring at the ignition key. Deliberately, I turned the key and started the engine. My mind swirled with thoughts; *If the timing had been better, the weather different or the tides had shifted a little in either direction.* I sat up straight. *Hell, no, it's simply us. We carve out our lives. It's us.*

I started the car, slammed the gear shift into reverse, shot out of the drive, and headed west. The highway rolled past as I sped through North Carolina, into South Carolina and Georgia. I drove with intensity, with one thought in mind. The sun began to disappear behind the trees as I crossed into Alabama. I flipped on the lights and tried not to let the black roadway hypnotize me. I stopped only for gas, pushing myself to stay awake as the centerline tried to lull me to sleep.

The sign read: "Welcome to Louisiana" instantly shaking the sleep that had almost taken over. Morning illumination was giving definition to the trees along the side of the road. In the semi-darkness, the light from an all-night café up ahead was a welcome sight. I pulled in, stretched my legs and walked in.

"Hi there. Have a seat and I'll bring you a menu."

"No need. Just a cup of coffee and three eggs scrambled light."

"No meat."

"Just toast."

The husky fellow with an apron tied to his waist moved to the table dropped the plate of steaming eggs in front of me and filled my cup again. "Been driving all night?"

"Yeah."

"You looked pretty beat when you came in." he laughed. You'll be okay for quite a spell now. My coffee'll wake the dead."

"I feel okay." I drained the last few drops from the cup, then dropped three dollars on the table. I walked into the cold air and took a deep breath. I was ready to go again.

*

My leg ached and moving it around under the steering wheel did little to alleviate the misery. I pushed on, trying not to think about the throbbing sensation that ran up to my hip. The sun was making its move again toward the horizon, almost hidden by the lowering clouds. The wind whipped at the car and small flakes of snow fell in a flurry across the windshield. The unending road, agonizing tiredness, the throbbing pain in my leg, or the changing weather didn't matter now. I saw the sign up ahead, moving back and forth with the wind: "Deerfield."

I braked to a stop, got out and leaned against the car, readying my mind and body to go to the door. The door opened and Leslie walked toward me. She stopped at the bottom of the steps and folded her arms against the wind. We were frozen there, waiting for something, anything. The tension was electrical. Her smile broke like a thunderclap, and I ran to her.

I held her tightly, ignoring the wind and snow flurries, oblivious to anything except the closeness of her body.

"I thought you would just appear at the door one day – that's the impulsive David I know."

"There's a reason – impulse, decision, rationality – call it whatever. Two souls met accidentally on a rainy day in San Antonio. Quickly, they welded into one. What we had – what we have – should be appreciated and treasured. It's too rare a gift to lose because we didn't try hard enough." I pulled her tightly to me. "Leslie, I'll do whatever it takes to make this work. God, I love you so."

Her breath was warm on my ear as she whispered, "I love you too. Maybe we've been shaken enough to realize what we were about to lose." She kissed me, then my cheek. Her breath was warm against my ear. "We'll make it."

The wind howled around us as the snow fell harder. I was never so warm in my life.

# EPILOGUE

It was a bucolic July morning, the sun just rising above the trees, casting soft shadows in front of me. I drove through the iron gates and parked off to the side of the gravel road that continued to meander around in an irregular circle. I opened the door and leaned against the car, surveying the expansive, well-manicured area that stretched before me. The gradual warming of the July sun would soon evaporate the dew that was still glistening in bright beads on the grass. Looking over this serene place, I wondered if this mission still had the attached importance for me. Had the feelings not diminished in twenty-seven years? I forced myself away from the car. Still mulling the question over in my mind as I walked. Why the urgent feeling of doing this after so long?

Moving through the cemetery, I searched for the family name between the discolored markers standing like sentinels. Shafts of sunlight streamed through the leaves in the old oak tree; some of its boughs almost brushed the ground, forming a protective arc above the tarnished headstones, stained by years of merciless wind and rain. I stood there in awe of what these granite markers represented—the resting place of vibrant human beings, families stilled forever beneath this sod. My eyes darted around to read the names on the nearby markers. I realized that these brief, carved notations in the head stones did not reflect their lives or the imprint on others they had touched. So much more needed to be told

I walked carefully, stepping lightly over the other headstones, until I stood in front of the large monument. As I ducked under the branches, a glint of light raked across the wide family marker which bore only one word. A name burned indelibly into my mind. There, in one corner of the plot, was a stone not yet corroded by time and the elements Bending down, I touched the granite, feeling its coldness move through me. I realized the grave is only a repository for whatever life gives up when it departs. My fingers moved across the letters. I had wondered many times what feeling would take hold of me if I came here to look down on this grave.

Kneeling there, I smiled at my reflections, wondering why we have such a tenacious tendency to look back on our past. *Is it vindication of decisions made along the way? Maybe it's a search for justification of our lives. Or is it a reconciliation of the past and present—a truce with life?*

Kneeling there, still looking at the tombstone, I continued to think about that year. In 1963, my life was in transition. The events of that year had a profound effect on me. It was a time when dreams became illusions, and I began the search for new ones. I look at things through different eyes now, and maybe that was why it was now comfortable recalling bits and pieces of scenes, remnants of fragmented events of that year. Some were vibrant, brilliantly clear, crystalline milestones. Others, less clear, were barely discernible.

I stared at the marker, wondering about the events in my life affected by the person lying here. Without realizing it, those passions had left the recesses of my mind, gradually disappearing just as echoes fade into gentle silence.

I rubbed my hand across the letters of the stone again, then stood, and read the inscription once more.

*Douglas Patrick Norwood*
*Lieutenant Colonel, United States Air Force*
*January 21, 1921-March 3, 1992*

The hostility and anger I harbored for most of the last 27 years was gone. My belligerence had been sapped by years of living. In 1963, life seemed vast, almost overwhelming. Over the years, it was cut down in size like whittling on a block of wood. By this stage of life, Seeing Colonel Norwood's grave was part of the shavings of life, scattered about, that no longer mattered. I now only felt indifference toward this person who epitomized everything I hated in a man.

The car door slammed behind me breaking the trance. I jerked around to see her walking toward me. She had sat patiently in the passenger seat while I made my visit. Leslie came up, put her arms around me and held our bodies close. She glanced down at the stone beneath me, and took my arm. "After the retirement ceremony at Delta yesterday, when you told me you had to make this detour, I cringed at the thought. Has this visit been as cathartic as you'd hope?"

"Even more."

"How do you feel?"

"Alright." I smiled as she touched my hand. "When I read about Colonel Norwood's death, there was no satisfaction, only ambivalence. But I needed to stand here, to look down on his grave and know I'd made peace with my life. Now it's truly behind me."

"I'm glad," Leslie said. "I think I knew that long before you did." She took my hand. We've been married for 36 years, and I've never been more in love with you than this moment. Let's go home."

CPSIA information can be obtained
at www.ICGtesting.com
Printed in the USA .
BVHW030558280819
556971BV00001B/5/P